About the author

Patricia O'Reilly comes to writing books via the route of freelance journalism, radio documentaries and plays. Hearing the story of Mary O'Connor while sitting in her aunt's kitchen as a child was the inspiration for *The First Rose of Tralee*. She has written 13 books, both fiction and non-fiction. Several of her previous novels are inspired by real life: *The Interview*, *A Type of Beauty* (listed for Historical Novel Society Award), *Time and Destiny*. She is a highly regarded writing tutor at UCD and elsewhere. She lives in Dublin.

Acknowledgements

Thanks to the staff of the National Library of Ireland, Dublin; the National Museum of Ireland – Decorative Arts and History, Dublin; Ordnance Survey Ireland, Dublin; the National Famine Museum, Strokestown, Co Roscommon; Kerry County Museum, Tralee, especially archivist Mike Lynch; The Society of Authors, London; and Members of the Historical Novel Society.

Thanks to Margaret Carroll who documented the history of our grandfather, his three wives and many children in 'The Family Tree of John Reidy (1853-1936)', launched on the occasion of the Reidy Gathering in October 2018 in Tralee; Fr AJ Gaughan; and June Considine for her friendship and support.

Thanks also to my family: husband, Xavier, my constant; son Peter for his gimlet eye; daughter Susanne marketing supremo; sister Pam, always encouraging; and my niece Zoe, full of ideas.

And most importantly: thanks to all the team at Poolbeg Press, special mention for Paula Campbell and my editor Gaye Shortland – without them this book would not exist.

To my many relatives from Tralee and beyond

She was lovely and fair as the rose of the summer,
Yet 'twas not her beauty alone that won me;
Oh no, 'twas the truth in her eyes ever dawning,
That made me love Mary, the Rose of Tralee.

'The Rose of Tralee' *(19th century Irish ballad)*

She was lovely and fair as the rose of the summer,
Yet 'twas not her beauty alone that won me;
Oh no, 'twas the truth in her eyes ever dawning,
That made me love Mary, the Rose of Tralee.

'The Rose of Tralee' *(19th century Irish ballad)*

CHAPTER 1

Tralee, County Kerry – 1840s

AS MARY PICKED UP the basket from beside the door, her father looked up from his worktable with a frown. 'Where d'you think you're goin'?'

Willie O'Connor had a hard, querulous tone to his voice, but she looked square at him.

'The market. We've no spuds.'

'No hangin' around the town.' He gave her a deep look. 'It's way past –'

'I know. Time I was wed.' She tried to keep her tone light.

It was the kind of comment he made when they were alone. The importance of her being wed consumed him and she dreaded where it might end. A shiver of anxiety ran up and down her spine. Marriage would condemn her to a life like her mother's and that of the other women of Brogue Lane.

Having had his say, Willie tied his leather apron around his waist and hunched to his morning ritual. Like his father and grandfather before him he had grown up on Brogue Lane, the heart of the shoemaking industry in Tralee, and had become one of the most skilled and respected shoemakers in the town. One by careful one, he placed the tools of his trade in a straight line along the table by the window: the awl for punching holes, the sole knife for shaping the soles and the size sticks that he used for measuring feet.

After a quick look at him, Mary pushed out the half door into the lane. She would take her time. She had no wish to spend the day under the scrutiny of her father.

✤✤✤

The wind whistled in and out of the market as Mary went from stall to stall in an unhurried way that was quite unlike her. She picked up and examined a potato from Paddy Joe's pile.

'It's the best, Mary – the best,' he assured her.

She nodded, returned the potato and moved up the line to a familiar face. She and Josie had sat beside each other in the schoolhouse. Now Josie had a small child propped up on a pile of sacks and her belly bulged with another. There was exhaustion in every line of her body.

Mary picked up a handful of potatoes from the stall and another and another until her basket was full. She placed it at the back of the stall.

'Keep it for me, Josie – I'll collect it on my way home.'

As she handed over the few coins in payment, she clasped Josie's hand warmly and tried to ignore the bleakness of her expression.

After dragging out the hours of the morning chatting to the stallholders, she made her way into town. It was beginning to snow. Soft flakes drifted downwards onto her upturned face. They frosted the buildings, nudged into cracks in the walls and webbed the corners of windows, transforming the brown muddiness of the street to a blanket of shimmering white.

The corner leading to Denny Street was black with people milling backwards and forwards. She pushed through the crowd. A gathering of townsfolk clustered around the entrance to the inn, their faces pale and thin and their expressions intent and sombre as they stood in a listening mass – men with throws of hessian across their shoulders, women swathed in black shawls, and mostly barefoot children, their limbs blue with the cold.

A voice echoed and resounded off the buildings, as though rolling into the heart of the town. '*Our country is worth struggling for. Cromwell, when pursuing his march of death and devastation amid viewing the beauty and fertility of our land, exclaimed, "Is not this a country worth fighting for?" He would say it was not only worth fighting for, but also worth dying for!*'

The richness and warmth of the tone so intrigued Mary that she rose up on her tippy-toes the better to see. Through the falling snow she saw a large man wearing a caped coat and the tall hat of the gentry. He was standing on a table at the entrance to the inn, his shoulders back, and as he spoke he used his hands for emphasis. She had never seen or heard the like of him.

She plucked at the sleeve of an old man who was bent forward, leaning heavily on a stick. 'Who's that? Who's he?'

'Shush, girl! That's Daniel O'Connell himself.'

So, this was the man they called 'The Liberator' and 'The Emancipator'. She had never thought to see him or hear him speak. But she knew of him. Everyone did. He was a legend, his name spoken in awe and his achievements talked about up and down the county – perhaps, she thought, throughout the whole of Ireland.

Weaving in and out of the crowd, the RIC constables were distinctive in their dark-green uniforms and wide leather belts. Occasionally one of them stopped for a word here, a comment there, a pat on the head of a small child. Although they carried truncheons, there was no threat in their presence.

Mary eased her way into the thick of the people, pushing forward, straining to catch every word, her father and the chores she should be attending to back at the cabin forgotten.

As the voice fell softer it became more persuasive. '*There is but one thing on which all welfare depends — Repeal! With Repeal of the Union you will be happy, with Repeal you will become rich, with Repeal you will obtain all that you desire and strive for!*'

Mary shivered at the power of the words and drew her thin shawl more closely around her shoulders against the raw cold of the January afternoon. The simple words with their ringing message of hope were compelling, holding the crowd spellbound until it erupted into loud cheers and stamping of feet.

Then the attention of the gathering fluttered, switching and swaying to focus on a young man with a head of golden curls who pushed forward, his green greatcoat swinging open and his linen shirt sparkling white against his throat. He jumped onto a chair, stood alongside Daniel O'Connell, leaned in towards him and said something to him before throwing his arms wide as though embracing the town.

'*I promise you!*' he shouted. '*Repeal of the Union will change our lives!*'

The crowd, including Mary, clapped hands and stamped feet.

The man was most handsome. She thought he might be the young master from West Villa.

She blew a little puff of hopeful breath at a passing snowflake, although she thought that for the likes of them — her mother and father, brother and sisters and all the other families living on the lanes – that Mr O'Connell's happiness and riches were not within their reach.

❁ ❁ ❁

Protected from the falling snow and secure in her black, glossy carriage, Margaret Mulchinock nestled into her furs.

It had long been her belief that no good came from such gatherings and that the crowd congregating along Denny Street had little in common except a sense of togetherness, although from the tightknit look of them their togetherness was powerful. Her heart went out to them and their courage. They were the withouts. Without food, without warmth, without work. Yet, haggard and hollow-cheeked, they had come in their droves from the cramped, black hovels of the labyrinth of laneways at the back of the town to listen to Daniel O'Connell.

She couldn't actually see O'Connell but she opened the door of her carriage slightly, the better to hear what he was saying.

'*There is nothing I would not do to prevent further suffering to my countrymen. When the hand of man is raised against you, I will defend you with every breath of my being!*'

As he spoke, the cadence of his voice rising and falling, she remembered the hugeness of his personality and the way his presence had commanded the drawing room when he had visited West Villa more than a decade ago. If she were a betting woman she'd wager that in the intervening years his charisma had grown.

A bout of cheering, followed by shouts of '*Aye!*' and '*Surely 'tis!*' stopped his speech for more than a minute.

Mrs Mulchinock leaned out of her carriage door to catch a glimpse of the great O'Connell.

And stared in astonishment. It was difficult to believe what she was seeing and hearing.

'*You've done that, sir — defended us with every breath of your being!*' The voice rang loud and clear. '*No one has ever done more for his fellow man — we applaud you!*'

It was William Pembroke, her eldest son, standing on a chair alongside Daniel O'Connell.

Her throat constricted, she watched in fearful fascination.

With stamping feet and loud cheering, the people responded enthusiastically to his endorsement of the man who had brought them Catholic Emancipation after centuries of religious oppression.

The two men acknowledged the adulation unsmilingly, standing still, their shoulders back. O'Connell pushed his chimneypot hat to a rakish angle that displayed his dark hair powdered with silver, and when William Pembroke raised his arms above his head and clapped, the crowd reacted with even more enthusiasm.

Then, as though deciding enough was enough, with a downward movement of his hands O'Connell sought to quieten his audience. As they settled he touched her son's shoulder, leaned in towards him and whispered something into his ear.

She watched as, in his unhurried way, William Pembroke buttoned up his greatcoat, jumped down from the platform and disappeared into the press of bodies.

Heart fluttering, she leant back against the carriage seat. If she hadn't seen and heard her son, she would not have believed what she had just witnessed.

CHAPTER 2

MARY COLLECTED HER BASKET from Josie and hurried through the squelching spurts of slush, her mind so full of what she had seen and heard that she was oblivious to the slap of her wet skirt against her bare legs and the squelch of her boots.

She caught up with the schoolmaster, head down, walking along slowly, as though he too was deep in thought.

As he turned towards her and halted, he tipped his hat. 'Were you there?'

She didn't have to ask what he meant – her heart was still beating at the power of Daniel O'Connell's presence and his words. 'I was, sir.'

'The O'Connell from Derrynane – Caherciveen – is one of us – he's a man of the people." Mr Foley, resting on his walking stick, spoke slowly. "A Catholic Kerryman educated in Dublin and Paris. Who read for the bar in London.'

'D'you know him, sir?' The master seemed to know everyone and everything.

'We've met. And it's beholden on every Irishman and every Irishwoman to at least know of him.'

Then, as she was about to ask about the other gentleman, he forestalled her.

'And good to see young Mulchinock taking an interest in the state of the country.'

At the entrance to Brogue Lane he surprised her by asking, 'And how's young Hannah these days?'

'Don't know, sir. Haven't seen her.'

Mary bit down on her lip. She hoped the rumours circulating around the town were no more than rumours. There wasn't a passing day when she didn't miss her friend.

As she walked on, newly observant after listening to Daniel O'Connell, she noticed that only a few of the thatched cabins, including theirs, were in decent repair – most were in varying stages of deterioration. *Hmm*. Riches.

She pushed in the half door of the cabin and adjusted her eyes to the interior gloom and her nostrils to the heavy air. Her brother Billy, going on thirteen, was scrawny-thin, with too-long arms and legs. He was hanging over his father's shoulder, nodding in time to the in-and-out of the curved needle. Any day now he'd start learning the trade. Her sisters, Brigid and Ellen, their school smocks grubby and their slates tossed aside, pushed and pulled at the string as they squabbled over a game of Cat's Cradle.

As she kicked off her wet boots and set them to dry by the fire they wobbled sideways, the leather tongues lolling drunkenly and the broken laces streeling.

She looked warily at her father, seated in his customary place by the window to catch the last rays of the weakening light, his features taut in concentration, his large knuckles bending to the task as meticulously he stitched a sole onto the leather upper of a man's boot.

'You were gone a long while.' He didn't look up from the boot.

Willie had the reputation of being a hard worker and his order book was always full, but he was negligent about collecting the monies due to him and there was many an unpaid-for well-shod foot walking the town and beyond.

'Not so long. It's snowing.'

'I hear there was a rally?'

'There was.'

She'd say nothing about Daniel O'Connell – her father did not consider politics to be a suitable subject of conversation for women. She threw another few sods on the fire and waited for it to smoulder before setting the pot of potatoes on the crane to boil.

Soon after, Nora pushed into the kitchen, wearily unwinding her sodden black shawl, revealing her dome of belly thrust pendulously forward. She was a dairymaid at West Villa, the Big House at Annagh, and had been in service there from the time she was a young girl.

'So you're here.' Willie's flying fingers barely paused. It was how he greeted his wife each evening.

'So I am.' That too was her greeting to him.

'Sit down by the fire, Mam.' Mary's heart went out to her mother. She looked drawn and grey-faced.

Nora sat heavily into the chair, spreading out her skirts to dry, and wrapped her arms around her belly, as though holding the unborn child in place, allowing the warmth of the fire to lap around her as she closed her eyes.

'It's too much for you, Mam,' said Mary. 'Walking there and back and the long hours you put in.'

'I'll be all right. It won't be long now. Please God, let him be born healthy.'

This child was taking its toll on her mother – she was bigger and bulkier than Mary remembered from previous carryings.

❀❀❀

Snowflakes a shade lighter than the snow-coloured sky continued to fall as Mrs Mulchinock, shivering as much from anxiety as from the cold, was driven home up Ballyard Hill to Annagh.

She was unnerved by what she had just witnessed. She had felt the message of hope that Daniel O'Connell had imparted with such fervour and sincerity strike at the heart of the townspeople, their passive adoration of him heightened by the relaxed presence of the RIC. But she had sensed ripples of unease too, masked as they were by the power, positivity and compelling words of O'Connell's speech. As she tried to think calmly, to make sense of the afternoon, she had to admit that she was most disturbed by her son's presence at the meeting and the public familiarity between him and the politician.

The more she thought of it, the more puzzled she was by her son's behaviour – publicly endorsing the views of a politician was not in keeping with what she knew of him – with what she thought she knew of him, she amended, because of recent times he had become secretive and evasive. Moody too. They were traits she had attributed to the grief they were all suffering since Henry's death – Henry, her fragile baby who had grown to a fragile boy and died before reaching manhood, his body worn out with fevers. Now she wondered.

That morning over breakfast she had read the latest edition of the *Kerry Evening Post*. On the first page a long, well-written article spoke of O'Connell 'weaving a lash of scorpions', as well as mentioning his 'truculent denunciation', and further down there was something about flinging aside 'all decencies of political warfare'. She had dismissed the article as radical writing. But now she wasn't so sure.

As her carriage turned into the gateway of West Villa, her breathing slowed and she began to feel calmer — her home had that effect on her. From her first sight of the house, some months before she was wed, she had been captivated by its compatibility to the land and the quiet refinement of its white walls. Situated on the western edge of the town, in the shadow of Slieve Mish and surrounded by the raw wilds of Kerry, everything about it appealed to her.

In the hallway she acknowledged the portrait of her husband with a little nod and a sad smile as she stood by the hallstand removing her foxfurs, stern black cloak and bonnet frilled with the finest of Carrickmacross lace, dyed to soot black as befitted her status as a widow.

Relieved to be home, she was nevertheless still uneasy. The knowledge that O'Connell possessed such commanding powers of persuasion gnawed at her.

As she moved towards the refuge of her small parlour, the bunch of keys and cluster of little bells at her waist tinkling her status as mistress of the house, William Pembroke walked through the hallway, his hair dishevelled and his boots and coat mud-splattered and wet.

Normally his presence brightened her life and her heart turned over at the sight of him — he was the image of his father Michael, the very echo of the man she had loved so dearly and whose death she had grieved for the past ten years. But today she felt only anxiety at the sight of him.

'Mother, dearest,' he greeted her with a smile, 'have you been out?'

'I have. And I saw you in town. In Denny Street.' She looked directly at him.

His pause was momentary and he answered easily. 'A well-attended occasion. Even Daniel's extempore speeches draw the masses.'

Daniel? That implied an intimacy. The words burst from her: 'Your poor father would turn in his grave at the thought of you being involved in politics!'

'You know I'd never do anything to dishonour the family.'

She wanted to believe him. But she had seen Daniel O'Connell's touch on his shoulder and that whisper into his ear.

'There's enough unease in the county, unruliness amongst the peasants and, from what I hear, the Whiteboys are back marauding,' she said anxiously.

'They're young lads, mostly harmless, and they have a point about the increases in rent.' His calmness sought to reassure, but it had the opposite effect.

She wouldn't enter into a discussion with him. Even thinking of the Whiteboys had her innards curling in revulsion.

He shrugged. 'I spoke for the crowd, congratulating Mr O'Connell – a gesture of courtesy. Do you not agree he is a powerful speaker?'

Her son's enthusiasm was worrying. He didn't conform, he'd never conformed – from babyhood he had been different to his brothers, his facility with words and rhyming being far removed from the family's farming background and commercial interests. They were even further removed, she would have thought, from anything to do with the hurly-burly of Irish politics. Although, in fairness, she couldn't fault his management and the success he was making of the family's drapery and haberdashery shop.

'Mr O'Connell is a powerful speaker,' she said. 'And in times of political unease such men can be dangerous.'

'He doesn't advocate violence. He's against it.' William Pembroke's defence was instinctive and his voice rang with pride.

She had thought she knew her son as well as she knew the beat of her own heart. But this? She was right to be concerned and her instincts were further confirmed by the way his face had lit up as he spoke. Her mind was full of worry as she wondered how best to handle the situation. The circumstances of her life had sharpened her survival instincts, and over the years she had grown cautious – she did not want to make an error of judgement by acting in haste.

Biding her time, she stood in front of the looking glass beside the hallstand, tidying stray strands of hair, tucking them into her indoor cap, smoothing the fashionable looping plaits she wore over her ears. She was proud of her hair, still luxuriantly brown.

The family, she decided, with a final pat to her hair, would be best served if William Pembroke were removed from the reach of Daniel O'Connell's influence – if influence he had over him. Her decision was sudden and she allowed that she might be overreacting, but she considered it better to be safe than sorry. That meant getting her son away from the county and as soon as possible – she'd heard tell that Mr O'Connell was speaking early next week in Listowel.

Adjusting the collar of her gown, which did not require adjustment, she turned from the looking glass.

William Pembroke was standing, arms clasped behind his back, looking up at the portrait of his father.

She saw no point in prevaricating. 'I've had an advice about a pair of carriage horses for sale. Would you be kind enough to look them over?'

As he turned towards her, his lick of hair flopped down his forehead. 'Of course I will.' He looked at her closely. 'And might

I ask where those fine horses are?'

'In Ballinasloe.'

'Ballinasloe? That is deucedly inconvenient, Mama. Can't Paudge go?'

'No. He can't be spared. I believe they're matching greys, seventeen hands high.' She gentled her tone, as though taking him into her confidence, and touched his arm. 'You know how reliant I am on you and your brother to look after our interests.'

She liked to praise, to acknowledge her sons' strengths and to pay lip service to their abilities, but at the back of her mind lurked the worry of what might happen to the family, the businesses and the household if she did not oversee and control them with a firm hand.

'While you're in Ballinasloe,' she said decisively, 'which I believe is a charming town, I would like you to pay my respects to your father's cousin and his family.'

'But I have business at the shop that needs attending to — there's a consignment of silk expected. I can't leave Tralee for a few days.'

'Monsieur Aubin is more than capable. Isn't that why you employ him? You need to be on this evening's coach.' Her tone brooked no argument.

William pulled out his timepiece. 'That's ridiculous. The Bianconi will be leaving from Benners in less than two hours' time.' He looked at her accusingly. 'You want me out of Tralee? On this evening's coach?'

'Yes, I do. It's for the best.' She would not stoop to a blatant untruth.

'Well, if I go tonight, I'd like to spend some time in Dublin first. Visiting suppliers, checking out various drapers.'

'And why don't you invite Rob to join you?'

William brightened. 'I'll do that.'

'That's splendid,' she enthused. 'Dublin is a most sociable town in the winter. And from there you can go on to Ballinasloe. I'll send word to hold the sale of the horses until you arrive.' She would ensure that those horses waited for her son. The longer he remained in Dublin, away from the influences of Daniel O'Connell and his politics, the better.

CHAPTER 3

MARY WAS AWAKENED by a cry from the outshot at the back corner of the kitchen where her parents slept. The sound was quickly muffled. During the night she and her sisters had spooned in and out of each other, and their lumpy mattress of straw was moistly warm and treacly comfortable.

As she stepped onto the floor, her toes curling in protest at the chill of the packed earth, it was beginning to get light in that grey cloudy way of winter's dawn. It was during the few moments after waking when night blurred into day that she felt most alive, with her thoughts leaping over fragments of what the coming hours might bring – although the fragments of that day were not looking promising. The cry came again, muffled this time, but lingering for longer and it was followed by sounds of rustling and whispering.

By the window in the kitchen and lit only by a weak flicker of tallow, Willie was pulling on his pants. 'It's your ma. I'm fetchin' Mrs Tangney.'

Mary took the candle from him and pulled back the curtain across her parents' bed. The stump of guttering light showed her mother's eyes huge with fright and a pool of red saturating the straw.

'It's happenin' again, *a stór*. I can't lose this one.'

Mary knelt down beside the trestle bed and wrapped her arms around her mother. 'You won't, Mam. He'll be all right. You'll be all right. Da's gone for Mrs Tangney.'

'This one is difficult. Contrary.' From the first quickening of the child, she had never doubted but that she was carrying a boy. 'What o'clock is it?' Racked by another spasm, she lay back on the bed, her breathing ragged. 'It's gettin' light. You'll have to go to Annagh for me today.'

Mary wondered if her mother was *ráiméis*ing, spouting out wandering thoughts that had little meaning, in the way of some of the old people of the lanes.

Nora plucked at her arm. 'Tell Mrs Mac I can't be there – not with bleedin' like this. She'll know to make it right with the mistress.'

As the midwife arrived with an armful of fresh oat straw and an atmosphere of authority about her, Mary was walking down the dark nothingness of Brogue Lane, the early morning blowing icy in her face, her breath hanging on the cold air. Part of her was glad to be escaping the ordeal facing her mother, another part of her felt she should be by her side to offer aid and comfort. As it was, she knew too much about the process of making babies, carrying babies, babies who bled out, babies who came away too early, babies who, if God so willed it, were born and babies who if He so willed it died.

As she turned the corner into the treelined avenue the scattering of stars was fading and the darkness began to leach away into the lightening sky. She stood savouring the stretch of the Big House, looking at the long windows, wondering at life behind their panes of glass, imagining awakening inside such a house each morning.

With a shake of her shoulders she returned to the present and walked on up to the house. On reaching it, she halted. Where should she go? Well, not, she was sure, up those fine stone steps, or through that handsome red door with the brass knocker and the knob that was bigger than a man's fist. But there did not appear to be another entrance. Why hadn't she thought to ask Mam?

Two black dogs came bounding out from the shadow of the trees. When they saw her they skidded to a stop a few feet from her and stood, growling softly. A young man, swinging a stick, and wearing a flat brown cap pushed to the back of his head, followed through. At his command the dogs sat silently.

'Where should I go?' Mary asked him.

'Who're you here for?'

'Mrs Mac.'

He pointed with his stick towards the side of the house. 'Round the back and down the steps, girl,' he said, adding as he appeared to notice her hesitancy, 'You'll be all right. Mrs Mac's all right.'

Mary wrapped her mother's shawl more tightly around her, grateful for its musty familiarity. At her mother's insistence her rope of hair was tightly coiled under her bonnet.

At the bottom of the steps at the back of the house, she pushed open a heavy wooden door and found herself in a dimly lit, narrow passageway with light and sounds coming from an open area at the end. As she moved forward hesitantly, her eyes darting from side to side, her hands were clammy with worry of what the day had in store for her.

A fat woman with chapped red cheeks, wearing a voluminous apron, came towards her, 'And who might you be?'

'Mary O'Connor, ma'am. My mother is Nora. She sent me for the day.' This was Mam's friend, Mrs Mac, who ruled the kitchen. On occasions she'd met her with Mam around the town.

'Why? What's up?'

'It's likely her time is near come.' It was what her mam had told her to say.

'*Harrumph!* Well, I never.'

Mary felt herself being scrutinised with critical eyes.

'You've grown. No point putting you in the dairy – you wouldn't be able for it – they'll have to manage. Best I keep you under my eye in the kitchen.' Shoes clack-clacking on the hard floor and skirt whooshing, she clattered back along the corridor.

The kitchen was big, bigger than Mary imagined a kitchen could be. A wonder with two ovens built into the wall, as well as the familiar fire on the hearth with a cauldron hanging on a sturdy crane and a large blackened bastible pot to the side. The floor had red and black flags and the walls were the gleaming white of recent lime-washing. A long table of scrubbed wood took up the centre of the room and chairs lined the walls. It was a warm, comfortable place.

Mrs Mac stood her at the end of the table with a bucketful of potatoes and a rough brush with a wooden handle. 'But first fetch the water from the yard – Lizzie'll show you.'

Lizzie was a small, skinny girl, with a pale, freckled face. Without speaking, she led the way out a door and into a porch where she picked up two buckets which she handed to Mary. The yard was a big square of frozen mud. The iron pump-handle was so cold that Mary felt the skin of her hands stick to it. As Lizzie instructed, she filled the buckets to the brim and carried them, sloshing water, back to the kitchen, with Lizzie again silently leading the way.

'Scrub the spuds – no earth to be left on them, mind,' Mrs Mac ordered. 'And when you're finished rinse 'em in the yard.' Her instructions were delivered in a precise no-nonsense voice.

Mary set to her task, raising her eyes occasionally to watch the constant activity – people scurrying in and out through the doors of the kitchen, carrying dishes, mops and brooms, baskets of turf, bundles of laundry.

Mrs Mac's movements were energetic as she banged about the kitchen, seeming to be in three places at once, kicking closed the door of a cupboard, retrieving a ladle, stirring a pot all in the harmony of one moment, exploiting time to the limit, making it yield double.

She ladled out thick, creamy porridge from the cauldron, set the wooden bowls on the scrubbed deal table and added a jug of sweet milk before going to the back door.

Three farmhands and the young man Mary had met earlier entered so quickly that they must have been lined up outside. A few minutes later two young women wearing blue dresses and striped aprons, their hair tucked tidily into stiff caps, came in, followed by a tall, thin woman wearing spectacles, dressed in a grey gown.

They gave Mary curious looks but said nothing as they bent to their bowls, and the sound of silence in the kitchen was broken by the clatter of spoons and slurps of satisfaction.

So far the morning was turning out better than Mary had expected. Around the town she'd heard tales of the hardship servants endured in Big Houses. None of that was evident at West Villa.

When everyone was finished eating and the bowls were

stacked at the end of the table, Mrs Mac put her hand on Mary's shoulder.

'And this is Mary. Nora is her mam.'

'Is it her time?' whispered Lizzie.

Mary nodded. 'I think so.'

The young man she'd met earlier rose from the table. 'You're in a good place here, girl,' he assured her, his eyes crinkling in a friendly way.

'Paudge is a great one for the *plámás*,' Mrs Mac said with a smile as the door closed behind him.

'Does Mrs Mulchinock know about Mam?' Mary ventured after a while.

By then Mrs Mac was by the fire, lowering the rungs of the crane to bring the kettle nearer the flame. As she straightened up, easing her back with the flat of her hand, she looked square at Mary and spoke in a kindly manner. 'Don't you worry. That's for me to deal with in time.'

She put Mary working with Lizzie preparing vegetables for the midday dinner.

'Scrape the carrots, peel the turnips and parsnips,' Lizzie whispered, pointing to each as she spoke. 'Pass them on for cuttin' up – the way she has to have 'em.' She gave a little giggle and a nod at Mrs Mac. Despite her earlier attitude, Mary warmed to her when she whispered, 'It's not too bad here.'

''Tis only for a while.' Not for the first time Mary wondered at how her mam was managing. She offered a silent prayer for her safety and the safety of the baby. She hoped Mrs Tangney would stay the day with her. But such considerations had to be fleeting, as she wanted to concentrate on doing whatever chores Mrs Mac pushed her way.

'Them vegetables done yet?'

'Almost finished, missus.' Lizzie grabbed a carrot from Mary and chopped it into neat little rounds.

Mrs Mac left the kitchen and Lizzie sighed.

'It's way too busy here,' she said. 'With the mistress and the young masters as well as Miss Charlotte.' She leaned closer to Mary. 'She has a husband in Cork, you know, but she's here most of the time with her little uns. Nigh on two years now. Florence – the snooty one with the spectacles – does for 'em'.

Mary didn't know much about the workings of the household – her mother was close-lipped – and she was happy to let Lizzie prattle on.

Mrs Mac came back into the kitchen, carrying a bundle of linen.

'Stop the blather. Get on with it. Have ye them vegetables ready?'

'They're all done, missus.' Lizzie pushed the basin across the table towards her.

'Lizzie, show Mary how to hang the sheets on the line. Mind you keep them straight.' She turned to Mary. 'If your ma's not up to it, on the morrow be back here on time.'

And that was how Mary O'Connor became part of the life of West Villa.

CHAPTER 4

WILLIAM AND ROB took lodgings in Sackville Street, Dublin's main street, known to be the widest and most cosmopolitan street in Europe. As soon as they had settled in, Rob disappeared to call on a young lady he'd met while she was visiting cousins in Tralee over Christmas.

William went walking. He'd visited the city on many occasions and its sense of extremes never disappointed. Wandering down Sackville Street he felt hope in the air, and he heard the word 'Repeal' breathed on many a frosted voice. When he stopped to buy a jam puff from a street vendor, he was drawn into a discussion.

'Don't you think the Irish parliamentary doors will soon open again?' asked a stylish-looking man in a caped greatcoat.

'It all depends on O'Connell,' William answered.

'From what I hear, he's working tirelessly towards it. He's some man.'

The vendor clicked his tongue in disbelief. 'There's talk of money dribbling back into the country. That I'll believe when I see it.'

'Given time the commercial pulse of the nation will strengthen,' William assured him, moving away.

Up Rutland Square he paused in admiration of the elegant Georgian houses, with muted stonework, graceful fanlights and wrought-iron lamps lighting the outside of the elegant doors.

However, behind the Square he wandered the alleys that *The Freeman's Journal* described as 'some of the worst slums of Europe'. The backstreets were a maze of blackened brick tenements and dunghill hovels. He made a hasty exit from a small square where men were fighting with cudgels and backswords. From the look of them and the viciousness of their blows, they were prepared to fight to the death. And he'd heard that bullbaiting and cockfighting were commonplace, as were pillories and public hangings.

It might be wiser in future to venture into this part of the city in the company of Rob. A lone stranger could find himself in trouble. Best to have a trusted friend at his back.

❁ ❁ ❁

William had been with Rob O'Sullivan on the night when first they met Daniel O'Connell. They were drinking thick black porter in a dark, smoky shebeen up the Rock in Tralee – William in an attempt to drown his sorrows and Rob keeping a worried watch on him.

At the time William was so locked into grief at his brother's death that he hardly knew which foot to place in front of the other. Although expected from babyhood, Henry's death brought back the sense of loss he'd experienced when his father died – with that had come the realisation that life, as he knew it, was over, and his dreams for the future were forever quashed.

Some of the shebeen's occupants looked to be equally locked into their own thoughts, sitting silently and morosely, staring into their tankards as they drank. Others were holding grunting monosyllabic conversations and a small group clustered around the fire were asking questions and receiving answers from a large middle-aged man wielding an unlit cigar, sitting on a too-small stool and holding a tall hat on his knee. His voice, as far as William could hear, was rich, melodic and compelling. He, and it, seemed to be out of place in the impoverished darkness of the tavern.

'That fellow's talking politics,' Rob said.

William listened, his interest piqued when he heard the words 'Act of Union' and something about, 'moving the Irish Parliament to London'. His mother had a habit of cutting short any sort of political discussion and Edward was too fully occupied with the businesses to be bothered, but recently William had begun to wonder about what the future held for Ireland, and he had become interested in reading the political commentators of the time.

Tankard in hand, he stood and moved over to the fire, Rob following.

An elderly man, with rat-tails of grey hair escaping from beneath his cap, was addressing the big man. 'So what are you up to now?' he asked.

He answered firmly. 'I'm campaigning for the repeal of this union and hoping for the recreation of an independent Ireland governing itself, with Queen Victoria as our queen.'

'Is that Daniel O'Connell?' whispered Rob.

The man caught the whisper and turned around. 'Yes, it is. And who's asking?'

Rob and William introduced themselves and in no time stools were found and another round of porter ordered as they joined the group.

'I feel the country's getting behind me,' said O'Connell.

William felt O'Connell's comment was slightly hesitant, questioning, without presumption, and William liked the man all the better for his attitude.

But there was no tentativeness about O'Connell's companions.

An elderly man wiped the back of his hand across his mouth. 'I'd think so. With them monster rallies – upwards of 100,000 people, I ask you!' He looked around and gave a satisfied little nod.

O'Connell pointed his still unlit cigar nowhere in particular. '"Monster" is a ridiculous adjective. But …' And he laughed.

Another man with a cultured accent said, 'We're with you all the way in the fight for Repeal.'

William found himself nodding. He listened intently to the backwards and forwards of the discussion on the benefits of holding a series of what the men termed 'more manageable meetings' in the small towns and villages throughout Ireland over the next months.

As Daniel O'Connell rose to leave, he beckoned to William and Rob. Surprised, they followed him outside.

As the three of them stood talking in the dark murk of the autumn night, it began to rain. Under the black canopy of an umbrella that had materialised from inside, with the roar of rain bashing down on its flimsy structure, Rob watched William come alive again.

❀❀❀

As the days passed in Dublin, from their windows the friends watched the world go by: fashionable ladies promenading the treelined mall, children trundling hoops alongside nursemaids wheeling bassinets, pie men selling hot meat pies, knife-grinders, bootblacks and matchsellers.

In his heart William was a poet and since the death of his father the lure of rhyming verse had battled with his sense of family duty. Despite the attractions of the city, a day seldom passed when he didn't sit at the small desk he had placed by the window, dip his pen into the black ink and move it across the white paper. The words dragged along the page, read sluggishly and lacked the rhythm of his verses that had been published to acclaim in *The Nation*.

His grieved for the past, grieved for those times when his thoughts had flowed effortlessly onto the page. Too frequently he was visited by the bitter sweetness of ruptured dreams ... Papa ruffling his hair ... an important guest visiting ... Papa, standing proud, saying, 'Our boy was scarcely out of petticoats before his mother and I recognised his facility with words, verse in particular. He is the poet of the family – his talent is to be nurtured.' And Mama, smiling, always smiling, nodding in approval and agreement.

For as far back as he could recall, the nurturing of his poetic talent was built into the family's plans. And, to prove it, for his thirteenth birthday his father introduced him to Paris. William had never forgotten the magic of the cobbled boulevards, the high buildings with their stylish wrought-iron balconies and the smart carriages with rattling wheels and the clopping hooves of horses.

He had looked forward to reaching the age of eighteen when it was planned that he would live in Paris until duty called him to return to the management of West Villa. With Papa he had walked the stylish streets of the area of Saint-Germain-des-Prés. They agreed on the suitability of taking rooms on rue Bonaparte, perhaps, behind the high walls of one of those *hôtels particuliers*. When he said he would write verse during the day, and by night drink absinthe and discuss artistic philosophies with like-minded people, Papa threw back his head in laughter.

After his father's death his boyhood hopes and dreams floated away on the tide of grief as he was caught up in the management of the estate and family businesses. Little did he know during those early days that he'd be overseeing crops, dealing with cattle, checking on vines, trying his hand at whatever his mother suggested. Always functioning on the fringe of failure. Until the shop. He had succeeded there, made it his own, and he drew pleasure from sourcing, stocking and selling the best of beautiful merchandise.

❀❀❀

Ballinasloe and the horses waited as the friends sampled the delights of political and social life in the capital.

Rob was a man of the now, thumping up the stairs, calling to William with an invitation for this soirée or that entertainment in some of Dublin's grandest drawing rooms, confiding with unabashed candour about his conquests.

'I have met the most enchanting creature,' he announced regularly.

'Another enchantress? You fall in and out of love with alarming frequency.'

'You should try it.'

William nodded and laughed. Rob never tired of pointing out to him the languishing glances he received from pretty young ladies, but he remained impervious to their charms.

'Well, perhaps the fun of a little flirtation?'

William laughed harder, but Rob wouldn't desist. 'Some day I predict you will fall madly, blindly and passionately in love,' he said.

❀ ❀ ❀

At a reception in the Stephen's Green Club, Daniel O'Connell made an unexpected visit, accompanied by a coterie of prominent Dublin barristers and men of letters – supporters who brought further credibility and gravitas to his campaign for Repeal of the Union.

He entered the first-floor drawing room like a current of fresh air, his presence invigorating everything and everyone, brightening and quickening the atmosphere. Sipping from a glass of whiskey, he moved easily through the throng, with a word here, a joke there, a clap on a back or a touch on a shoulder.

The brilliance of the evening's conversation was like a shower of intellectual fireworks creating responsive sparkling in the laughter bursting through the cigar smoke.

O'Connell draped his arm around William's shoulder and whispered, 'Will you and young O'Sullivan step into the library in about ten minutes' time? In the meantime – enjoy yourselves.' He gave a roguish laugh before moving off as though there was nothing more on his mind than a pleasant evening of socialising.

William worked his way through the crowd towards Rob who was leaning against the wall casting smouldering glances at a young girl in flounces of pink.

En route, a smothering, mothering society lady, wearing a particularly livid shade of maroon, and well known for her penchant for young men, ensnared him. She had a tenacious grasp on his arm, a flirtatious look and a determination to have her say.

'It's amazing the way politics divert gentlemen from their normal interests.' Her voice was loud enough to draw knowing glances in their direction.

William cursed inwardly. The last thing he needed or wanted was attention such as this.

'And thank the Good Lord for that,' intoned her companion, Mrs Power, with a kindly look at William.

Mrs Power was a wealthy, childless widow who had taken him under her wing. She turned up regularly at entertainments and political meetings. He rather liked her. He enjoyed her easy company and the way she shared her admiration of Mr O'Connell with him, although he was cautious about his politics when conversing with her.

At last he escaped the women's clutches and, raising his eyebrows at Rob, he gestured towards the door. The girl in pink was forgotten as Rob joined him in the library which was packed with young men, many already known to them. All eyes rested on the imposing figure in the fashionable brocaded coat standing at the fireplace.

Daniel O'Connell's voice, modified to suit the room, was no less compelling than when he'd held in thrall the men, women and children of Tralee.

'I want it known that I wholly reject the use of violence in the pursuit of political objectives,' he declared.

With his barrister supporters he spent a short while with individuals, setting out his plans, offering suggestions as to how best rallies and meetings could be organised and mounted, stressing the importance of secrecy during the stages of planning, refining the meaning of Repeal so that everyone had an understanding of what with their help he planned to achieve.

William and Rob were to organise the rally in Tralee and at the same time to assist in promoting the re-election of Daniel's eldest son Maurice as a Member of Parliament for Tralee.

One of the barristers murmured, 'It's about time the power of the Denny family there was broken.'

Puffing on a generously sized cigar with a map of the town and its environs laid out on the table before him, O'Connell listened to suggestions for the site of the rally and shook his head after each one.

Eventually William said, 'Denny Street worked well in January?'

O'Connell smiled and nodded. 'Yes, that's the place. Take your time planning. A Saturday afternoon? Autumn, do you think? Remember there's a garrison of soldiers stationed in the barracks – they're an active presence and their officers are always spoiling for a fight.'

'I hear there's talk of the removal of the military and shutting up the barracks,' a barrister said.

O'Connell considered that with a frown. 'A population of some 11,000 inhabitants without a single soldier and a town left short of considerable income?'

'The police force is considered sufficient for any emergencies,' said the barrister, 'although no doubt it'll have an impact on the town's finances and I'm hearing talk of a shortage of about £12,000 a year.'

On a lighter note Rob assured them, 'The military have never troubled us – isn't that so, William?'

'Your families are not only important landowners – you also have commercial interests in the town,' said O'Connell. 'It's the peasantry we need to worry about. They have nothing and yet they have much to lose – they are the people you need to inspire.

And they still have the RIC to contend with.'

'Will you speak, sir?' asked William.

'I hope to, but if I cannot be there it will be up to you, the organisers, to bring the message to the people.'

William looked around at the gathering of young men – a good twenty by his count. 'I'm no politician,' he said.

'No politician, that is true,' said O'Connell, 'but I should say you're a more valuable commodity.' He cast William a look of considering fondness. 'You, young man, have a statesmanlike attitude. Ireland has a plethora of politicians – but our best men do not go into public life – we are represented by mediocrities.'

'So now it's up to you, William Pembroke Mulchinock.' Rob draped an arm around William's shoulder.

'No, it's up to you, Robert O'Sullivan. You've the gift of *plámás*.'

'Forget the jokes and *plámás*. It's truth that inspires. And I am relying on everyone here this evening.' O'Connell's eyes swept the four corners of the room before he snuffed out his cigar and left, with his bevy of barristers bringing up the rear.

Flushed with excitement at the thought of playing an active part in the politics of Ireland, William tried to assess the other men, his co-conspirators in changing the course of Irish history. If – no, *when* – the Act was repealed it would not only herald the end of the Irish tithe system, it would introduce universal suffrage and secret ballots for parliamentary elections. With the implementation of these changes, Ireland would be a different place – a place, hopefully, for the harmonious living of all creeds and classes of its people.

❀❀❀

In between political meetings and entertainments William visited several of Dublin's smartest drapery stores located along Grafton Street and Anne Street, and in a small establishment on Pembroke Quay he enjoyed a glass of Guinness porter with a young woman who did the most exquisite embroidery. He took copious notes and made little sketches of what he considered to be the most fashionable of gowns, paying attention to styles, shapes and colours and the use of trimmings.

He and Rob made a series of appointments with their tailor in Dame Street. William ordered a frock coat in black barathea, some waistcoats in the latest shades of brocade shot through with gold threads, three pairs of fashionably cut trousers in a pale colour and a new greatcoat in dark green, trimmed in velvet and with a caped collar. Rob's order was for half a dozen waistcoats with jewelled buttons.

CHAPTER 5

THE LINGERING SPRING FROSTS made life harder than usual. Morning after morning Mary rose before dawn. Well before anyone else was stirring she tiptoed across the kitchen. Using a small rake she tidied the embers of the previous night's fire, scraping them into a circle before setting down three fresh sods of turf which she arranged like spokes of a wheel, and stood quietly waiting for them to catch in the tentative way of turf. Before leaving for West Villa she would set a cauldron of thin oatmeal onto the fire so that when they woke the family could break their fast.

'Mary!'

Billy had come up behind her so suddenly that she jumped.

'There's something I have to tell you,' he said. 'It's bad.'

She straightened up and nodded, wondering what could be worse than their present situation and what had got Billy up so early – he was such a slug-a-bed.

'I saw Hannah yesterday.'

'How is she? Did you get talking to her?' From what she could make out in the gloom of dawn Billy's expression was sober.

'She weren't in condition to talk to anyone – limping something awful she was, and her face all bruises. She said not to tell you. But sure I have to. The two of ye were always so thick.'

'Was it Hennessey, d'you think?'

He shrugged. 'Who knows what that divil'd do?'

Mary had long been uneasy about Hannah. It was months since she'd had sight of her. She determined that she would make time to visit. First chance she got. And hope Hennessey would let her see her.

But even with the best of intentions days turned into weeks and she didn't get around to climbing the hill to the Hennessey cabin.

❀❀❀

Nora was no better or no worse, existing fragile as an injured bird, her belly growing larger by the day. Mary fretted about her: four of her last six carryings hadn't been born – well, not properly born, and the two who came into the world hadn't survived for more than a few minutes. The O'Connors were used to dead babies, but they were not used to their mother being so unwell.

Mrs Mac was full of kindly concern, asking after Nora, pressing an occasional round of bread or slab of currant cake on Mary as she left after the day. Mary suspected Mrs Mac's main anxiety was ensuring the smooth running of the household, and she understood that. She had become absorbed into the workings of West Villa, acquired the blue serge dress, striped apron and cap of the indoor servants, and she was growing proficient at meeting Mrs Mac's exacting, but fair, standards of household management. It was a comfortable house, and Mary grew to understand that when money wasn't an issue comfort was attainable.

The weather was so cold that year that the iron handle of the pump was frequently frozen and on a particularly frosty morning as Mary pumped up water from its source of darkness, the palm of her hand stuck hard to the handle and, already creased and chapped, began to bleed. She looked at it in dismay, wrapped her apron around it, and, ignoring the stains of blood, began pumping again.

'Here, let me do that.' It was Paudge, who was accustomed to walk through the kitchen and around the yard with an air of authority.

His movements were quick and economical and in no time the buckets were filled to the brim. As she bent down to take them, he reached forwards and picked them up as though they were thistledown and carried them to the porch.

On her way back to the lane that evening he caught up with her on the boreen and handed her a small earthenware pot covered with a circle of white linen.

'Goose fat for your hands. It'll heal 'em.'

Before she had a chance to reply, he whistled to his dogs and turned back towards West Villa.

❀ ❀ ❀

Mary pushed in the door of the cabin with a heavy heart.

During the hours of her absence at West Villa her mother always appeared to have grown frailer, her father more silent,

Billy more restless and Brigid and Ellen unhappier. And the midwife, Mrs Tangney, knees splayed, would be seated by the fire, nursing a proprietary air about Nora and the unborn baby. Although Mary was grateful for the way she cared for her mother, she was relieved to have the door closed behind her each evening and was always pleased to see the back of her.

'What has you crying?' she asked her sisters as she unwrapped her showl on an evening when she was back earlier than usual and grateful to be inside. The wind was wet-lipped, howling around the cabin, gusting down the chimney and hurling rain against the windows.

'It's her.' Ellen pointed at the door through which the midwife had left. 'She tells us awful things.'

'Like what?'

Brigid's defiant head-toss didn't hide the quiver of her lips. 'About a gentleman what lives in a fine house. When he has company he makes bold children dance on red-hot sods.'

'In their bare feet.' Ellen eyes were huge with fright.

Brigid spoke slowly, quietly – she had a good way with words. 'She says we're bold.'

Mary stood her sisters in front of her, out of earshot of her parents. 'Don't you be minding Mrs Tangney's goings-on. Sure isn't she one of the best storytellers around? Her guff is only stories.' Keeping her tone light, she succeeded in calming them, although she was outraged at the midwife's insensitivity.

'Not bold?' asked Ellen. 'Are we?'

'No, Ellen. You and Brigid are the best girls ever.' In the circumstances she justified the fib.

The child looked at her dubiously. She wasn't used to being called a 'best girl'. 'So we wouldn't ever have to dance like that?'

Mary ruffled her hair, 'No. Never.'

'Is that what gentlemen do?'

'No, Ellen. Gentlemen don't have children dance on hot sods.'

'Even with shoes?'

Mary was exasperated. 'No. That's just one of Mrs Tangney's silly stories.'

'Does she have to be here?'

Brigid and Ellen only ever referred to Mrs Tangney as 'she'.

'If she wasn't we could sing stories to the babby with Mam.' Brigid had another thought. 'Does Mam always sing to the babies before they come out? Did she do it before I came out of her?'

The child looked so vulnerable, so wishing.

'I believe she did,' said Mary. 'Mam likes to sing.'

Their mother had a fine voice, but Mary had not previously heard her sing to her unborn, and these days she was uneasy at the faraway expression on Nora's face as she stroked her belly and crooned.

'While she's here, we can't sing.'

'For now, Brigid, Mrs Tangney needs to take care of our mam, but only until the baby comes. And I promise she won't tell you any more stories.'

They nodded, their small faces solemn.

❀❀❀

Over the weeks the family waited and there were many false alarms and certainties that the birth was imminent, but they came to nothing and an air of expectation permeated the four corners of the cabin.

On an evening when wave upon wave of wind battered the cabin, Mary was sitting on the bed holding Nora's hand. She had become the strong one of the family, the one who had outside work and wages – small but regular. Spending time with her mother gave her time to think, allowed her thoughts to roam backwards and forwards, and being at West Villa was opening her eyes to possibilities.

The lanes had a hold over their inhabitants. No doubt of that. The cabin with its heartbreak of dead babies was home, and the history of Brogue Lane was buried deep within Mary, a bloody splinter in her soul – residing there as though by some ancient force, strengthening her feelings of love and compassion for her parents, sisters and brother. But none of that prevented her from hoping. The thought grew and lingered that she could better herself. She was certain of it. Be a teacher? Introduce children to learning? She wasn't sure of how or in what way that might happen, but Mr Foley should know.

The storm rattled on, pausing for a time, then beginning again. Smoothing back the damp hair from Nora's forehead Mary murmured softly, assuring her that all would be well.

Nora touched her belly, 'He's taking his time, this one, but Mrs Tangney says it won't be much longer.'

As a new spasm took her, the air was punctuated by splintering cracks of thunder. Mary held her hand tighter, rubbing gentle comfort until the pain passed. Keeping time with the claps of thunder the spasms advanced and retreated, as though this child was deciding to come into the world, then deciding against it. Mary suspected that was not usual. But then, as she knew, there was nothing usual about her mother's babies.

'Is there anything I can do?'

'No. Nothing, *a stór*. It will be over soon. Just you look to the others.'

Mary blinked back her tears, her heart stirring with compassion and pity for the lot of her mother. Without comment or complaint, Nora bore child after child. Unlike the women of the lanes who dropped their babies shouting, screaming and cursing their menfolk, Nora's birthing was done in silence.

❀❀❀

The O'Connor child was finally born with a bellow at about ten o'clock on a frosty night of black ice.

Nora's face was wreathed in happiness, the difficulties of the carrying and birth forgotten.

Willie looked as though his heart might burst with excitement, nodding and smiling with each bellow. He had the well-pleased look of a man who had succeeded in his Catholic duty of fathering another son. He held the featherweight child delicately, out from his rough shirt, cupping his tiny frond-like fingers in his immense palm.

Mary was weak at the knees with gratitude. The baby was born. A son and robust of voice.

'We'll call him Liam,' Nora said, reverently taking back her child. In readiness she'd had Mrs Tangney lay strips of old sheeting, salvaged by Mrs Mac from West Villa's linen cupboard, on the bed. Centering the baby in the folds of the material, Nora wrapped him loosely, rejoicing in the flailing movements of his tiny arms and legs, gazing in awe at his button nose and rosebud lips.

'*Come and see!*' Willie called out to the children. 'Before I'm off out to wet the babby's head.'

Ellen and Billy pushed through the curtain, looking solemnly excited. Brigid followed them, her face scrunched up in that grumpy way of hers.

'Do you want to hold him?' Nora asked Mary.

'Yes.' It was a reluctant affirmation squeezed from between Mary's lips. With the birth of the baby she realised that her hopes of bettering herself were reduced – in all likelihood snuffed out. When her mother returned to work in the dairy at West Villa, she would be back in the lane raising the child.

'Let him rest with his mother for a while.' Mrs Tangney determinedly held on to her air of authority. 'And he's to be swaddled.'

'We'll swaddle him later.' Nora handed over the bundle of baby to her eldest daughter.

The tiny, defenceless baby touched Mary in a way she hadn't thought possible and didn't want.

As Mrs Tangney clucked disapproval, she missed the look of love, understanding and compassion that crossed between mother and daughter, but Willie caught it and he was warmed by it.

Mary's expression softened at the way the baby rested in her arms, and she pressed her lips to his forehead. She had never imagined herself with child … but holding this wee fellow …

Then, as he moved his legs and balled his little fists his breath stuttered – fluttered like a weak candle flame before stopping.

'*Oh, no! Please God, no!*' The cry burst from Nora.

Mary was puzzled. She held out the bundle. 'Mam, he's not …'

'Hush, give him to me.' Nora reached towards Mary.

But it was Mrs Tangney who took the child. She held him upside down by his legs and smacked his bottom. Once, twice, three times. Except for the sound of the smacks, the small space was full of silence. Then she laid the baby on the end of the bed, held a finger to its neck, turned around and shook her head.

Nora's cry was one of raw grief that echoed off the walls of the cabin and spun out into the lane.

'I'm sorry, so sorry,' Mary said.

Nora's words of comfort were bleak. 'It isn't your fault, *a stór*.'

'He's gone to God,' said Willie in that pious way of his.

'Some God!' Nora said bitterly. 'That has women go through the bearing and birthing of a child, and then to take him.'

'Hush, don't talk that way.' Willie made the Sign of the Cross.

'It's the only way I can.'

Willie stared the wall.

Brigid and Billy looked with round-eyed hope at their mother, as though she could make things right.

Unchecked tears ran down Ellen's cheeks.

Mary averted her gaze to the floor.

The O'Connor children were young in years, but they were old in knowledge. It had happened too often – babies hoped for, but not born properly – not like this one – this was a proper baby. They knew babies brought additional hardship – less food, less space and all that went with poverty – but babies brought happiness too.

They stood fidgeting, unsure of how to react to the drama of birth and death in such quick succession. The atmosphere in the small stuffy space was potent with grief.

'God help us all.' Mrs Tangney made the Sign of the Cross. 'In the name of the Father, Son and Holy Ghost.' She heaved a sigh, 'Sure 'tis the will of God. His will. He'll bless ye with more. Aren't ye young enough and strong enough, yet? Sure haven't ye plenty of time?'

Mary wanted to slap the woman her across her mouth to shut her up. She was the midwife. She should know better. She had been privy to Mam's lost babies who were little more than lumps of raw liver, delivered the dead babies that looked perfect, and babies who died as soon as they were born. But what did she know of true grief? Nothing. All of her ten babies had not only survived birth and childhood but they were growing into healthy adults.

'*Away out, all of ye!*' Willie suddenly yelled.

Mary shepherded her brother and sisters away from their mother. It was better to have them out of the range of such naked sorrow.

Mrs Tangney lingered beside Nora, her black apron enveloping her plump figure. Rummaging deep in the recesses of its pocket she drew out a small bottle with a plug of cork that she eased off with her thumb and forefinger. She tipped some of the liquid into her palm and using the fingers of her other hand she incanted a sorrowful prayer as she sprinkled drops over Nora who was too locked into her cocoon of sadness to pay attention.

'What're you up to? *Out! I said out! Get out!*' Willie spoke more sharply then he intended and pushed her away from the bed.

'It's holy water from the holy well. And I'll baptise the wee lad … just in case …'

Willie raised his hand as though he might strike her, but then stepped back and, shoulders slumped, said, 'Well, get on with it so.'

Mrs Tangney bent over the baby, shook a few drops of water over his head, made the Sign of the Cross on his forehead and incanted, '*I baptise thee, Liam, in the name of the Father, the Son and the Holy Ghost.*'

She reached into the bed, picked up a small square of linen and, expertly juggling child and cloth, wrapped the baby. 'I'll look after –'

'No. You won't. Give him here.' Willie's voice was rough with emotion.

With a crimp of her lips she handed over the baby, looked from Willie to Nora, shrugged and scuttled out.

When he and Nora were alone, Willie knelt by her side and reached for her hand, but she turned away from him and scrambled towards the wall as though she wanted to disappear into it. Their tiny son lay abandoned at the end of the bed in the tussle of soiled sheeting.

Willie looked at the child with dread. What he had to do wasn't easy. It never was. Previously he'd wrapped what had come away early from Nora in the paper that came with his supply of best leather. At night when he was on his own, he'd burned the parcel at the back of the fire. For a long time afterwards he'd be haunted by the crisp white of the flames as the paper caught light and the blueness as they reached upwards, as well as the crackle and crunch of devouring heat. Up to now he'd allowed Mrs Tangney to deal with the babies that were full term.

But not this little fellow. He couldn't hand him over to her.

Something had changed in him. And it frightened him. The fire was gone from his loins. For some time past he'd no longer wished to draw comfort from Nora's body. No matter what that banshee of a Mrs Tangney said, he believed Liam was the last child he'd sire – perhaps it was his punishment for his fondness for the drink.

He reached into the bed for the child, lifted him out and held him against him, this time cradling him awkwardly and closely against his shirt. As he stood lost in helplessness with his son, Mary pushed back the curtain.

Her eyes were red from crying, but she carried two mugs wafting the steam of strong tea. She was a good girl. He said nothing as she balanced the mugs on the narrow shelf by the bed. He handed her the baby. 'Take him away outside. I'll be out after I give this to your mother.'

Nora took the mug from him. 'Keep him near us, Willie. Don't send him to Rath.'

Willie nodded. 'I promise. He won't go to the cemetery.'

The kitchen was cloaked in despair. There was something about this baby that had touched each of the O'Connors in different ways. Perhaps it was as simple as the crooning certainty of their mother that a life would be born.

Standing with her back to the fire, Mary held the child close. Already he was growing cold.

'Come, Brigid and Ellen, look at him. He's lovely.'

'I don't want to. He's dead.' Brigid's lip curled.

Her head down, Ellen sidled up to Mary. She was crying softly, each sob a tiny hiccup that shook her narrow chest, rocked her little body and made it hard for her to breathe. She put a small grubby hand on the baby's wrapping.

'Why did he die?' she whispered.

Brigid answered, 'Because God wanted him. That's what they say. What they always say whenever a baby dies. And Mam's babies always die.' She turned back to the table and with an arc of her arm swept the learning slates to the floor.

Billy surveyed the broken slates in dismay. 'Wait 'til Da sees what you've done!'

'I'm sorry, I'm sorry. Don't tell. Please.' Brigid hurled herself at Mary, grabbing her skirts, almost toppling her over.

'Sure won't he see?' said Billy. 'He's not an *amadán*.'

'Hush, Billy. Give Brigid a hand to gather up the broken pieces and take them away. *Do it now*.' Mary's voice rose sharper than she intended. Her father had enough to bear.

The night through the small window was black dark, that impenetrable darkness in which the moon was no more than a blurred coin of sad light. Sitting in the sagging chair, holding

Liam close to her chest, Mary rocked backwards and forwards, willing God to rebreathe life into him.

Willie rested his hand on her shoulder, his touch unfamiliar and unexpected. She was unused to him showing his feelings.

She turned to look at him and by the flickering light from the fire she saw his tight-lipped grief, and air of hopelessness. This was a night bleak with sadness. Willie took his hand from Mary to touch the baby – his finger tentative, unsure.

Billy shifted from one foot to the other, Brigid chewed on her thumbnail while Ellen wove a short length of string in and out between her fingers.

Mary tightened her hold on the child. 'What'll you do with him, Da?'

Willie was a small, bandy man, but as he squared his shoulders he seemed to straighten and to grow in stature. He looked around, his gaze lingering on each of his children in turn.

'Ye all know I have to deal with this. And I will.'

He walked the few steps across the kitchen and lifted the lantern from its hook, lit it and left, shutting the door carefully behind him. Next came the crunch of a tool being removed from its resting place against the wall, followed by the sound of dragging footsteps as he moved away from the yard and out of hearing.

Collective breaths were drawn in the kitchen.

Ellen dropped the string and knelt by Mary's side. She poked a gentle finger at the baby's cheek. 'He's lovely, isn't he?' she whispered.

Mary rested her hand on her sister's head. 'Yes, he is,' she whispered back.

'What'll happen him when he goes to God? Do you know?'

Mary bit back the standard answer of the baby being with

God, and Jesus loving him. 'I don't know. That's up to God.'

'It's not bloody good enough,' announced Billy, savouring the English swear word which in other circumstances would earn him a clip around the ear. 'The boys are right.'

'Don't, Billy. This is hard enough for Mam and Da. It's hard for all of us. The quicker tonight is over the better.' Mary stood up, awkward with the bundle of baby, and faced Billy. 'Who are these boys? And what do you mean about them being right?'

The hardness of Billy's expression was new. 'The Whiteboys,' he said, 'and they're the boys to enforce justice for the little people of Ireland.'

Enforce justice! Mary's heart curled in fright at the mention of the dreaded Society. And the implications of Billy being involved.

Willie came in from the dark, his boots rimmed with icy mud. Without a word he took the child from Mary's arms and disappeared back into the night. For a moment through the open door the gleam of the moon and a star or two lifted the blackness, but nothing could lift the air of hopelessness in the cabin.

CHAPTER 6

MRS MULCHINOCK CHECKED her appearance in the looking glass in the hallway. She made a minor adjustment to her bonnet, picked up a folder of papers, nodded farewell to the portrait of her husband and hurried down the steps to her carriage.

She was going to the County Court House, to a committee meeting about the Poor of Tralee, chaired by the Provost. In the folder was a list of ideas and notes that she'd drawn up. As she sat back, listening to the clip-clop of the horses, admiring the fresh greenness of the hedgerows rich with birdsong and the way the sunlight danced off the leaves, she was remembering ...

❀❀❀

Her beloved Michael had shared every aspect of his life with her — it was unexpected that a husband would, and it hadn't been that way with her father and mother. For her part she was interested in his many ideas and plans for the working of West Villa, interested in the family's commercial interests in the town and in the activities of the town itself. She participated in the more mundane aspects of his daily life and was a willing listener, soaking up his hopes and dreams and mixing into them ideas of her own.

And she had plans, carefully laid plans that she kept to herself until she was satisfied with every detail. Only then did she call to his office, a small, characterless room situated at the back of the dairy. She was on official business and there was a new sense of purpose about her every movement.

He looked up with a welcoming smile. She knew he enjoyed being surprised by her and her occasional midmorning teabreaks. But instead of being accompanied by one of the serving girls carrying a tray, she came alone, holding a sheaf of papers.

'If you're not too busy, I'd like to talk to you?'

'Never too busy for you, my love.'

She came around to his side of the rent table and spread out the papers.

'You're a good teacher, Michael Mulchinock, and I've been thinking.'

He looked at her fondly. 'Thinking?'

'Yes. Thinking that if we grew barley and oats in the top fields, instead of potatoes, we could export. Get some of our tenants to help with the planting and harvesting. The English are paying top prices for quality grain.'

'We can't leave our tenants short. Their diet is mostly made up of potatoes.'

'We wouldn't. They could still grow their potatoes and have a bit of an additional income. Last year we grew way too many potatoes. And it's not the first time the surplus rotted.' She handed him a sheet of paper with lines of figures in her neat writing.

He studied it. 'This is certainly worth looking into. You never cease to surprise me, Margaret.' He put an arm around her waist. 'Any more plans for change?'

She looked around the bleak space. 'Yes.'

He threw up his hands in mock horror.

'Instead of working here, why don't you use the parlour? It's so much more comfortable.'

'But that's your room.'

'Yes. And we'll work in it together.'

Margaret found a new fulfilment, attending local fairs where she and Michael bought and sold livestock, reorganising the vegetable garden, laying out a flower garden and creating a comfortable home – as well as taking a lively interest in the welfare of their tenants, encouraging them to learn to read and write, to send their children to school, and setting up linen-making and weaving for those who were interested.

❀ ❀ ❀

'You are becoming quite the businesswoman,' Michael remarked one morning as they made their way back to the house from the dairy, having sampled the latest batch of cheese.

She laughed at the idea of being called a businesswoman.

As they crossed the yard, Mrs Mac came running out to meet them.

'Ye have a visitor.'

'Who is it?'

It was unusual to have an unexpected caller so early in the morning.

'It's Daniel O'Connell himself, sir.' Mrs Mac was all smiles.

Michael looked at Margaret with raised eyebrows.

'I've put him in the drawing room.'

'Thank you, Mrs Mac,' said Michael. 'Will you kindly tell him we will be with him shortly.'

Margaret turned to Michael. 'I want to change my gown.'

'And I'll get my coat.'

Standing with his back to the fireplace Daniel O'Connell cut an imposing figure, but he was all smiling affability as he greeted them, the hugeness of his personality and the command of his presence dominating the room.

Margaret gestured to him to be seated and he sank back into one of the sofas, comfortably crossing his legs, while she and Michael sat opposite him on matching upright chairs.

'Will you take tea?' she asked.

'Thank you kindly, but I won't. Not this morning. I'll come straight to the point. I am here to ask for your help and support in my campaigning for Catholic Emancipation. I have –'

Michael raised a hand. 'My wife and I know and admire what you're doing for Ireland. And what you've achieved. We're honoured that you've considered us. But campaigning for you would a big decision for us. We would be obliged if you would allow us time to think it over.'

'Very well.' Daniel O'Connell rose to his feet. If he was disappointed at the outcome of his visit it was not obvious. 'I wish you good day and thank you for your time. I shall await your answer.'

Michael and Margaret walked him through the hallway to the front door. They watched as he went down the steps, and for a man of his bulk he mounted his horse nimbly. With wave of his arm he was away, galloping down the driveway.

'That was unexpected,' said Michael.

'Yes. Most unexpected and I'm glad you asked for time.'

'There's no stopping his campaigning. He's a good man with the best interests of the country at heart, and he has the Duke of Wellington and Sir Robert Peel on his side. We'll give it thought for a few days, but I consider it better not to become involved in the quagmire that is Irish politics. Our family never has.' Michael spoke firmly, stating his position, before asking, 'What do you think, my love?'

'I'm inclined to agree with you. In public Papa claimed to be apolitical, but in private he held strong opinions on the disruption to the country caused by politics.'

'So we are agreed? We'll continue to stay out of politics in public – whatever our opinions may be in private?'

'Agreed.'

And that is what they 'regretfully' conveyed to Daniel O'Conell about their position.

After the death of her husband, Mrs Mulchinock passed no comment on the Whiteboys, even to her children. And God knows she had reason to, as all the evidence pointed to members of that society being responsible for her husband's untimely death.

When Michael's horse had returned without its rider to West Villa a frantic all-night search was instigated, but he wasn't found until the following morning, lying half-submerged in a watery ditch, and three days later he was dead from a fever. During the hearing the magistrate decided that Michael Mulchinock Esquire had been thrown from his horse. According to an eyewitness who refused to be identified, the animal was frightened into rearing by a band of marauding young men with blackened faces and white shirts.

His burial in the graveyard on a bleak November morning was

etched on her soul and the heartbreak of her keening remembered for many a day by those in attendance.

During the lowering of the coffin and the lonely sound of the scattering of earth on its lid, Edward stood beside her, impassive. On the way out from the graveyard he took her arm. It was an unexpected gesture as he was the least tactile of her children. She put her other hand over his and gave it a little squeeze.

'Mama, I'm not returning to the Academy.'

She stopped walking and turned to look at him.

His eyes narrowed. 'I am needed in our businesses. I see no point in spending any more time learning Roman history and parsing French verbs.'

She hadn't thought that far ahead, hadn't thought how she'd keep going, but, despite her firm belief in the importance of education, Edward's announcement gladdened her. Unlike William and Henry he was not academic but, as he had proven time and again, he had an instinctive grasp of business matters and a love of the land that bordered on the obsessive.

That evening she took down the journal Michael had gifted her and ran her fingers across the cover of green-tooled leather. At the time she'd laughed as she opened the package he'd ordered from London, saying, 'I have no need to write down memories – as long as I live I'll not forget.'

And she wouldn't forget – but writing what was in her heart might ease the pain of hatred, and her loathing for the Whiteboys Society, a pain that was too deep-rooted even to share with her confessor. In her neat hand she wrote on a thick creamy page towards the middle of the journal: *Whiteboys: an organisation whose stated purpose is to protest against unfair landlords but who seem little interested in anything but violence. They roam the countryside, their faces blackened, wearing white shirts over their outer garments – they are murderers, more involved in crime than causes.*

She sobbed until she could sob no more. And then, enveloped by the dark hopelessness of her life, she retired to her bedchamber and refused all contact.

A few days later Mrs Mac knocked on the door. When there was no reply she opened the door and stepped inside without invitation. She carried a pot of steaming beef tea, and a cup and saucer of the finest china. She set the tea on a small table, then fussed around the room, opening the shutters, tending to the fire.

All the while Margaret lay on the bed, keeping her eyes tightly closed, feigning sleep. She was pleased to hear the opening door heralding Mrs Mac's departure.

But, before she stepped out into the corridor, Mrs Mac turned around. 'It's time to get up, ma'am. The place, the children and the business all need attending to. And Master John has called to enquire about you on several occasions. All the way from Cloghers House he came.'

Close as Michael and his brother John were, and kind and pleasant as John was, it had never been Michael's wish to have him involved in their businesses, and she would adhere to that. She was fond of her brother-in-law and admired how efficiently and capably he ran his businesses. The thought that, out of the goodness of his heart, he might consider taking over what she and Michael had so carefully built up and nurtured was the impetus that had her throwing back the bedcovers and placing her feet on the floor.

She stood up shakily, stripped off her nightgown, had a quick wash in cold water, buttoned up her bodice, stepped into fresh pantalettes and laced her corsets before putting on her new mourning gown of unflattering black bombazine. She dressed her hair in a perfunctory manner and added a small plain cap before hanging her bunch of keys around her waist. Then she went down the stairs and into the parlour.

She unlocked the bookcase, took out the pile of ledgers and opened the one on the top of the pile. The last entry was in Michael's meticulous, upright writing. Seeing it was nearly the undoing of her, her thoughts separating, falling off and away from her, but she pulled herself together and ran her index finger slowly and lovingly over the debit entry, whispering, '*I will*, Michael. *I will* follow our dreams.'

And she started there and then by prioritising jobs appertaining to the various businesses, making 'To Do' lists in her precise writing. After an hour she sat back. She had to get on with life as best she could. She had to push the sadness to the back of her mind, but she also had to hold close to her heart memories of the love she and Michael had shared.

It had been Michael's idea to set up a drapery shop on the Mall, and shortly before his death he had acquired a building of old staircases, twisting corridors and dim corners. Despite her lack of knowledge of the clothing industry, she decided to implement his plan, as a memorial and in honour of him. She'd carry out the minimum of renovations, install a few young girls as sales assistants, take advice on stock and hope for the best.

The realisation that the success of the family and their thriving businesses rested on her shoulders sharpened her attitude and rendered her rigidly determined. She was swift to put down her elegantly booted foot when she considered it necessary, as was the case with William Pembroke.

'There is no easy way to say this,' she said to him softly as they walked through the small copse of copper beech trees, 'and I am sorry, but despite your very obvious literary talents and the plans your father and I had for you, living in Paris can no longer be countenanced. You are needed here.'

He flexed and closed his fingers, stopped walking and looked at her the way he used to as a small child when he wanted her to make something right. 'What about Uncle John?'

His voice was hopeful, but when she turned to look at him she saw that his eyes were bleak.

'What about him?'

'Well, he's Papa's brother ... perhaps, he could ...'

Her voice softened further – she was killing his dreams and it was breaking her heart. 'No, son, we must look after our estate and businesses, and leave Uncle John to his.'

She knew that a part of her eldest child died that afternoon. She also knew that he was aware of his position as eventual heir, and she would make sure that she prepared her children for the carrying out of the duties attached to their station in life. She would ease him in gently, giving him charge of the gardens and the glasshouses.

Some days later, heavily veiled and dressed in the deepest of mourning, she had the carriage drive to the bottom of Ballyard Hill. Accompanied by her four children, she walked deep into the back laneways of the town. They were slick with dung, soot hovered in the air and the smell was of cesspits and rotting fish. Raucous women screeched, men slumped against walls, barrow-boys with jaunty caps and bold eyes swaggered, but the worst and most enduring sight of all was a young boy scooting along on stumps, reverting to fists and back again to stumps, all the while humming some happy-sounding tune.

West Villa's tenants had always been well cared for, but it was a different story for too many of the people who lived in the town.

During the particularly harsh winter of 1828 with the added misery of a poor potato crop, Michael had said, 'Our business interests are turning a goodly profit now, and I believe it's our duty to care for those less fortunate souls in the town.'

She had agreed without hesitation, 'There's much to pity.'

'We should draw up a list of families.'

'I already have.' She moved some papers on her desk and located the single sheet on which she had listed twelve impoverished families that needed clothes, food and boots.

'I should have known.' His smile was affectionate. 'But I'll deal with this. The lanes are no place for you.'

With his death the lanes became yet another place for her, and from her first visit there she had determined to take Michael's place on the committee for the Poor of Tralee.

At the end of a particularly narrow alleyway a woman in a filthy frilled cap, stationed in a darkened doorway with a knot of children behind her, stepped out, blocking their way, accosting without words.

Mrs Mulchinock nodded, touched her shoulder. 'I don't believe we've met?'

The woman's eyes narrowed. 'No, ma'am, but me cousin works in your dairy.'

'Ah, would that be Nora O'Connor?'

'You know her?'

Mrs Mulchinock inclined her head graciously and asked after the woman's children, how many, what ages, were they healthy and did her husband have work? As she spoke the woman's attitude thawed somewhat and they parted affably.

Mrs Mulchinock was aware of her children's differing reactions to the misery of the poverty they'd seen that afternoon. William was curious – it was obvious from the intent way he had watched and listened to the various exchanges. Shoulders hunched, Edward had turned away to face a stone wall. Charlotte too had stood aside, distancing herself, and had given a few sniffs – but Henry had remained by her side.

As they moved off, Edward said, 'Really, Mama, you come up with the strangest ideas of how to pass an afternoon.'

She rounded on him. 'There is much to pity in these lanes. Tomorrow you and William Pembroke will call on that family with food and clothing. I suspect all is not as well as she makes out. Kerry people are proud – they may hide their hunger and poverty, and the terrible diseases that inflict them. Typhus, diphtheria and cholera are everywhere. And it is beholden on people like us to give.'

She gave and continued giving. It was the way she was.

❀❀❀

The memories continued rolling until the carriage drew up at the Court House.

As she went up the steps, a cold February sun was shining. She paused by the side of a young woman leaning against the wall, with a child by her side. The woman looked at her in mute appeal. Mrs Mulchinock moved her shoulders uneasily inside the warmth of her fur-trimmed cloak as she took in their shivering appearances.

'Go out to the house,' she told the woman. 'Tell Mrs Mac I sent you and ask her to give you food and clothing.' It wasn't the first and it wouldn't be the last time she'd made such a gesture.

The meeting convened slowly and, when called upon to speak, she stood up, looked around the richly panelled meeting room and at the prosperous committee members, all men.

'Our town has a population of about 11,000 persons. Too many of them are starving, their children growing up never knowing a full belly. We need a workhouse where they can find refuge and be cared for.'

She felt her plea was heard, given due consideration and noted in the minutes of the meeting, but on the way out the Provost took her to one side.

'Your idea is worthy, m'dear, but with talk of the military withdrawing from the town we won't have the funding for a workhouse.'

Her disappointment did not deter her. She would continue to implement the plans that Michael and she had made with such hope and optimism.

❀❀❀

On one of the first warm days of the summer, she sat reluctantly at her desk checking figures – she kept a close watch on the finances of each business. Easing out the tightness in her back and shoulders, she stretched her arms above her head and, taking a moment's respite, she looked out the window and saw Charlotte sitting tucked away in a corner of the garden.

When she opened the door and called out to her, she watched as her daughter rose reluctantly, dragged slowly along the path and entered through the glass door.

'What is it, Mama? What do you want?'

'You're idling while everyone else is busy.'

'I'm not idling, I'm reading a novel.'

'It's the time of year when there's much to done and every pair of hands is needed. It'll likely rain later and Mrs Mac's jelly needs potting.'

'You expect me to scythe, Mama? Or to watch quinces dripping through muslin?'

'If you choose to remain here rather than return to your husband, which is where you should be, you must contribute.'

Charlotte's face crumpled, and unchecked tears spilled down her cheeks. From babyhood whenever she considered she was being thwarted she had a habit of dissolving into easy tears. 'Are you trying to get rid of us?'

'West Villa will always be your home.' That was both a diplomatic and a true comment.

Charlotte dabbed at her eyes and blew her nose. 'I presume you've something in mind for me, Mama?'

Until that moment Mrs Mulchinock hadn't considered how her daughter's general lack of ability could be best employed but, inspired, when she spoke it sounded as though she had thought the matter through.

'Yes. I have. You can help out in the soup kitchen.'

Charlotte bit her lip and looked wary. 'I don't think so, I don't believe I could ...'

'Now is the time to learn. I will leave the matter in your hands. We can discuss the details later.' She was pleased at how decisive she sounded.

'But there's Anne and Margaret ...'

'Yes, and you have employed Florence to take care of them.'

By then Charlotte was redfaced and outraged. 'I suppose I must.'

'Yes, you must.' Her confirmation brooked no argument.

Like the proverbial duck to water, Charlotte adapted to the soup kitchen and to everyone's surprise, herself included, she became a well-liked presence.

❀ ❀ ❀

Life continued. Paperwork was the bane of Margaret Mulchinock's life. Daily, to keep abreast of it she needed to spend several hours at her desk. Over the past decade the businesses had thrived. They included a prosperous farm with fields set in oats and barley, most of which went for export; a modern dairy; a herd of rare *Buinín* cattle, indigenous to Kerry; vegetable and flower gardens; a hardware store on Castle Street and the drapery shop on the Mall.

She had found a solution for the struggling drapery shop more by accident than design. After William Pembroke had failed to find his feet in other areas — the dairy, the gardens, the cattle, the crops — she had finally lost patience and castigated him for his incompetence. As a last resort she had put him in charge of the drapery shop, almost as a punishment for his 'misdeeds' and, to her surprise — and his — he found his forte.

She wished happiness for her children and she sought to accommodate their differing personalities. She didn't like to admit it and would never do so publicly, but William Pembroke was her favourite. From the dawn morning when he had slipped from her body and into her arms, it had been so. While she didn't doubt his love for her and she was aware of the satisfaction he drew from management of the shop and his well-received verses, he had an air of lonely restlessness about him.

After his father's death, his devastation was inconsolable. It was heart-breaking to see her once lively child so listless, so disinterested, head down, hands shoved in his pockets as aimlessly he roamed the house and grounds or sat by the range in the kitchen.

That situation went on for seemingly endless months until the morning when Henry, delicate from birth and regularly laid low with fevers, followed her to the kitchen. As she was discussing the week's menus with Mrs Mac, Henry limped up to where

William Pembroke was sitting in the old *sugán* chair. He squashed in beside him and rested his head on his chest.

'The poor craythur. He'll be all right now,' Mrs Mac had decreed with a nod.

And he was.

When Henry was well enough, he and William Pembroke played ball, spun tops, flew kites and rode together; times when he wasn't so strong they played games of chess, read and swapped secrets. Often Rob O'Sullivan from the neighbouring demesne joined them for much-argued sessions of croquet and cards games that ended up more fun and repartee than competitive.

Henry's death turned time back to the days after Michael's death. But by then she was stronger, better able to cope, to keep a brave face for her family and friends, and there was no keening from her at the graveside. But on many an evening she joined Mrs Mac in the kitchen and they sat companionably together, the firelight flickering, Mrs Mac's knitting needles clicking and her occasional murmur of 'God rest the poor wee craythur' bringing a modicum of comfort.

Mrs Mulchinock shook her head and looked down at the spread of ledgers. Rambling thoughts. Daydreaming. Although, frequently, it was during those times that she was visited by her best ideas.

As she set about itemising lists of goods for payment, a light knock on the door of the parlour was followed by a thump and the door swung open.

Her eldest granddaughter stood on the threshold, a red-faced tiny figure of indignation.

'Grandma, I hate Florence. And so does Margaret.' The child had never been a shrinking violet about her feelings.

'Anne, you mustn't hate anyone. And you know you shouldn't

leave the nursery. Florence will be so worried about you.'

'No, she won't.' The seven-year old advanced confidently into the room, her hands clasped into tight balls of little fists swinging by her sides. She gave her grandmother a considering look. 'She hates us too.' Adding, 'Margaret says she does.'

Mrs Mulchinock resisted the urge to laugh at the thought of her sweet little namesake, all of five years of age, having such strong feelings. From babyhood Anne had been determined and strong-willed in a way that made it impossible to ignore her.

From Charlotte's occasional comments about the lax attitude and disinterest of their nursery maid, Mrs Mulchinock suspected the child might be correct – although it was unlikely she was right about the 'hate'. She sighed. She did not relish further involvement in her daughter's problems.

Anne perched confidently on the arm of a chair, her hair unkempt and her boots unbuttoned. Swinging her legs backwards and forwards, she looked around the room, her eyes darting hither and thither. Eventually she nodded approvingly. 'It's nice here, Grandma. Nicer than the horrid nursery.'

'Back you go, young lady.' She spoke sternly, ignoring the child's look of disappointment. 'And I expect you to behave yourself and to be good for Florence.'

As the door closed behind the reluctant child, she picked up her pen again.

The complexities of running the family's various businesses and her children and grandchildren kept her occupied during daylight hours. But nights were the loneliest of times. Sleep became an extraordinary state where parts of her brain seemed to rest and other parts worked busily, setting out lists of what was necessary that she hadn't been able to sort out in the daytime.

But, now, those bills demanded her undivided attention.

CHAPTER 7

WILLIE STOOD UP and thumped his worktable. He flattened his skimpy fringe of hair against his forehead, his habit when addled, rammed on his old felt hat and went out into the laneway.

He wondered would Nora ever be herself again.

A tankard of porter would help his thinking.

He had waited a goodly while after Liam's death before trying to talk to her about Mary, remarking on several occasions, 'It is way beyond time she was wed.'

But Nora had refused to be drawn. Turning away from him, her answer was always the same, 'Lave it for now, Willie. There's plenty of time.'

He had been remiss about letting the matter drift, but now he was determined to negotiate a good marriage. He had a few prospects in mind, but he wanted to talk them over with Father Sheehy. It didn't do to rush something as important as the making of a match – such matters were better served with detailed planning.

Last year he had avidly followed the negotiations Mr Cluskey made for his daughter, although he was taken aback at Nora's violent opposition to young Hannah marrying Mr Hennessey.

'It's wrong, tying her to that old man.'

He had sought to soothe her with, 'That remains to be seen. All this going-on about love is nonsense. The best marriages are ones of compatibility.' The word 'compatibility' rolled off his tongue with fervour. He didn't like seeing Nora upset, although he was consoled by Father Sheehy's assurance that women weren't logical and didn't have the type of minds suitable for negotiating.

In the end, despite Hannah's tears, ranting, objections and protestations of her love for young Danny Stack, she had married Mr Hennessey. And rightly so, Willie thought. He considered it a good match. His Mary was beautiful inside and out. Even he, her father, was aware of the effect she had on those she came in contact with. If it wasn't for Nora's attitude he could have the matter dealt with and Mary married. He should have no trouble negotiating a good bride price for her.

❀ ❀ ❀

Through the open half door, Mary saw her mam sitting at the table, head bent. Seeing her looking so vulnerable gave her an uncomfortable feeling and she lingered outside, reluctant to disturb her, or to have to face into yet another problem. Mrs Tangney puffing up the Lane changed her mind and she darted inside.

'Are you all right, Mam?' Mary unwound her shawl.

Nora lifted her head from her hands. 'The lot of women. And it's all before you, *a stór*.'

Mary put a few leaves of tea into the teapot and wet the tea. She gave the pot a good shake and stirred the contents with the handle of a handy knife before pouring and passing a cup and saucer to her mother.

'What are you up to at all? Tay and the good delft off the top shelf?' Nora, taken by a fit of coughing, rooted in the pocket of her apron for a scrap of cloth that she held over her mouth.

Mary sat opposite, warming her hands against her cup. 'Why not, don't we deserve it? Mam, is everything all right?'

'Why wouldn't everything be all right?'

'Because it often isn't.' Mary's reply was bold

Her comment jerked Nora to awareness. 'You've changed since you've gone to the Big House.'

'Of course I've changed. I'm seeing a different life, a life I didn't know existed.'

'A lot of good the seeing of it'll do you.'

'No harm knowing there's a better way of living to be had.'

'For them that can have it, I suppose. But it's not for the likes of us.'

'Oh, Mam. Why not? Why shouldn't we be able to make our lives even a little easier?'

Nora moved her shoulders in an agitated sort of way and gave a click of annoyance. 'I'm quite out of sorts.' It was an unusual admission for her to make.

A child every year or two was the lot of most of the women on Brogue Lane. 'Steps of stairs' Mary had heard the schoolmaster say – not that any of the families had stairs in their cabins.

'You wouldn't be out of sorts if you weren't constantly carrying and dropping,' she said.

'What do you know about it? It's a woman's lot. Always has

been and always will be.' Nora pursed her lips. 'I don't know how I'll manage without you when you're wed.'

Mary laughed. 'You needn't worry. I've no plans to be wed.'

Nora took a sup of tea. 'Your da says you and your ideas will be the death of us.'

'Well, whatever Da says or doesn't say, your lot won't be mine.' Her voice firm, Mary looked squarely at her mother.

'God help you, but it will. Your father is looking to make a match for you within the year.' Nora reached across the table and rested her hand over her daughter's.

The shiver of something crossing her grave ran up Mary's back. 'I've told Da I've no wish to be married. I'll not be married off like Hannah. It's wrong, Mam, that daughters scarcely more than children can be wed to old men for the sake of money, land and livestock.'

'It's the way of life. Always been so and always will.'

'No, Mam. It's not. And it shouldn't be.' Her face flushed, Mary leaned forward. 'Under the old Brehon Laws women could choose who they married and they were equal to their husbands. They could own property. Be physicians, scholars and lawyers. And not only the gentry.'

'You can't change the way things are.'

'I can, Mam. Given a chance I know I can.'

'How can you change anything, *a stór?*'

'Teachers can inspire change.' She threw her arms wide and high above her head and laughed. 'I want to be a teacher.'

Nora closed her eyes, as though to shut out what she was hearing. Willie was right about the schoolmaster filling Mary's head with nonsense. Her daughter, a teacher – a *múinteoir!*

When she opened her eyes again they were bright with tears. 'Shush, *a stór*, no good comes from that sort of talk.'

❀❀❀

As the O'Connors rose from their knees after finishing the nightly ritual of the Rosary, the Sorrowful Mysteries that evening, Nora kissed the crucifix tenderly and Willie made an extra solemn Sign of the Cross.

Then there was a rap on the top section of the half door.

Mary pulled back the flap.

'*Dia dhaoibh* – God bless all here,' Father Sheehy peered into the kitchen.

When Mary opened the lower section of the door, he stepped in briskly.

'*Dia is Muire dhuit* – bless you too, Father,' Nora and Willie chorused.

Nora began the bustling that was her form of hospitality and put the kettle to boil, while Willie drew out a chair, gave its seat the swipe of a cloth and gestured to the priest with a grandiose wave of his arm.

Father Sheehy sat down heavily. He was a corpulent man with a bulbous nose and pale-blue eyes.

He looked around the kitchen. While it was clean as could be, thanks he was sure to Nora's insistence and Mary's industry, the smell of the poverty without lingered, heavily and oppressively. He noted that the few good dishes were stored on the top shelf of the dresser, the lower shelves cluttered with chipped, everyday mugs and bowls. The drawers burst with odd spoons and knives. Buckets and basins, stained with use, rested at the base of the dresser. The food press and meal bin were wedged into a corner – he guessed that they were seldom used as the O'Connors, like most of the families in the lanes, lived a hand-to-mouth existence.

His gaze lingered on Mary. 'Well, Mary, we'll be looking for a husband for you any day now.'

Mary tossed her head, tendrils of hair working loose from their tidy confines of the morning. 'No, *we* won't.'

Father Sheehy's lip curled. He read Mary's emphasis on the word 'we' as brazenness. Young Mary O'Connor was getting above herself – she'd had that trait since she was a wee one. And, now that she was off working at the Big House, he feared for her mortal soul. She was too lippy and forward for a girl and she had too many ideas and opinions. That's what came of a bit of learning and coming under the influences of the gentry.

'Willie, you and I'll have to work on a match for Mary. It's about time she was in the care of a strong man.'

Mary gave another toss of her head. 'I wouldn't want ye to waste yeer time. I'm in no hurry to marry. Perhaps I'll never marry.'

Willie clenched his teeth and tightened his lips. 'We'll discuss this another time, Father,' he said, as loftily as though it were a parliamentary matter.

'A strong man, indeed!' Mary said. 'I have no need for either of ye to choose a husband for me.'

Nora caught a hold of her arm and whispered, 'Don't be going on so – don't say anything more, *a stór*.'

'Father will take a little sup, Mary.' Willie looked towards the priest, 'Right, Father?'

The priest nodded in a pleased way. Willie had an air of expectancy about him and Nora looked worried, but Mary scotched any thoughts they might have had about the jug at the back of the cupboard.

She stood, straight, formidable. 'Mrs Mulchinock takes her tay black. Without milk or sugar. She says the taste is purer. Will you try some her way, Father?' It was more of a statement of fact than a question.

It was obvious from the priest's moue of disgust that he'd prefer something stronger, but he answered in an affable way. 'Thank you, I will so.'

While Mary tended to the making of the tea and took down the willow-pattern cups from the top shelf of the dresser, the priest asked Ellen and Brigid about their schooling.

'It's all right,' Brigid said. 'We're learning money sums.'

'Sometimes we sing,' Ellen said.

The priest leaned towards Willie. 'I often wonder what is the point of education for young lassies. All young girls need is the ability to satisfy their husbands, rear the children God blesses them with and keep house.'

Mary slapped down a cup and saucer before the priest. The cup was half full of pale amber liquid. Weak it might be, but hot judging by the steam rising from the rim.

The priest looked at Billy who was sitting by the fire, flexing his fingers. 'Billy's grown to a grand lad,' he complimented. 'Any day now you'll be taking him into the business, Willie.' He took a sip of tea. 'That reminds me. Boots. Any sign of them?'

'Yes, Father, just a final bit of stretching and they'll be ready. Comfortable as a pair of slippers they'll be.'

'There's nobody can turn a pair of boots like you. You've a name for it not only in the town but about the countryside too.'

Arms on her hips, Mary looked down at him. 'Da was showing me the leather for your shoes. It's soft as velvet – there'll be no stopping the style of you.'

The priest didn't comment, taking another sip from the cup.

'He got the leather for a good price too,' Mary went on, 'and if you talk to him nicely he'll likely give you a bit of discount.'

Nora's breath caught in her throat.

Willie stared at his daughter.

Father Sheehy dabbed at his forehead with a square of snowy white linen. He turned away from Mary and looked at Willie. 'Should I offer you a little on account?'

Before Willie could say yea or more likely nay, Mary answered, 'Yes, Father. Times are hard, and even with me at West Villa it's difficult to make ends meet.'

With all eyes on him, Father Sheehy reached into his side pocket and pulled out a tan leather purse which he placed on the table. 'How much?'

His displeasure was obvious from the tightening of his lips and the unflinching way he stared around the kitchen, but nobody said anything. All eyes rested on the purse.

'Why don't you pay four shillings now,' Mary said slowly, 'and when you collect the boots you can pay the balance.' She suspected Father Sheehy was getting a bargain.

The priest reached for the purse and opened it with a loud click. Slowly he extracted three coins, plucking them delicately from the interior with thumb and index finger. One by one he laid them on the table. 'I'll leave it at the three shillings. And pay the balance later.'

Willie averted his eyes.

The priest got up and the family all rose to their feet.

At the door, he turned back and looked at Willie. 'And as soon as you have this pair for me, I'll be ordering another. And so will my curate.'

Willie nodded. 'Thank you, Father.'

The priest went to leave again but did an about-turn back into the kitchen and pointed his index finger at Nora. 'And isn't it about time you were churched? Your purification and the blessing of God would benefit the whole family.'

Nora bit down on her lip.

The priest set his hat firmly on his head and pushed out the door.

There was a thick silence in the kitchen, broken only by Nora moving around the cups and saucers on the table until Willie turned on Mary.

'How dare you disrespect me in front of the priest!'

'It is you who disrespect us. From the sounds of it willing to give him his boots without proper payment.' Mary spoke slowly, enunciating each word. 'You are worthy of his money. You put in the hours. He's not short and we are. He should pay you a fair price and if you ask for it he'll respect you all the more.'

Willie drew in a tight breath, stared at Mary through narrowed eyes, and with a slump of his shoulders muttered, 'I doubt that would earn his respect.'

CHAPTER 8

WHILE MARY WAS WALKING back from West Villa the rain that had drummed down all day finally stopped, leaving the fields a soggy grey as the watery sun slipped below the horizon. Her boots were clogged with mud and the hem of her skirt crusted with more mud.

'*Mary!*' a voice called.

At the sound of her name she stopped and turned around.

'*Wait! Wait for me!*' Panting, Danny Stack came to a running stop a few feet away from her. 'I saw you from the top field.'

'Danny! How are you? How've you been keeping?' In truth she was shocked by his appearance. In the bedraggled young man before her there was no sign of the handsome youth of less than a year ago.

'How's Hannah? D'you know?'

There was an air of desperation about him, one of pleading too. He was thin, stick-thin, his trousers held up by a thick belt, twig-like wrists sticking out from his grubby shirt. He looked as though he hadn't had a decent meal or a good night's rest in an age.

'I don't know, Danny. I don't see her and more's the pity. I miss her so.'

From the look of him Danny had gone through enough suffering without telling him about the state of Hannah when Billy had seen her.

Danny moved closer, grasped her sleeve. 'You have to get a message to her.'

His intensity was scary.

'I don't know that I can. Anytime I've called, Mr Hennessey sends me away and from the look of him he'd like to give me a belting with his stick.'

There wasn't a glimmer of reaction from Danny at the idea of Hennessey hitting Mary. 'You have to.' His eyes burned with passion.

'I'll try, Danny. Do my best. Come and have a bit of supper with us this evening?' With a few spuds and a drink of buttermilk inside him he might be calmer.

He shook his head. 'Nah — I won't. But thanks. Just go an' see Hannah.'

'What d'you want me to say?'

'Tell her to be ready to leave.'

'Leave? Leave Mr Hennessey? She can't. She's wed to him!'

He nodded. 'She can.'

'Danny, you can't.'

'It's the only way. I should've never let her go.'

'You'd no choice.'

'Get her to meet me in the usual place on Tuesday at six o'clock. I'll wait every week until she comes.'

Mary frowned. 'Tuesday?'

'It's when Hennessey meets his cronies in that place up the Rock. They play cards and drink.'

'Danny, are you sure? Mr Hennessey isn't a man to be trifled with. What if he finds out? It's Hannah, not you, who'll pay the price.'

But Danny wasn't interested in listening to reason. He touched a finger to his forehead. 'Thanks, Mary. I'll never forget this. Hannah and me'll never forget.' He jumped over the low hedge and, fleet of foot, ran across the fields back the way he'd come.

'Be careful! Don't do anything!'

A blackbird soared upwards on a thread of song and her words were whipped away on the evening breeze.

The usual place … That was the fairy ring with its sentinels of hawthorn bushes where Mary used to keep watch while Hannah and Danny met. Those meetings occurred little more than a year ago, but the memory belonged to another life – when Hannah lived four cabins down the lane from the O'Connors. For as long as Mary could remember she and Hannah had been part of each other's lives.

Mrs Cluskey had pointed features and a hacking cough and Mr Cluskey was a herring-thin grump of a man. From babyhood Hannah, their only child, was a mischievous beauty with a wild streak.

The girls spent most of their waking hours together – after school doing the household necessities in O'Connors' and then playing hopscotch, hopping from one square to the next. Or they skipped – with one end of a rope tied to a stake, they inveigled whoever happened to be passing to turn the other end. Jumping high, with whirling hair and fluttering skirts, their feet thumping the dust, chanting at the top of their voices '*Eeeny, meeny, miny, moe* ...'

When they were older, arms encircling waists, they'd walk together to Clahane of a summer's evening, to the dance platform. From a distance wafting on the breeze they'd hear the lilt of fiddle music and the thump of dancing feet, and Hannah, lifting her skirts, would run towards the sounds.

She moved with abandonment, her head thrown back, her sheet of hair the colour of autumn chestnuts touching her waist, as she danced 'The Walls of Limerick', 'The Siege of Ennis', jigs and reels, her feet thumping in time to the primitive beat.

Mary was without Hannah's uninhibited ways, although she was the one both young and old men watched.

On their way back to the lane by the light of a wide-awake moon, the nights would be cool rather than cold, the girls' shivers an automatic reaction to the steps of the dances, the notes of music and the boys who tried to steal kisses from them, as well as to the glitter of moonlight on the fields and the stars pricking sharply through the darkness.

When Hannah and Danny met their attraction was instant, and their love for each other grew boundless. He was a handsome youth with an air of success and a pair of flying feet on the dance platform. They courted in secret for the best part of a year during which time, unbeknown to Hannah, her father was brokering a match for her with the widower Hennessey.

Once Hennessey got the idea into his head of making Hannah his bride, the romance between her and Danny was doomed. Shortly after his second wife died he put his eye on Hannah, and he watched, patiently biding his time as she blossomed into womanhood. He wasn't the type of man to stand for having his prize plucked from him by a young spalpeen like Stack.

If he was a day, Jamie Hennessey must have been sixty years of age, and his lameness checked each step he took like the jerk of a chain. But he knew what he wanted and bald-headed he went for it, and he had grown the reputation of being a man it was better not to cross. He owned land set in oats and barley, a three-roomed cabin, several pigs, a goat, some hens and a milking cow, and every now and again he'd mention his 'interest' in the business of shoemaking, Cluskey of course being a shoemaker.

When Mr Hennessey and the matchmaker called to the Cluskey cabin, Mr Hennessey carried a jug of poteen and a determination to begin the process of brokering. Despite not having a farthing of a dowry for Hannah, Ben Cluskey knew from the way Hennessey cast his eyes around and licked at his lips how much he wanted his daughter, wanted her so bad that he, her father, would be able to drive a bargain in his favour. Best of all, though, was the knowledge that Hennessey had the money and the willingness to pay for her.

The deal was the talk of the lanes and beyond. Cluskey boasted to anyone who'd listen and most did, especially Willie O'Connor who hoped to learn a trick or two about brokering an equally financially beneficial match for Mary.

From her parents' whispers Mary picked up on the negotiations – her father rubbing his hands at the amount of the bride price Hennessey was rumoured to be willing to pay – her mother silent, until her opposition to the match burst from her in a most uncharacteristic fashion.

No matter how often Mary warned her of what was happening behind her back, Hannah would throw her arms wide and laugh at the idea of being wed to old Hennessey. 'My da wouldn't do that to me.' Hannah was like that, disbelieving of anything she didn't want to hear.

'It's no joke, Hannah. Your da was in with my da and I heard them talking. Better you and Danny speak to him before it's too late,' Mary urged.

When Danny finally called on Mr Cluskey his linen was fresh and his hair combed. He spoke of his love, promised to care for Hannah and asked for her hand in matrimony – yes, he actually used the word 'matrimony'.

Mr Cluskey remained seated by his hearth and heard him out in silence – he had not invited him to be seated. Hannah stood alongside Danny, proud, with flushed cheeks. Mrs Cluskey sat in the corner and coughed and coughed.

As Danny finished speaking Mr Cluskey stood up, threw back his shoulders, stamped his feet and spat out the word '*Love!*'. He said a match had already been made for his daughter and he forbade Danny to have anything more to do with her. He finished by telling Hannah to 'Get out and go see to that hen that's on the cluck!'

Hannah continued to meet Danny in secret and Mary watched out for them. But as the time drew near for the bride price to be paid over, Hannah grew more and more distraught.

'Tell your da you won't marry Hennessey – run away with Danny,' Mary urged.

'I can't. Da says we're blessed to have someone like Mr Hennessey wantin' me, savin' him and Ma from the side of the road.'

On the evening when the match was to be finalised, it was growing dusk as Mary pushed through the door of Cluskeys' cabin. Hannah was bent over the cauldron of potatoes, her face hot from the flames, the hem of her skirt dribbling in the ash. Her feet were bare, her features set and stern in a way that no young girl's should be.

Her father snapped, 'Clean yourself up, girl. They'll be here soon.' When Hannah didn't react, he roared, '*Now!*' Seeing Mary, he scowled. 'And you. *Out.* There's no place here for you.'

Hannah stepped away from the pot of potatoes, put her feet into a pair of boots drying by the fire and lifted the lantern off its hook by the door.

'What are you doin'?'

Hannah looked levelly at her father. 'To see to that hen. If I don't, nobody will. Come, Mary.'

'She'll hold till the morrow.'

'No. She won't. She'll be gone off the cluck.'

'Get cleaned up and dressed.'

'I'll do as I am. Good enough for that auld man.'

In the yard the girls turned right along by the low wall, ignoring the clucking, scratching and the soft ruffle of feathers, moving slowly until they came to the place where the yard dipped down towards the stony field with its scattering of spiky hawthorn trees.

The October evening was cool and a full moon crept sinister shadows over the spindly branches and scarce foliage. People were nervous of the power of the hawthorn, full of superstition and piseogs about the revenge of the fairy people. Not Hannah though. This little clearing was the place where she'd known love.

A low whistle answered Hannah's one. She lowered the lantern to the ground and Mary watched as she moved towards the sound. A figure emerged from behind a nearby tree and came running towards her. They embraced, Hannah's head falling naturally to Danny's shoulder, his arms tight about her slender figure.

Eventually they drew apart. Mary, watching out from the brow of the field, released her breath. In the black stillness of the night lit by moon shadows, the intensity of feeling between them heightened the enormity of what lay ahead for Hannah

Mary had always noticed that whenever Danny looked at Hannah the light of love shone from his eyes. She knew that it was love, the way things should be between a lad and his lass who wanted to be wed.

Her heart coiled with fear as she remembered how she and Hannah had gone over the terrifying story of the Blasket Island girl. That young girl was promised to a widower with land, but she and the schoolmaster had fallen in love. When her father found them lying together in the bracken, he dragged them apart. Her uncles held the man down while her father tied her hands behind her back, carried her to the shore and put her face downwards in the bottom of a currach. He rowed out into the Atlantic with her uncles following in another boat. Some distance from land, he took the oars and crossed over to the currach manned by his brothers.

Hannah liked to believe that by some miracle the girl was saved, but Mary pictured her face down, hands bound, rocked by the waves and chilled by the wind until death.

A swaying lantern emerged from the cabin and Mr Cluskey's roar of '*Get back in here, girl!*' echoed on the night air.

Wanting to alert Hannah, Mary moved closer to the copse of hawthorns.

Danny was speaking, pleading. 'Has he made his final bid?'

Hannah's voice was barely above a whisper. 'I don't know. I haven't seen him. Oh, Danny!'

From listening to her da Mary knew that Mr Hennessey and Mr Cluskey planned to 'consolidate' – Hennessey's word – their shoemaking businesses. They'd had discussions on getting new customers and there was talk of 'investment money', no less, coming from Mr Hennessey's son who was an important man in America. Loftily, when they'd a few sups taken, they'd expound on how the traditional business of shoemaking was fast changing.

'To think, Danny, this is our last time ...' Hannah's voice was reduced to the softest of whispers floating on the breeze.

Mary didn't want to listen, but she couldn't stop. She was part of their heartbreak. Every shadow threw a scare into her and she was fearful of what the night would bring. One way or another, she knew enough about the ways of the time to know that no good could come of whatever decision was made.

'I shouldn't be torturin' us with last looks and kisses,' Hannah whispered.

Danny turned his head sideways and pressed kisses into the chestnut of her hair. 'You said you'd run away wi' me.'

His voice had risen and Mary held her breath in frightened anticipation of them being discovered.

'That was afore the roof went. Afore the agent said we had to pay more rent. And Mam's coughin' blood.' Her voice too had risen.

'*Shush! Careful! Ye'll be heard!*' Mary's warning was a hiss.

Danny drew Hannah back into his arms and held her face upturned to the moon. For him it was simple. He loved Hannah and she loved him. No matter what the circumstances, they should be together.

But Hannah was weighed down with daughterly responsibility.

'I'm sick at the thought of you being bought by old man Hennessey.' In a swift movement Danny drew her closer to him and kissed her hard. 'I can make a bid for you. Bid thirty pounds, I can.'

'Thirty pounds! Where did you get it?'

'Don't matter. It's enough that I have it.' He patted at his chest.

'Oh, Danny, I can't. The thought of my marriage has lifted the dread from Mam's heart.' With a banshee of a cry Hannah raised her skirts and ran, gasping and staggering, up to the break in the wall, and back onto the lane.

At the time it was whispered around the lanes that even if Hannah's father got her as far as the church, she would run to Danny from the altar before the sacrament of matrimony was carried out.

But she didn't. Wearing her Sunday gown, she knelt without moving throughout the ceremony. When it was over she walked unsmilingly down the aisle, slightly ahead of her new husband, with her hands clasped so tightly by her sides that her knuckles showed white.

After the marriage, neither bride nor groom was seen around. The men sniggered about old Hennessey being busy and if Mary was within earshot she glared in their direction.

Some weeks after Hannah was wed, as there was no word from her, Mary walked to the fourth cabin down the lane. She rapped on the door, her knuckles resounding on the wood. After what seemed an age, Mrs Cluskey opened the top section, but only the merest crack.

'*Dia dhuit.*'

Mary's greeting was answered with a fit of harsh coughing. 'Who are you? What do you want?' She peered at Mary uncomprehendingly as though she'd never seen her before.

'It's Mary, Mary O'Connor. I'm wondering how Hannah is?'

'She has a husband now.'

'I know. Mr Hennessey. But have you seen her? D'you know how is she?'

Another spasm had Mrs Cluskey backing into the darkness. Mary waited. After what seemed an age, she returned. She leaned out towards Mary, looking up and down the lane, and her cheeks were damp.

'Don't know. Haven't seen hide or hair of her. She's wed a while now.' She brought her lips together in a tight line, as though stemming her flow of words. And with that she slammed over the upper half of the door.

On several occasions Mary had trudged up the slope of the hillside to Hennessey's cabin that was more than three times the size of any of the cabins on Brogue Lane, but each time he had turned her away. He looked older and more repulsive than she remembered and her heart grieved for Hannah and Danny and what might have been.

❊❊❊

As Mary walked up the hillside evening sunshine cast long shadows from the trees and hedges bordering the sweep of the mountain, and a blue-and-silver ribbon of a narrow stream curled and looped, threading its way across the stony fields. Mrs Cluskey had been laid in the ground the week before. She left life as she had lived it, without fanfare. No wake and a skimpy funeral service where Mr Hennessey had kept a hand clamped to Hannah's arm.

When Hannah opened the top of the half door, her eyes widened in delight and her smile was disbelieving. Putting a finger to her lips she stepped outside and closed over the door carefully, soundlessly, before clasping Mary to her in a quick hug.

'Come quick! He's nodded off.' She grasped Mary's arm and pulled her into the yard behind the cabin, scattering hens and ducks as she stepped over the low stone wall. They sat on the grass, their backs against the wall, as they had on so many other times against so many walls, in so many places.

Neither spoke until they spoke together.

'Mary!'

'Ah, Hannah!'

Mary's heart was breaking at the unfairness and cruelty of life.

'Are you all right, Hannah?' She was relieved to see there was no sign of bruising.

Hannah pulled a *duidín* – a pipe – from her pocket and sucked on it, unlit, as Mary had often seen the old women of the lanes do. Mary didn't know whether to laugh or cry.

'He beats me. When he says I misbehave. *Misbehave!*' Her voice rose on the word. 'I hate him.'

Mary remained silent. Better silent than saying the wrong thing. Eventually she said, 'Danny wants to see you.'

Hannah jumped up, her face breaking into a smile, her eyes sparkling. 'Danny, *mo chroí!* How I want to see him. Not a day passes when I don't think of him, wished I'd run away with him that night. But I couldn't, you know I couldn't.'

She sat down again and Mary put her arm around her shoulders. 'You did what was right at the time. That's in the past. What's done is done.'

'Now that Mam is dead I want to see Danny. And right this minute. But how can I? I'm a prisoner. He keeps me a prisoner. Never lets me out of his sight. Locks me in when he goes out.'

A rough voice called out through the upper half of the door, *'Hannah, Hannah! Where the divil are you?'*

Hannah put her finger to her lips, *'Shush!'* She stood up. Her delight had vanished, but there was a new sense of purpose about her.

'Danny wants you to meet him in the usual place on a Tuesday. At six o'clock – the first Tuesday you can make it,' Mary whispered, pulling on Hannah's skirt for emphasis, the way they used to when they were girleens. She wasn't sure if Hannah heard, as Hennessey was slapping his stick against the door.

'*Hannah – by God – get back in here! I'm warnin' you!*'

'*I'm comin'. Hold your whisht! I'm out lookin' for the eggs!*'

Hannah's voice rang loud and clear, and, Mary was consoled to hear, it was without fear. Hannah gave a little skip, wrapped her arm around Mary's shoulders and whispered into her ear, 'I'll do it. Break down the door if I have to. Tell Danny I'll be there. Six o'clock. First chance I get.'

Without a backward glance she stepped over the wall, leaving Mary to make her way down the mountain by crawling along the lee side. She was a long way from the Hennessey cabin before she dared to stand up.

CHAPTER 9

AS WILLIAM WAS CONSIDERING it was about time to part from Rob, take his leave of Dublin and undertake the journey to the West, they received one of the coveted invitations to attend at the Viceroy's 'Drawing Room'.

Since the 1600's Dublin Castle had been the focus of Anglo-Irish hospitality. It was where the most powerful of the Ascendancy class were entertained. The six weeks preceding St Patrick's Day on the 17th of March were known as the 'Castle Season'. This was when the Viceroy resided in the Castle along with his personal staff, chaplain, gentlemen-at-large and aides-de-camp. The festive splendour of those weeks was said to surpass the best of London's ceremonial celebrations.

Well in advance, the hotels and boarding houses in the city were booked out, and on the evening a stream of carriages and jarveys conveyed the invited guests to the Castle where windows blazed with light, staircases and corridors were dressed in scarlet

and banks of spring flowers filled every gap. The ascension of
Queen Victoria to the British throne four years previously had
brought a feeling of hope and a new lightness to the celebrations.

Nearly a decade ago Charlotte had been one of the debutantes,
and up to two years ago William, Edward, Henry and Rob had
attended, with Edward insisting it was the perfect place to broker
business deals, exchange commercial gossip and inveigle
introductions to the most marriageable of the debutantes.

'If your philandering with young matrons becomes public it
won't endear you to prospective fathers-in-law,' Rob had said.

Edward turned on him. 'I plan to fulfil the Mulchinock destiny
by marrying a suitable wife, as will William and Henry.'

'And what's a suitable wife?' Rob asked. Turning to William,
he laughed. 'And how do you feel about fulfilling this destiny that
Edward has mapped out for you?'

William shrugged – along with the power of the land, talk of
family destiny was one of Edward's favourite conversations.

'Tell me more, Edward,' Rob goaded in his humorous way.
'Go on – about your suitable wife.'

Edward took himself seriously. 'She'll be from a wealthy,
Catholic, landowning family. And I expect William Pembroke and
Henry to make equally appropriate marriages – three good
dowries would further consolidate the family holdings.'

Rob raised his eyebrows in amusement as he looked after
Edward's retreating figure.

William always supposed he would marry some day, but it would
be for love – loving and being loved in return. He wanted a close
relationship like that of his parents – he carried within him
memories of the way they were together: the lights and reflections
of love in his father's eyes and the dazzling happiness of his mother.

But this year it was only William and Rob in attendance at

Dublin Castle, resplendent in the most flamboyant of their new waistcoats.

The Rooms may have flaunted the style of the Empire, with centuries of the traditions of British rule lurking within their walls, but the music was unexpectedly modern – formal quadrilles, perky polkas and the godless waltzes, damned by the clergy from pulpits throughout the land as 'riotous and indecent' for provoking within its participants an illicit enjoyment.

Margaret Mulchinock had insisted that her children learn to waltz. She said she'd settle for efficiency, although she would favour dazzling. William was the only one whose dancing dazzled, and to her chagrin he was the one who least liked to dance.

Sipping from a bowl of champagne, he watched the proceedings, drinking in the surroundings, committing to memory the sights, sounds and scents. Lost in his world of memories from the past and thoughts of the future, his musings floated randomly between words, music, dance and the politics of Ireland.

He visualised writing sturdy, blocky words of substantial verses in pencil, whereas the more delicate of his visions would best respond to the loops and curlicues of pen and ink.

But his visualisations were mere hopes.

Henry's death had left him bereft of the ability to forge verses. Despite forcing himself to sit down and write, he had continuing difficulties about committing poetic thoughts to paper in any orderly or, indeed, disorderly fashion. Hopes of further publication had become an untenable dream. But the atmosphere of the Castle was palpable and he believed he could feel it heightening his creativity. Surely the reds, blues and gold decorations, softened by floral arrangements and lit by flickering candles and sconces would inspire?

He was more of an observer than a participant, watching the

young girls resplendent in the pastel, bell-skirted gowns popularised by the young queen; the matrons and chaperones with elaborately coiffed dangling curls – ridiculously named 'spaniel curls'; the menfolk strutting like peacocks in brightly coloured jackets and extravagant ruffles of lace; and the officers magnificent in dress uniform – blue trousers and scarlet tunics decorated with saw-edged silver embroidery.

He was relieved to be on his own – Rob, already a little tipsy, was happily prowling the ballroom.

Unlike Rob he didn't flirt with the young debutantes and unlike Edward he had never flirted with young matrons. Indeed, never having been in love, never having flirted, William was uncertain about relating to what Rob called 'lovely lassies'. Although he carried a memory of one girl: an unknown girl that he had seen only fleetingly at dusk on a dance platform – dark-haired and pale-skinned, she had danced with an inner joy he'd never forgotten.

'My dear, dear boy! Are you all on your own?' Mrs Power interrupted his thoughts. Her black gown was resplendent with lace, braid and ribbons, but as befitted her status as widow her frivolities were dark. 'Come with me. I want to introduce you to dear, dear friends of mine.'

She was the kind of woman who did not take no for an answer and it was hard to ignore her disarming friendliness. She led the way, darting sideways to greet old friends whose lineage she described in detail as they circumnavigated the ballroom, searching, until she found those dear friends.

As she rushed at them in delight, William stood to the side.

The woman Mrs Power was greeting with effusive enthusiasm was handsome in a substantial way and well-corseted in brown taffeta. Her husband, presumably, tall and thin, had his hand on her shoulder and nodded at her every word. Their daughter, presumably again, dressed in delicate blue and with a head of bouncing ringlets, was flirting from behind her fan, her eyes dancing with amusement and her eyebrows saucily raised. The object of her attention was a handsome officer in a scarlet dress uniform, smiling at her appreciatively while keeping a wary eye on her father.

Mrs Power turned back to William.

'My dear, let me introduce you to my friend William Pembroke Mulchinock Esquire. William, dear, these lovely people are the Keogh family from Ballinasloe.'

William bowed over Mrs Keogh's hand.

That her interest was instantly aroused was obvious from the perk of her head; she ruffled her taffeta skirts and positively clucked approval. 'Well, well! What a coincidence!' She addressed her husband, 'Dearest, this must be your late cousin's son from Tralee? There cannot be two gentlemen with such a distinguished name.'

Her husband harrumphed. 'Indeed, yes. Delighted to see you again, young man.'

William couldn't remember ever having met him.

Their daughter rested her fan on the table and smiled prettily at him.

'And, William,' said Mrs Power, smiling, 'this is their daughter Alicia.'

The girl curtsied as he bowed.

Mrs Keogh was delighted at the coincidence of Mrs Power introducing him to them and remarked how small a place Ireland was.

'Indeed,' said Mrs Power. 'And it happens that William will soon be travelling to Ballinasloe on business!'

On hearing that, Mrs Keogh promptly invited him to stay with them.

CHAPTER 10

THE DAWN RAIN was insidious, without let-up. When Mary woke to the sound against the window, delicate, like the tapping of a baby's fingers, she pushed thoughts of the dead child to the back of her mind. Liam's birth and heavy after-bleeding had taken its toll on her mother who was so frail that she had no choice but to remain in the cabin trying to regain her strength while Mary continued at West Villa.

Each morning as the light eased over the fields and hedgerows, Mary's heart lifted as she turned the corner of the driveway and saw the house; in the evenings, she looked back for a last glimpse, marvelling at how its appearance had changed from dawn to dusk. She wondered would she ever get beyond the many duties in the kitchen, ever get to open doors and step into the drawing and dining rooms, the parlour and the bedchambers. She was envious of Florence who spent her days upstairs, caring for Miss Charlotte's daughters – caring for their clothes, looking to their meals and teaching them reading and writing.

She hadn't known of the existence of the gardens until the morning Mrs Mac paused from kneading a round of dough, looked at Mary and said, 'Fetch me a goodly few sprigs of lemon thyme from the herb garden.'

Rather than admit she didn't know where the herb garden was, what lemon thyme looked like or where she might find it, Mary walked in what she hoped was the right direction.

It was good to be outside in the soft cold air, beyond the horizons of the kitchen's white lime-washed walls, away from the heavy air of cooking, washing and boiling. She stood for a moment, with closed eyes, enjoying the rich smell of brown earth, the sunshine and snap of spring. Eyes opened, she looked around at the trees in bud and little flowers bursting from the ground, recalling what Mr O'Connell had said about happiness. She remembered back to the beginning of the year, to the touch of those snowflakes on her cheeks.

There was Paudge, his back to her, bent down examining something caught between the stones of the wall. She liked him, liked the way he helped her.

The other afternoon when she'd looked up from applying a paste of finely powdered whitening to a handsome circular dish, he was standing in the doorway of the back pantry.

'Do you know what that is?' he had asked, indicating the dish.

'No, I don't, but isn't it lovely?' She rubbed at the dried paste and watched the shine of silver emerge.

'It's a called a potato ring.'

She lifted it up, turned it around and examined it. 'For the spuds?'

'Yes, for the gentry's potatoes.' He was smiling as he spoke and she laughed with him.

Now Paudge turned around, holding a small plant by its stem, scatterings of earth falling from its roots.

Paudge was drawn to Mary and confused by his feelings for her. The circumstances of his life had taught him the benefits of being in control and planning. He would not rush Mary, but he was planning to get to know her better and, with that accomplished, he hoped to make her his bride.

His eyes crinkled. 'You've escaped from the kitchen?'

She explained about the lemon thyme.

He disappeared and returned with a fistful of the greenery to find her looking at the neat drills, rows of seedlings, the bare barks of climbing fruit trees and the long wall of glasshouses. Her expression, as she looked around, was one of wonder.

'There's so much of everything. It's lovely. So lovely.'

'What's lovely?'

'Well, everything.' The wave of her arm was all-embracing. It was her response to the neatness of the flowerbeds, crunch of the gravel pathways, and the air of orderliness about the garden.

He handed her the herb and watched as she raised it to her nose and caught its pungent scent.

He was bemused, unsure of his next move, but wanting to keep her with him.

'Have you seen the mistress's flower garden?'

She shook her head.

He led the way along criss-crossing paths and through gates of delicate wrought iron into a walled garden with wide flowerbeds filled with bushes waiting for leaves and blossoms – towards the front of the beds clusters of blooms in bright yellows and whites stood straight and proud.

Mary clasped her hands – in a gesture of delight that squashed the lemon thyme. Sometimes, West Villa was too much to absorb.

The lanes were not places for such bounty – nobody even knew of flowers like these.

'Do you know what they're called?' she asked.

Her eyes were dark, the colour of the night. She had an appeal about her that would have him happy to answer her questions forever. He had never felt this way about anyone before, and certainly not a slip of a girl like Mary O'Connor.

'Most of 'em.' He was pleased with his knowledge.

'What's that? There.' She pointed to a trumpet-shaped, yellow blossom on a slender stem.

'A daffodil.'

'A daff-o-dil.'

He'd never heard it spoken that way before.

'All those daff-o-dils. Hundreds of 'em. Can I smell one?'

Mrs Mulchinock was sitting by the window. Her spring garden gave her untold pleasure and she planned to capture the likeness of some of the daffodils in embroidery.

Her mind was pleasantly at ease as she considered the precision of her silver thimble on her finger, the flash of her needle with its silken thread flying in and out of the length of linen held rigid in the tambour frame. As she worked, she planned how she would use satin stitch and a little cross-stitch to recreate the blooms.

She looked up and, gazing out the window, saw Paudge by the bed of daffodils – dear Paudge, who knew the workings of West Villa better than anyone. It was unusual to see him in the flower garden at this time of the day.

She had been wed a few years when he had come to live

permanently at West Villa, and the small, scared boy had touched her heart. He was a welcome addition to the household. For generations his family had been associated with the Mulchinocks, filling the roles of stalwart labourers, indoor servants, wet nurses and foster parents.

Since the beginning of the century the custom of fosterage had mostly died out. But when Michael had to travel to the continent on business, it was inconceivable that he'd go without his wife or that she would countenance a separation. Paudge's grandmother, Peggy, had stepped in to foster six-week-old William Pembroke, forging a never-to-be broken bond between the families.

When Peggy, her son, daughter-in-law and several children had been taken by the fever some three years later, nine-year-old Paudge came to live at West Villa. Over time he'd grown from a frightened child to a steadfast, reliable and dependable young man. Mrs Mulchinock was fond of him, and he repaid her with unstinting loyalty.

But who was that with him? The girl was bent forward, leaning over the daffodils, with Paudge hovering beside her. The girl stretched out her hand and looked to be stroking the trumpet of one of the blooms, then stretching in further she buried her nose in the blossom. As she straightened up Mrs Mulchinock saw she was wearing the blue dress and striped apron she provided for her maidservants. Strange. She had never seen the girl before and, even from this distance, she knew she was not someone one would forget.

She crossed the room to the door and pulled firmly on the cord of the bell.

❀ ❀ ❀

'Daffodil flowers should have a scent,' Mary said.

Paudge smiled in agreement, although he had never given thought as to whether or not they should.

Mary opened her fist, saw the squashed herb and groaned, 'Oh, no! Mrs Mac!'

'We'll get more,' Paudge assured her. Then he looked at her solemnly. 'I would like to get to know you better, Mary.'

She tucked a stray curl back into her cap as she considered what he had said.

Paudge was different to the other local lads – he didn't hang around corners. She couldn't imagine him asking her for a 'little kiss' or patting her bottom. Paudge knew a lot but his knowledge was different to the schoolmaster's. He seemed to know everything that was to be known about the inside and outside of West Villa. How agreeable it would be to learn more!

Her answer was solemn. 'That'd be nice, Paudge.'

❀ ❀ ❀

'Who is the strange girl in the garden and why is she wearing a maidservant's uniform?'

Mrs Mac, eyes cast down, took a deep breath before answering. 'It's Nora's daughter. Poor Nora's still not herself.' She blessed herself piously. 'We had to keep the household running what with Miss Charlotte and the little dotes still visiting.'

She was pleased with her explanation, but Mrs Mulchinock was unimpressed.

'You cannot take it upon yourself to hire staff.'

'No, ma'am.' Mrs Mac carried out a rapid think-through of how much she could safely reveal about the circumstances of the O'Connors. 'On occasion Willie O'Connor is known to take a sup too much, the rent is up this quarter and their thatch needs redoing. They can't afford to lose the money!' Her voice rose. 'Nora's been poorly since her last little one died.'

'And who is paying the girl?'

Mrs Mac hung her head. 'I had a bit put by.'

Mrs Mulchinock gazed at her, deep in thought, then said, 'That will be all.'

Mrs Mac bowed her head and turned to leave.

But Mrs Mulchinock spoke again. 'Is the girl competent and does she have a strong constitution?'

Competent wasn't a word that Mrs Mac would use to describe any of the servants. If pushed she'd have to admit to not quite knowing its meaning but, now that she was being asked, she supposed Mary was the one servant who could be described as 'competent' – it was a word that seemed to fit her. And as for a strong constitution – Mary was young, without a husband and she did not appear to have inherited her mother's poorliness.

'Yes, ma'am, she's competent and has the constitution, but in my opinion good looks are all right for the gentry but servants fare better if they're plain-lookin'.'

'Well, yes, Mrs Mac. Now this conversation is to be kept between ourselves. The household has functioned well over the past weeks and for that I give you credit. You will be reimbursed.'

Mrs Mac bobbed her head, 'Reimbu ...?'

Mrs Mulchinock's voice was kindly. 'Let me know how much you've paid the girl, so that I can repay you. And thank you.'

Mrs Mac allowed herself the flicker of a smile as she closed the door of the parlour and stepped out into the hall. She had achieved a well-functioning household!

Mrs Mulchinock sat back, thinking through the situation. Nora was obviously too poorly to carry out her duties and from the sound of it she was unlikely to be well enough to return to the dairy in the near future, if ever. Edward had replaced her in the dairy within weeks, but only on a temporary basis, he'd assured her. Nora had been a loyal servant for many years. The poor woman was worn threadbare by all those pregnancies, torn by her constant confinements, lost teeth and lost blood.

Mrs Mulchinock appreciated loyalty and she would ensure the O'Connor family didn't go short and, anyway, for some time she had been thinking about taking on another upstairs maid.

CHAPTER 11

ON SUNDAY MORNING Nora and Mary picked their way down the lane, along the streets, by the slight light of a crescent moon and a scattering of stars. Nora had a goodly sized tallow candle in her pocket.

The church of Saint John the Baptist was just off Castle Street and its heavy door was closed – there was still half an hour to go until early Mass, but Nora had insisted on being early. They hugged the wall, in an effort to shelter from the sharpness of the pre-dawn wind, the black silence broken by a screeching cat and a hissing goose.

Mary had known that after every baby Mam was churched. She thought it a strange word, a word she didn't understand, and she wondered why this churching was so important. Whenever she asked about it, her mother brushed aside the question. As they waited in the chill, she tried again.

'Why do women have to be churched?'

'To wash away the sin of childbirth.'

'*Sin of childbirth?*' Mary's voice rose.

'And to thank God for the safe delivery of a child.'

'But Liam …'

'The ceremony is a blessing after recovery from the birth,' Nora said firmly.

'But you've not recovered, Mam.'

'It's a purification.'

'Purification.' It wasn't a word bandied about on the lanes, but Mary knew its meaning. 'What has to be purified?'

'Don't, Mary. Not now. We can't fly in the face of God. It's in His hands.'

She should have known. It was pointless

Eventually Father Sheehy arrived and unlocked the door. He was carrying a lantern and the hem of his cassock touched the ground. Two shivering young boys accompanied him. The five of them entered the church, the priest moving ahead, followed by the boys, with Nora and Mary trailing after them. Gradually pinpricks of light pierced the gloom as the boys lit candles and lanterns.

Mary and Nora waited. When Father Sheehy emerged from behind the altar he was wearing a crisply laundered white surplice and a stole over his cassock, and he carried a small silver pail of holy water. He gestured to one of the boys who lit Nora's candle from his.

Nora knelt and Mary, keeping her distance from her mother, knelt too. The priest marked Nora's forehead with the holy water and made the Sign of the Cross, sonorously intoning, '*In nomine patris, et filii, et spiritus sancti*', followed by a few mumbled prayers. Throughout, the candle trembled in Nora's hand. And then it was over.

Nora remained kneeling, tears streaming down her cheeks. As Mary took the candle from her, she was unsure as to whether her mother's reaction was at the loss of Liam or emotion from the ceremony.

Mary had no dithering thoughts about the ceremony. How could the Church encourage families who had nothing to have child after child, yet regard childbirth as unclean? It was not her parents' way to question the Church or its teachings. But surely there had to be more to life than the grinding hardship of the lane? There certainly was at West Villa.

❀❀❀

As Mary walked back to Brogue Lane on a balmy May evening, Danny caught up with her. It was more than a month since she'd gone up the hill to Hannah, and there was no mention of them around the lanes or in the town. She'd worried, each day expecting to hear that they'd fled together. The circumstances of their running away would be the talk of the place.

'I've the plans all sorted for Hannah and me. We're going to America next week.' He gave a whoop of joy and the light of hope was back in his eyes.

'Oh, Danny.' She was happy for them, but sorrowful at the thought of never seeing Hannah again.

'He's been beating her.'

'She'll be out of it now. Gone from him. I'm glad for the both of ye.'

He crossed his heart with his right hand. 'I'll see nothing bad ever happens to her again.'

She believed him. 'How are you going?'

'Sailing from Blennerville to New York.' His face lit up. 'We couldn't leave without telling you. When we're gone it's better if you don't let on to know anything.'

He was buoyed up with such optimism and excitement that she worried he'd be indiscreet.

'We're not lettin' on to a soul of our plans, but we'll write you a letter, let you know.'

'Oh, Danny. I wish you both the best – you know that. But be careful. Hennessey is not a man to take lightly to being crossed.'

'I know. I wouldn't like to be around when he finds out Hannah's gone. And with me.' He reached out, gave her a quick, unexpected hug, and ran on ahead of her, disappearing around the corner.

CHAPTER 12

BALLINASLOE WAS A FAR CRY from Dublin or Paris or even Tralee, but it had its own quaint charm. William had a good eye for horseflesh – the pair of greys were superb specimens and he arranged for them to be transported to West Villa.

As there was rumour that a Repeal rally would be held in Galway sometime in the near future, he accepted the Keoghs' invitation to remain on as their house guest. He ignored his reservations about Mr Keogh's fervour about his various businesses, Mrs Keogh's endless chatter and fussing and the way Alicia hung on his every word. He was not used to such attention.

Hector Keogh had always pined for a son and, after years of living in a household of women, he was enjoying the rapport of having a young man around the place. He was impressed by learning and cleverness, and initially he was impressed by what he perceived as young Mulchinock's wide-ranging knowledge of businesses.

His wife was impressed by their guest's family background, his conversational ability and elegant manners.

Within hours of meeting William, Alicia was so impressed by him that she hadn't given any further thought to her officer.

William had a quiet charm, he could hold his own in any company and he was fluent at discussing his family's business interests. He had Edward to thank for his familiarity with farming methods and his mother for his knowledge of the administration involved in profit and loss accounts.

He was tired, still grieving the death of his brother, worn out from months of living the conflicting life of a political supporter while having to keep his activities secret from his family.

And so he settled easily into relaxation in Keoghs' stylish household, basking in their open admiration of him and comfortable in a pleasant way. He enjoyed the unfamiliar sensation of freedom — he was beyond the control of West Villa, Mama and Edward. Even Daniel O'Connell — he and his supporters were unlikely to visit Ballinasloe.

He never moved far from home without his well-furnished writing-case holding pens, pencils, India rubbers, a selection of seals and sealing wax in red and black. Shortly after arriving in Ballinasloe he wrote a three-page letter to his mother, giving her an edited version of his stay in Dublin, waxing lyrical about the entertainments at the Castle and informing her he would remain in the West for the foreseeable future. Then, pulling out another sheet of paper from his case, he wrote a short note to Edward explaining how he planned to take the opportunity, courtesy of his host, of viewing the operational practices of some of the more successful businesses in the town of Ballinasloe and beyond.

He took meticulous pleasure in the craft of letter writing. And in these two letters his words were sequenced to his satisfaction —

the tone of the letter to his mother was appropriately affectionate, and to Edward it was business-like, with a touch of brotherliness he hoped. From his case he chose the small seal engraved with his initials, folded over the pages and lit a taper.

Resting his elbow on the table to keep his hand steady, he held the stick of wax between thumb and forefinger so that it barely touched the point of flame. He turned the stick around until it was softened on all sides, inserted a little of the wax under the turnover of the letters and dripped a blob onto the outside of it. Then he pressed down the seal in the middle of the wax. It was a meticulous process, one that he took pleasure in.

He sat back with the contentment of a job well done. How pleased Mama would be to receive such a long, newsy missive, and hopefully even Edward who was disapproving of what he called 'unnecessary jaunting' would be appeased.

While in Ballinasloe he planned to devote time to writing verse, hoping to recover his previous fluency with words. But finding a quiet corner in that household proved to be difficult.

'What are you doing?' Alicia would ask if she came upon him.

'Writing verse.'

'Oh. Why?'

That was the signal for him to give up and gossip with her.

Despite writing several series of rhyming lines, he was displeased with the end product – the words were never quite as perfect as he hoped.

On a morning of driving rain and sheeting wind, as he sat by the fire with the latest edition of the *Freeman's Journal* resting on his knees, his host bounced into the room.

'The very man. I hoped you hadn't gone out. You'll want to view the cultivation of my potato crop.'

Viewing fields of potatoes in the rain was the last thing

William wished to do, but his innate good manners won out.

From the comfort of the carriage, against the dourness of the intractable landscape with Mr Keogh keeping up a running commentary, William watched the bending and stooping of the men, women and children, their movements sluggish and their shoulders shawled with rain as they tended to the tubers.

'It's hard work,' he observed.

'Hard work is good for them, good for them. The native Irish peasant is a naturally lazy breed.' Mr Keogh leaned forward and tapped William's knee with his cane, 'It would be more lucrative for me if I planted grain. Much better export potential. Soft I am. Too soft. That's my problem.'

After living with the Keoghs for a few weeks, soft was not a description William would apply to any of the family, especially not his host.

'Are they tenants?'

'No. Tenants, as such, are bothersome. Those labourers,' he cast an expansive arm towards the miserable fields, 'are mostly old men and women and the very young – not suitable to be employed by Lord Clancarty. They work for the right to a small plot of land on which they can grow enough potatoes to feed their family – a family of two adults and four children consume about thirty pounds of potatoes a day.' Mr Keogh sat back into his seat with an air of satisfaction at imparting such statistics.

'That's not much, as many of them have little else to eat,' William commented. 'It's a hard life.'

Mr Keogh raised an incredulous eyebrow.

'I'll wager it's as hard for the peasantry in Ballinasloe as it is in Tralee,' William continued, ignoring Mr Keogh's expression. 'I presume you dispense charity?'

'Mrs Keogh can be soft like that. But I say most of them are work-shy good-for-nothings.'

'I disagree, sir. The Irish peasant has little opportunity for betterment – ongoing potato famines, the population explosion, outbreaks of typhoid, cholera and dysentery, and the country is still caught up in the economic disaster of the Napoleonic Wars.'

Hector Keogh was not a man to take to being contradicted. He grunted displeasure as he tapped on the partition of the coach. The coachman picked up his reins and they returned to the town.

With increasing frequency Mrs and Miss Keogh kidnapped William to escort them to afternoon teas, assuring him earnestly that such entertainments were the latest thing in London. In the best of the West of Ireland's drawing rooms he ate finger sandwiches, triangles of ginger cake and lemon tartlets, and sipped tea poured by hostesses who presided graciously over silver tea urns.

Alicia was a sweetly pretty girl with a polite manner and a penchant for flounced pastel gowns. He parried her flirtatious personality with light-hearted good humour, considering her in much the same way as he did his young nieces – female, deliciously bothersome and to be humoured at all times.

And he was good at that – emerging from the newspaper or closing over his notebook and laying aside his pen when she wanted to gossip or discuss the latest style in bonnets or trimmings from London or Paris. He merely nodded when she confided to him that occasionally she not only used visage powder, but also a touch of rouge.

One afternoon she rather surprised him by asking, 'Tell me, William, do you plant potatoes?'

He was puzzled at the question and laughed. 'No, I don't.'

She tossed her head, 'Not you personally, but your tenants – do they plant potatoes?'

'Yes, they do. And I believe some of the servants who live at West Villa also plant potatoes – we make land available to them. Potatoes are an important part of diet in Kerry.'

'Do you export them?'

'No. As far as I know they're grown more for consumption. But we export most of the barley and oats grown at West Villa. Satisfied?'

She looked at him from under her lashes and nodded.

CHAPTER 13

'MAMA, MAY I talk to you?'

Charlotte advanced into the parlour and sat down without waiting for an affirmative.

Mrs Mulchinock prodded her needle with its wisp of yellow thread into the piece of linen and rested the embroidery frame on her knees.

'What is it, Charlotte? Everything all right in the soup kitchen?' She was edified by reports of how well the kitchen was doing.

'It's not the kitchen — that is running efficiently. It's Florence. She's quite impossible. She cannot manage the girls.'

'Two little girls shouldn't take much management.'

Charlotte waved an airy arm. 'They do — there's much to be done.'

'You did insist on employing Florence. And you did interview and approve her.'

'I know.' Her voice was brusque. She didn't need her mother to so pointedly make her aware of her failings.

'What do you want me to do about it?

Charlotte leaned forward. 'If I were to dismiss Florence, could I borrow someone to take care of the girls — just as a temporary measure?'

'Borrow? I don't think so, dear. There's really nobody.'

As Mrs Mulchinock spoke, she remembered Mary O'Connor. She had done nothing about her. She had intended to call her upstairs, have a closer look at her, but with William Pembroke away she'd been busier than usual.

Charlotte dabbed at her eyes and sniffled.

Mrs Mulchinock wanted nothing more than to get on with capturing the stately yellow daffodil in silken threads. 'Give me a few days to think about the matter.'

❀❀❀

Mrs Mac, her hands on her hips, cap awry, chapped cheeks glowing, was more flustered than usual, issuing orders in a barking voice — 'Lizzie, the potatoes. Paudge, when you've a minute, please could you see to the range?' Her attitude to Paudge, as always, was one of respect, courtesy and politeness.

'There you are. At last.' She sighed gustily as though Mary was trailing in hours late. 'The mistress is lookin' for you — she wants to see you. No dilly-dallying. You're to go to the upstairs.' The word 'upstairs', as always, was uttered with reverence.

When Mrs Mac was all ado as she was now, Mary knew it was a waste of breath to point out that she was more than half an hour early.

'What does she want from me?'

'Maybe you're going to be let go,' muttered Lizzie, banging the pots on the table.

Mrs Mac snapped, 'Stop that nonsense, Lizzie!'

'Where will Mrs Mulchinock be?' Mary wasn't used to being so summoned.

It was Paudge who answered. 'Her parlour. Where she does the books. I suspect it's good news for you.'

Mrs Mac caught the fondness of his smile and it had her wondering.

Mary straightened her cap, took a clean apron from the shelf and, thanks to Paudge's words of encouragement, climbed the stairs with a sense of expectation.

Going to the upstairs was a hushed experience. Each foot she placed on the creaky steps seemed to whisper to her that she was a stranger, that the house did not know her well enough to accept her. She paused to look around the spaciousness of the hall – the bright red walls and the black-and-white floor tiles, and to admire the handsome master, looking out at her from his golden frame.

She tapped on the door of the parlour and entered.

Mrs Mulchinock looked up from her desk which was covered with tidy piles of papers. She put down her pen, turned around and Mary felt her scrutiny, but she was too fascinated to be nervous. She had seen the comings and goings of the mistress and Master Edward and Miss Charlotte and the little ones. She had seen the gentry in their carriages. On horseback. Walking. At Sunday Mass. But never before had she been so close to a lady or to a gentleman in their surroundings.

Standing still as a statue, she absorbed details of the mistress – her pale, china-white skin, pearly ovals of nails and small, delicate hands – unlike her own swollen, reddened and chapped ones.

Her gown was black, but with the shining richness of the material it was so different to the clothes worn by the widows of the lanes that it scarcely seemed like mourning at all, and when she moved her skirts rustled and whispered. Her indoor cap was little more than a small scrap of lace with delicate streamers, and gleaming combs held her loops of hair in place.

The room had an air of blueness about it, so much blue – light blue like the mid-morning sky and the deep blue of dusk – walls, rugs and curtains, as well as the furniture shining in the sunlight – small round tables, chairs with soft seats and bookshelves lined with books. The room was a lovelier place than she ever imagined a room could be.

Close up, Mrs Mulchinock decided, the girl was even more impressive than when she'd viewed her in the garden: she was neat and clean, waited to be spoken to and she did not appear to be intimidated or nervous. She was not surprised at Mrs Mac's championing of the girl and she had been right about her good looks.

'From tomorrow, you will be working upstairs.'

'Does this mean I can stay?' Mary's heart gave a leap of pleasure and she smiled as though the world was hers. *Upstairs.* She would be away from the repetitious drudge of kitchen duties. She could walk through the handsome hallway, into the mistress's parlour, open doors and look into the other rooms, see what she knew would be beautiful things.

'Yes. You may regard yourself as in service.'

'Even when Mam is better?'

'Yes.'

'And back in the dairy?'

'Yes, Mary.' There was a touch of asperity in Mrs Mulchinock's voice.

'And what are the wages for the upstairs?'

Mrs Mulchinock was taken aback. She had never before been asked such a question and she certainly hadn't expected it from this young girl, but she seemed competent and she certainly knew her own mind.

'Ten pounds a year, Mary. That's a good wage. A bowl of oatmeal in the mornings and a bit of dinner at noon.'

'Yes, ma'am.' Mary didn't know whether or not it was a good wage. But she did know the family needed money. Her father had not received payment for several completed orders, the rent was due and the last heavy showers of rain proved how much that thatch needed repairing. She was too proud to go into family circumstances, but she took an unprecedented chance. 'Not so good for an upstairs maid, ma'am. And living out.' Every extra shilling she could bring back to the cabin would ease living for the family.

'And what would you consider appropriate?'

Mary was unmoved by the touch of sarcasm. 'Could you make it a little more, ma'am?'

Mrs Mulchinock frowned. 'No, I could not.'

Mary was unfazed by the refusal – she'd expected it, but she'd felt she had to try. 'My thanks to you, ma'am. I'll like being upstairs.'

'Like?' Mrs Mulchinock's glance was sharp.

Mary was looking around with wide eyes. 'Oh, yes, ma'am. Life here is so different to where we live – it's different enough to be in another world.'

What an observation for a servant to make! Mrs Mulchinock was nonplussed, intrigued by the girl's attitude. Liking duties or situations was not something one anticipated from one's servants. From what Mrs Mac had told her, she doubted that Nora would ever be well enough again to take up her duties. Unknown to Edward she had made arrangements to pay her a small quarterly stipend. She would delay further decisions – from experience she knew that problems, if left alone, frequently sorted themselves out. She settled for, 'That's all for now, Mary.'

After the door closed she wavered. She hoped she had made a right decision about employing the girl and bringing her upstairs.

CHAPTER 14

THE COPPER BELCHED STEAM, its load of bed linens and tablecloths bubbling away, fogging the kitchen windows.

In the corner Mary leaned over the washboard, scrubbing at the muddy hemline of Miss Charlotte's petticoats. Despite being soaked overnight in lye, the soap wasn't shifting the stains, but it was cutting into the skin of her hands which was raw and cracked – how she envied Mrs Mulchinock her smooth white hands!

She hated washday and was glad it was only a once-a-week occurrence.

Being upstairs at West Villa was one of the nicest things to happen to her. She hadn't told Mam, hadn't said anything about being moved from the kitchen – she couldn't bear to see the frown of worry lines along her forehead, knowing she was fretting about losing her own position.

Mary squeezed the excess water from the petticoats and dropped them into the copper, prodding them up and down with the tongs. When she pulled them out they looked considerably cleaner.

Dreaming of the upstairs rooms and their contents enriched her thinking and compensated for the unending hardship and drudgery of washday. Elbow-deep in rinsing water as she sloshed clothes up and down, her thoughts wandered.

As she had suspected, upstairs was a different world to the world she knew, and she was particularly taken with the books in Mrs Mulchinock's parlour. As she went about her parlour duties she'd look longingly at the bookcases, wondering what it would be like to open the glass doors, reach in and take down a book and then to sit on the blue velvet chair with the buttoned back, to open that book and to read it, but she never did, never had the opportunity as the parlour was mostly occupied and it was a place of continuous comings and goings – Mrs Mulchinock at her desk or embroidering by the window overlooking the garden, Mr Edward discussing business, Mrs Mac consulting about household matters, Miss Charlotte and her daughters in and out.

Feeling almost invisible, she went about her tasks.

But the spaciousness and elegance of the bedchambers, with their mahogany wardrobes, colourful rugs, commodes, feather beds, soft pillows and cosy quilts were a different matter. When she was doing out those rooms, she had them to herself.

One day on an impulse she had opened the door of the grand wardrobe in Miss Charlotte's room and lifted a dress of rosy pink off a hook. As she held it up for inspection, the silk rushed to the floor and sprang out in a womanly shape. She stood entranced, imagining the pleasure of wearing such a garment before rehooking the dress, closing the wardrobe and picking up her feather duster.

On another occasion she discovered several copies of a

magazine that had words in a foreign language written stylishly across the top of its cover. She didn't known the meaning of the words but she'd sat into an elegant chair and lingered, turning the pages slowly absorbing the beauty of the pastel pen-and-ink drawings of gowns and bonnets and petticoats, forgetting time, oblivious to the fact that she should be washing windows and dusting furniture.

Before leaving the room she ran her finger over the title of the magazine and committed its letters to memory. Later she'd written them down and when she'd asked its meaning from Mr Foley, he'd pushed his spectacles back up his nose, raised his eyebrows and translated slowly: 'Nouveau Journal des Dames' – 'New Magazine for Ladies'. Now you know more about French fashions than I ever will.'

She'd asked him about becoming a teacher 'A real teacher,' she added.

He'd taken his time before answering. 'There's a training college in Dublin.' After another pause, he said, 'I'll make some inquiries.'

Mrs Mac was asking, 'How many more loads, Mary?'

Mary's back ached and her swollen hands burned as one by one she dunked the petticoats for starching in cold rice water.

She rattled off a quick assessment, 'Two tubs of soaking linen, sheets and pillowcases, towels, the mistresses' undergarments, and Master Edward's neckties. Four loads at least, missus.' Luckily, Florence did the children's clothes in her own time. 'Yuck!' Mary raised a petticoat dripping jellied starch.

'Get along with ye! Out to the yard,' Mrs Mac ordered, 'and bring that lot.'

'Yes, missus,' Mary and Lizzie said in unison.

Slithering on the soapy slime of the floor, they carried out the tub of dripping clothes.

Mrs Mac with a proprietary air stood guard over the mangle that had arrived from the town two days previously and was now tucked into a corner of the porch. It was one of those new-fangled, labour-saving devices that Master Edward favoured. Though if asked she'd have said there was nothing wrong with having the girls give the clothes a good wring-out. Still, she fed the articles one by one through the wooden rollers. She had Lizzie turning the handle and Mary easing the garments into the basket. She put on a fine performance demonstrating the workings of the mangle with a frown here and a sigh there. She finished with a flourish of authority. 'When I have a bit of time, I'll show ye how to use it, but until then ye are to lave it alone.'

As Mary was hanging out the sheets in the yard, lifting them high to the line, ensuring they hung straight, with corners aligned, as Mrs Mac insisted, she saw the shine of fine leather boots and confident stride of a man coming into the yard. She peered around the sheet and saw it was Master Edward. He paused for a moment, looked around and clicked his fingers.

Paudge led out a horse from the stables. It was a handsome animal, shiny sleek and as black as night.

Mary moved sideways, half-hidden by the billowing linen to watch the skittish animal dancing on the cobblestones with Master Edward soothing it as though it were a child.

'Whoa, there. Easy now. Take it easy.'

Master Edward was dark with a ruddy complexion and deep creases on either side of his mouth. His hand ran up and down the animal's neck until it stood motionless as though waiting for the next caress.

The sheet behind which Mary was standing swayed outwards and upwards.

Edward, in the process of leaping onto the saddle, stopped short. 'Hello,' he said after appraising her for a moment. 'And who are you?'

Mary resisted the urge to bob a curtsy and looked directly at him. 'Mary O'Connor, sir.'

'And you work here? Of course you do. I believe I've seen you in the parlour?'

'I'm mostly in the kitchen, sir.' Her response was automatic. In the kitchen Mrs Mac was in exclusive control. Nobody exercised such control upstairs. Her instinct warned her to be wary of the man before her.

'Give Mrs Mac a hug from me.' With that he gestured to Paudge who bent down, locked his hands, and Edward sprang from them into the saddle.

With a snort of anticipation, the horse left the yard, rearing for the freedom of the open fields.

'So, you've nothing better to do than to stand around starin' at Master Edward?' Mrs Mac missed little and she had an inbuilt sense of when anyone was 'idling' as she called it.

Mary tried and failed to imagine the outcome if she were to carry out Master Edward's instructions.

'Isn't it well for some? Sure the clothes will hang themselves.' Mrs Mac drew closer, but her voice became kinder. 'And a word of warning to you, Mary O'Connor – no familiarity with the young masters. No good can come of it for the likes of us.'

'I know, missus.'

'Stay out of his way, girl. If you know what's good for you.'

As Mary moved back into the porch Paudge caught up with her and took the empty clothesbasket from her. 'Wait here,' he told her.

A minute later he reappeared.

'I've told Mrs. Mac I'm taking you to get some flowers for the mistress's room.'

He took a trug and scissors from the porch and led Mary in the direction of the flower garden.

'Isn't the mangle a great invention?' he said over his shoulder.

To keep up with him she had to walk quickly. 'It is,' she agreed, somewhat puzzled, as she had already put fresh flowers in Mrs Mulchinock's room.

Paudge placed the trug on the gravel pathway, leaned in, cut a few red tulips, and placed them tidily in the trug.

Then, straightening up, he reached towards her and took her hand in his.

She pulled away from him, reclaimed her hand and stepped backwards. 'Paudge, what are you doing?'

'I want you to know I've grown fond of you, Mary. Very fond of you.'

'And I like you too, Paudge. You've always been helpful.' She chose her words carefully, relying on instinct, as she had no previous experience in handling a situation such as this.

He caught her hand again. She frowned and, although she left her hand lie in his, she looked beyond him to the flowerbeds.

She liked him. She did. There was much to like about him. He helped her out in many ways – whenever he was around he pumped the water and carried the buckets from the yard to the kitchen. He had shown her the best way of black-leading the range, explained about the candle table and, best of all, he took the chamber pots from her and emptied them down the stinking holes of the outside privy.

She looked at him.

'I think about you a lot,' he said.

Mary watched him, cautiously trying to make sense of the

situation — unsure, biting on her lower lip. First Master Edward and now Paudge ... what a day ...

She was relieved when he released her hand.

'Maybe we'll dance at Clahane some evening?'

'Maybe we will,' she agreed with more politeness than enthusiasm.

CHAPTER 15

THE KEOGHS DOTED ON their only child. Ignoring Alicia's more obsessive traits, they made a point of granting her every wish – the only proviso being that it was socially expedient. After less than a week Mrs Keogh had decided that William would make a perfect husband for Alicia, but she bided her time and when she conveyed her decision to her husband he was non-committal in that annoying way of his.

Unbeknownst to his wife, initially Hector Keogh had been thinking along the same lines, but the ups and downs of his life had taught him a cautiousness that she hadn't learnt.

Despite the Mulchinock family's reputation as astute purveyors of a variety of businesses in Kerry, Hector was not a man to accept information without checking. He made some discreet enquiries about William's prospects, the diversity of the family's ever-expanding businesses and the status of the Mulchinocks within the county and beyond. The information he received back was much as William had already conveyed. However, it also confirmed his reservations.

Violet Keogh was increasingly lavish in her compliments regarding William, remarking to anyone who'd listen 'he's so well brought up' and 'knows how to conduct himself', as though he were a child rather than a young man in his prime. She went as far as professing her admiration for his mother's astute handling of her late husband's business interests.

The situation rested until the evening when Alicia and William had taken the carriage to attend a recital by Miss Rossini Collins, a well-know violinist who was giving a classical concert in the town hall.

Mr and Mrs Keogh sat relaxing in the small parlour at the back of the house.

Violet tinkled on the pianoforte that Hector had ordered some months ago from Aldridge's in Dublin's Duke Street when Alicia had expressed a desire to learn to play. It had arrived two weeks ago and Alicia had not so much as cast a glance at it, much less run her fingers across its keys.

Hector, his legs stretched towards the fire, was reading and rereading an article titled 'Emigration to Australia' in the latest edition of the *Connaught Journal*. Finished, he raised his head, removed his spectacles, rubbed his eyes and crumpled the paper in annoyance.

Violet, who was awaiting her opportunity to get his attention, stopped playing and turned around on the stool. 'Dearest – I need to talk to you.'

'Listen to this, my dear. More than 140 persons from this area are on their way to Australia for agricultural work, including several strong young women.'

'About Alicia and William –'

'Emigration on this scale is going to affect my business interests.' He tapped the paper. 'This is not good. Not good at all. This mass emigration of our healthiest workers to Australia will be to the detriment of our economy.'

She was not interested in emigration. She rushed in with, 'I believe Alicia would be happy to be betrothed to William. He is the eldest son and will eventually inherit the bulk of the family's estate.'

He put his spectacles back on and lifted the paper.

On observing that her husband was more interested in reading about Australia than discussing their daughter's happiness, she raised her voice. '*Dearest.*'

There was threat in the term of endearment that he knew better than to ignore. He dropped the paper to his lap, removed his spectacles again and placed them on the side table.

Nodding her approval at having his attention, she continued, 'Surely you've noticed how Alicia's eyes light up in William's company? How she asks for his opinion on gowns and bonnets and how interested he appears in even the trivialities of her life?'

'I must say I haven't,' he said, stalling. Before answering in either the affirmative or the negative he would need to further analyse the pros and cons of Alicia marrying into the Mulchinock family.

His wife warmed to her topic, 'Why, dearest, only the other afternoon William was most attentive when Alicia drew his attention to the delicacy of the embroidery on her new cream kid gloves.'

Hector nodded.

'You must have noticed the care with which he replies to Alicia's questions. And as we both know she asks a lot of questions!' Violet gave a little laugh – Alicia and her endless questions was a joke they shared. She fiddled with the amethyst brooch centred on her lace collar. 'He's quite devoted to our daughter. But I have one reservation about the match.' She left that reservation floating in the comfortable air of the parlour.

Her husband waited, newspaper crackling impatiently between his hands. He had twenty years of marriage to the sweet girl who had turned into such a formidable wife. When she made such a statement it was beholden on him to pay attention. From past experiences he knew how much she enjoyed creating suspense.

'And what's that?' he eventually asked.

After what seemed an interminable length of time she said, 'We must ensure his willingness to settle in Ballinasloe.'

'That is an imposition too far, my dear.'

His wife wailed, 'I cannot conceive the thought of Alicia living so far away from us in Tralee!'

'As you've rightly said, William will inherit someday. He'll have to live in Tralee.'

He spoke so firmly that she knew the matter was closed.

Hector had kept his growing doubts about their guest's long-term interest in business matters to himself – initially, he had mistaken the boy's natural politeness for commercial enthusiasm. But he had come to the conclusion that their guest, pleasant as he was, was more of a gentleman scribbler than an ambitious entrepreneur – he liked the word 'entrepreneur', the sound of it and its connotations, and he took every opportunity of applying it to himself.

He pulled out his pocket watch. 'It's time to retire.'

'Shouldn't we wait …?'

He rose, put the guard in front of the fire and snuffed the lights as his wife closed the piano.

She tried again in their bedchamber, but he further expressed his reservations about William.

'In my travels I have come across such alluring men and women, in Dublin and London. Perhaps we have been taken in by the boy and his charming manners?'

Violet sat up in bed, a barrage of pillows at her back, and indignantly pulled her silk wrapper around her shoulders.

'She has her heart set on him.'

'Has she actually said so?' Hector was worried. On occasions his wife and daughter developed opinions and considered themselves capable of making decisions without discussion with him.

'Yes.'

'Specifically?'

'Well … perhaps not in so many words, but it's expected a match will be announced soon.'

'Who expects it?'

'Everyone.'

'Who is everyone?'

His wife waved a languid hand that embraced life beyond the four posters of their marital bed. Already her mind was buzzing with thoughts of tea parties, shopping expeditions and the all-important trousseau. 'You know, dearest, society.'

'Society is not everyone. And society's opinion is not a yardstick with which to assess our daughter's happiness.'

'Why don't we discuss it with her?'

'That is out of the question.' He put on his nightcap and climbed into bed. 'As far as you and Alicia are concerned the matter is closed. I will handle it from now on.'

❀ ❀ ❀

Next morning, after a night of disturbed sleep and a scarcely touched breakfast, Hector, making quite a production of consulting his pocket watch, asked William to step into his office in half an hour's time.

The young man found the older man sitting solemnly behind a huge partner's desk, going through contracts and smoking a cigar.

William waited as his host continued riffling papers. This was obviously not an invitation to luncheon or a request to accompany him to one of his premises. He wondered about the reason for the summons. Wonder began to turn to unease. Something was amiss. And he was still standing. When he cleared his throat, it rasped in the silence.

Mr Keogh raised his head from his paperwork. 'Before I take this matter further, I want to ask you a question.' He paused, took another drag from his cigar and watched as the smoke curled up from between his lips.

William waited. What matter was his host referring to? Was there something under discussion that he was unaware of or that he'd forgotten about?

Hector Keogh Esquire was a man who prided himself on coming directly to the point. He had thought long and hard about how to handle the situation.

Apparently a betrothal to William was what Alicia wanted and he had never denied his only daughter. His wife wanted a betrothal too and, now that he thought of it, he had never denied her either. But a betrothal was a serious matter that needed to be assessed from all sides. It was not a frippery, not as simple as purchasing a ridiculously expensive new carriage, acquiring invitations to Dublin Castle, or gowns from Paris.

He did not wish to think of the repercussions if he failed. He was sure failure was the likely outcome of this meeting and its

Machiavellian nuances pleased him. During breakfast when every morsel lodged in his throat, instead of his usual habit of hiding behind the newspaper he had watched William's attention to his daughter.

Dammit, his wife was right. The boy was courteous and charming and his daughter was smitten.

He'd have to give the young fellow the option.

Putting his doubts to the back of his mind, he waved to the chair opposite. It was time for blunt talk. 'Sit you down. Should we begin by discussing the matter of your betrothal to my daughter?'

William was barely seated when he jerked backwards in surprise. He said nothing as his mind ran through the implications of the question that had to be answered.

How had Mr Keogh, who he considered to be a man of limited imagination, made such a mistake? How had he reached such a conclusion? From where could he have got the notion that he wanted to marry Alicia? Had he given any hint to that effect? Had he done or said anything to Alicia that might be so construed?

No. He had never hinted at a betrothal. Indeed, he did not believe the word 'betrothal' had ever been mentioned by either of them or her parents during the weeks he had spent in Ballinasloe.

Truth be known, he was beginning to find Alicia's clinginess suffocating and, compared to the intelligence of his mother, he considered Mrs Keogh to be vacuous with little in her life but constant rounds of socialising and gossip.

But how best should he handle this situation?

By nature William was kind. Why, he did not have it in him to kill a cockroach. Only a few days after Christmas, Edward had laughed and his mother ruffled his hair when carefully he cupped in his palms a scaly black beetle that was running across the carpet, opened the window and gently placed it on the sill.

He looked across the desk at his host and answered his question as best he could with, he hoped, frankness and compassion.

CHAPTER 16

DUSK WAS FALLING as Paudge took a deep breath and knocked on the door of the parlour.

Mrs Mulchinock looked up from her paperwork and gave him a warm smile as he entered.

'The complications of profit and loss, Paudge.'

'Sure isn't the bookkeeping second nature to you now?' he said as he began to light the lamp.

'Well, except for the creamery accounts.' She stood from her desk and loosened her shoulders.

Unusually for him, he fumbled with the chimney and the wick. Finally, when the light was casting a warm glow round the parlour, he asked, 'May I have a word with you, Mrs Mulchinock?'

She gestured him to a chair and took the opposite one.

He sat, leaning towards her, hands clasped around his knees. He cleared his throat, bit on his lip.

'What is it, Paudge?' she asked gently.

The circumstances of his upbringing had taught Paudge to fend for himself, to keep counsel and to be circumspect. He had put much thought into the best way of ensuring he got to wed Mary O'Connor. In his neat cabin, sitting by a small fire night after night he did his planning, deciding on this, dismissing that, settling for something else. Eventually he had come up with a course of action that appeared to be without flaw.

Mary's reaction to his admission of fondness for her had left him disheartened and deflated. But he was not about to give up – Paudge had reached his present position of indispensability around West Villa by determinedly learning and knowing as much as he could about the management of the estate, and by exercising care, caution and humility. In all aspects of his life such attitudes stood him in good stead.

'If I was to court Mary O'Connor would I have your approval?' After careful consideration he had chosen to ask permission rather than declare intent.

'Indeed you would, Paudge. She's a capable girl and she'd make you a good wife. And it's about time you settled down.'

He had expected her permission, but the warmth of her tone and her enthusiasm surprised and pleased him. He cleared his throat. So far so good. Now for the question that had caused him the most difficulty.

'Before I call on her father I'd like to know my long-term prospects at West Villa.'

'West Villa is your home – you'll always have a home here.' Now her surprise showed.

'I appreciate that. But when I marry I'd like to have some independence ...' His voice trailed off. He had ambitions and, with Mary by his side, he had hopes of bettering himself, perhaps setting up on his own.

'What do you mean by independence?'

Knowing Mrs Mulchinock, he should have anticipated questions, but he wasn't prepared.

'I have a few ideas …' Even to himself he sounded unsure.

'I'd have to discuss anything like that with Edward.'

Paudge wondered if he'd overstepped the mark.

'Have you spoken to Mary?' she asked.

'Not yet. But I've told her I'm fond of her.'

❀ ❀ ❀

Until Mary went into service she had little understanding of a life beyond the lanes. Brogue Lane was her heartbeat, the blood flowing through her veins – its lines of cabins strung with generations of sorrow and joy – as though the walls and thatches were living entities holding their inhabitants in thrall. Part of her was comforted by the familiarity of the lanes, another part of her craved escape from the obligations and way of life they imposed.

Now the world she knew was one of extremes – the small cabin on Brogue Lane and the big house at Annagh. She had little knowledge of anything else, but she saw being a teacher as a step towards freedom. If asked about the best part of her life – and she never was – she would answer, 'It's learning.' She thirsted for knowledge. She was desperate to disengage, to untangle from the clutches and expectations of an arranged marriage and a life, as she saw it, without prospects.

Her flights of imagination were without boundaries, although frequently they were swayed by what she observed at West Villa. Her knowledge of the family's way of living was limited but her interest in the packages of books coming from London, the newspapers lying about and the scatterings of magazines was never-ending.

She wondered about the shop on the Mall with its windows full of dazzling gowns, ribbons and lengths of lace. She wondered what it would be like to wear such finery, to feel the softness of those materials against her skin, a ruffle of that lace tickling her wrists. Sometimes, when she looked in the window, she saw the man they said was a Frenchman, fixing a button here, checking a bow there, and she'd heard there was a seamstress from Paris who was seldom seen about. She wondered about them and their lives.

Then she would shake her head at her foolishness but in her heart she knew it wasn't really foolishness at all – more like one of those desires that Mr O'Connell had spoken of.

Unable to resist any longer, one morning she opened the glass doors of the bookcase in Mrs Mulchinock's room and ran her finger across the spines of the leather-bound books . . . so many stories . . .

A few days later she'd placed her feather duster on the table, reached into the bookcase and removed a book. It was a novel called *Pride and Prejudice* by Jane Austen. She sat into the blue velvet chair, opened the book at the first page, ran her hands across the print, feeling the texture of the paper. As she read the opening lines, '*It is a truth universally acknowledged, that a single man in possession of a good fortune, must be in want of a wife,*' she breathed deeply and was assailed by the pungency of the words. She could have sat there for hours, reading, if a stir in the corridor hadn't alerted her.

She'd been happy in the schoolhouse, a one-windowed room at the back of the lanes with an earthen floor and a roof of rushes. Mr Foley had a shelf of books, but they were functional rather than elegant. As well as reading, writing and Irish and English grammar, Mr Foley taught maths and a little Latin and Greek, and he shared with his pupils an endless supply of stories, lines of verse, titbits of history.

'What's your best story, sir?' one of the boys had asked one day shortly before going-home time.

'Well, now ...'

Mary remembered how Mr Foley had looked at the eight of them, slowly casting his eyes over the five boys and just three girls – Hannah, Josie and her.

And then he had brought to life the story he called 'The Salmon of Knowledge', and as she listened to him and imagined the happenings, she forgot the cold and hunger.

'Any questions?' he asked.

Her hand shot up.

'Yes, Mary.'

'Is it really true?'

'What do you think?' He looked into each face in turn, giving them the chance for discussion.

The children sat silently absorbed in the wonder of how it would be to know everything after only the lick of a finger that had touched the flesh of the salmon.

'It's just a story, isn't it, sir? I don't believe it,' she said.

'And what, Mary O'Connor, do you believe?'

'To know we must learn.' She wasn't sure where that came from or why she said it.

Mr Foley didn't comment but, from the way he looked at her and his little nod, she was sure he agreed with her.

❀ ❀ ❀

Mrs Mulchinock had the reputation of being a fair employer, and the Big House at Annagh was regarded as being a good place to work. Mary was aware of the glances of envy cast in her direction and how the same envy stunted many a greeting as she passed through the town. She was blessed – she knew that. Regularly she counted her blessings in the same way as she counted out the prayers on her beads during the nightly ritual of the rosary.

During the brightness of the day she held those blessings close to her. With spring turning to summer as she walked to and from Annagh, she was enchanted by the power and beauty of nature – the blur of bluebells and carpets of buttercups, the hedgerows bursting with blossoms and the thrill of birdsong in the high blue of the sky.

But the darkness of nightfall brought fluttering anxieties.

Her main fear was being forced into marriage. Her father was not a cruel man, but he had a foolishness about him, and he was easily swayed by the likes of Father Sheehy, and Mr Cluskey swaggering along the Lane, boasting and bragging about the dollars in his pockets, courtesy of Hennessey's son in America.

As always thinking of that match brought Mary back to Hannah and Danny. There wasn't a whisper about them and not a sign of Mr Hennessey around the town. They must have got away safely, across the wide ocean to America.

Twilight fingered the outside air with grey as Mary pushed in the half door.

Slowly Nora straightened up from the fire where she was tending to the pot of potatoes. She held onto the back of the chair in an effort to ease out the pains she was learning to live with and looked at her daughter.

'I'll not be going back to the Big House again.'

Mary unwound her shawl. 'Are you sure, Mam? Give yourself time. You'll get better.'

'No, Mary, I won't. Mrs Mac called this morning. And I hear you're gone to the upstairs.' She gave a worn smile. 'I am proud of you, *a stór*. Why didn't you tell us?'

'You're better off here for now.' Mary ignored her mother's question. 'I'm bringing in enough for us to manage.' She grieved for her mother but exulted that she'd be spending her days at West Villa rather than back on the lane.

'It's not right.' Willie's voice slurred. On getting an order from the new curate earlier in the day, they had celebrated the deal with half a jug of poteen. He was stitching on the uppers of the boots now, his curved needle and waxed thread flying in and out of the leather.

Billy was hanging over his shoulder, asking his interminable questions. When could he make a pair of shoes? Could he have a go at using this awl? Why was that strip of leather so soft? Well, maybe he could thread the needle?

When Willie O'Connor had drink on him he ignored his son — he ignored everyone and only spoke to complain. Now he fixed Mary with a sour look and gave a grunt of displeasure.

Once it was obvious that his father wasn't in the mood for answering his questions, Billy said, 'I'll be slippin' out for a while, so.' As he spoke his eyes slithered sideways and his behaviour was so uncharacteristically nonchalant that Mary feared he was on his way to no good.

❀ ❀ ❀

It was late when the groan of the door on its hinges marked

Billy's return. It groaned again, although more gently as he closed it over.

Mary exhaled a breath of relief. He was back. Safe. She listened for the shuffle of his footsteps to the corner where he slept, but instead he came and stood over her, looking down to where she lay with Brigid on one side and Ellen on the other.

'*Psst*, Mary. Get up. I've got something to tell you.'

Careful not to wake her sisters, Mary eased away from the warmth of the bodies spooned around her. Throwing her shawl across her shoulders, she stepped over Brigid who grizzled grumpily. Barely awake and scarcely aware of the sleepy slur of her footsteps on the earthen floor she joined Billy where he was standing by the fire, his back to the dying embers of the turf, his thumbs stuck into the waistband of his trousers.

He had lit a stump of a candle and its flame ran shadows like grasping fingers across the ceiling. In the dimness of the half-light, Billy's expression was serious. He caught at her hand and his whisper was barely audible.

'Mary, there's something I have to tell you. But you can't let on to know. Or ever tell anyone where you heard it.'

Mary felt the tightening of fear across her chest. 'Billy, what is it?'

'Promise me first.'

'I promise.' What could he know that was so serious? Something to do with the Whiteboys? Her fear was strangling her. 'Tell me.' She placed the palm of her hand on his cheek, the way she used to when he was little and frightened.

'It's Danny and Hannah.' His voice shook.

'What about them? What about them, Billy? Answer me.' The news couldn't be good and she wanted to scream, but she kept her voice to a whisper.

'They found 'em. Washed ashore at Blennerville.'

'*Oh, Billy! No. No.* It can't be them. They should be well gone to America.'

'So you knew?'

She nodded.

'Hennessey must have found out. They were tied to each other. Face to face. Lying on the stones.' His voice broke.

Mary had no control over the way her belly voided, scattering vomit down her shift and over her bare feet. Her knees buckled and she sank to the floor.

Billy squatted beside her and put his hands on her shoulders. '*Shush*. Never talk of this. Never let on to anyone that you knew anything about it. Hennessey is capable of anything – everyone knows that.'

Mary shook with silent sobs. 'Billy, how do you know? Where did you hear?'

'At the meeting tonight.'

'The Whiteboys?'

He nodded.

'For God's sake, Billy, be careful.'

He was a subdued figure. A boy no longer, within him she saw the man he was fast becoming.

'I will. We take care. We always do.'

❀ ❀ ❀

There was open-mouthed gossip aplenty around the town the next day when the discovery of the bodies became public.

Young Danny Stack and Hannah Cluskey – in death she was no longer referred to as Hennessey's wife. Initially it was presumed their drowning together was an appalling accident, but the way they were found lying on the cold grey stones of the harbour, bound together and facing each other put paid to that rumour. Sadness at the loss of such young lives settled like a pall over the town. Everyone had an opinion, everyone knew something, but Mary was the one who knew the most and she was the one who said nothing.

There was talk and rumours of the RIC inspector leading an investigation. Muttering suspicions for the deaths pointed towards Mr Hennessey. Reportedly he was seen limping from the station after questioning, others saw him stumbling along the Rock of an evening, while someone else came across him halfway up the mountain, waving his stick and cursing.

But in the end all the surmising about him, his movements and reactions turned out to be little more than fleeting, unsubstantiated rumours. The tragedy tore at the heart of the community, but eventually, as happens, people ran out of speculation.

CHAPTER 17

THE SHOCK OF THE LETTERS Mrs Mulchinock had received that morning had her head reeling and her thoughts swirling. She stood up from her desk – there was no way she could concentrate on the new regulations from the creamery or the costings for reroofing the stables.

She opened the double doors leading to the garden and stepped out, tightening her shawl across her shoulders and tucking her hands into its folds of silk as she sought to steady herself, to tell herself that the news could be worse, although she found that difficult to imagine.

The weather contributed to her sense of unease. The last days of April were as capricious as the rest of the month. The warm breeze and sunny skies of yesterday had disappeared – the clouds were heavy and grey, and the wind sharp and biting. For once her flower beds with their explosion of colour – stately tulips in reds, yellows and striped pinks, perky blue forget-me-nots and the appealing orange and maroon faces of early pansies offered no solace.

She tried not to dwell in the past – she knew that her survival and the survival of her family and their business interests were best served by living her life in the present. Each morning she made lists of tasks to be done and decisions requiring action, doggedly throughout the day she accomplished them and before retiring for the night she took pleasure in crossing them off her list.

It was too cold, the greyness too penetrating to remain outside. She returned indoors and stood with her back to the fire's peaty flames, feeling the warmth through the wool of her skirt.

Perhaps she should spend a little time with her embroidery? But the perfection of the half-worked scattering of purple and yellow pansies created in meticulous satin stitch on the square of cream linen gave her no pleasure.

The letters had every fibre of her being aching for Michael – it was a long time since she had been consumed by such a craving.

Just this once she would permit herself the luxury of wallowing in her past.

Unlocking the drawer of the bureau, she removed her green-leather journal, ran her index finger over its cover. Up and down her nail traced the gold lettering. It was years since she'd read the story of Michael and her, but she had drawn comfort from knowing of the existence of her personal record of happier occasions.

Evenings, after the day's work was done, had been precious times for them. They would sit by the fire reading, chatting, curled into each other in one of the blue velvet chairs.

After his death, she had sat night after night recalling that fatal

Friday, until every detail of it was stamped on her brain like the faces on bad coinage. Evenings became raw, lonely times, her grief so painful that she feared for her sanity.

In desperation, during the purpling twilight of a January evening, she had started to write. As she had told him, she wouldn't forget, she couldn't forget every nuance of their lives together, their story, but she hoped that writing it down might bring him close, might ease a little of her pain.

As she dipped her nib into the ink holder and began to write the story of Margaret McCann who fell in love with a young gentleman called Michael Mulchinock, she felt the presence of her husband, the parlour filled with him.

While she reminisced and wrote, Mrs Mulchinock, widow, mother and mistress of West Villa, reverted to the young Margaret McCann. Moths hurled themselves against the lamp and fluttered around the candles, but she paid no mind to them. For the first time in a long time all else was eclipsed by the purer sense of purpose and the words she was writing. She no longer distinguished between dreams and memories, each bleeding into the other, laying down layer after layer of recollections as she filled the pages slowly and lovingly, savouring each memory, imagining memories that weren't quite hers, but that might have been.

March 1818. King George III was on the throne.
Margaret McCann was one of the most vivacious of the young ladies presented during the Season at Dublin Castle.

Vivacious!

On an occasion when Mama had insisted she accompany her on her calls, Margaret overheard her mother's special friend, the dowager refer to her as "vivacious". She hadn't felt right applying the word "vivacious" to her young self until now, and the thought of the innocent she was then brought on a gentle smile.

Margaret's father, a prominent member of Dublin society, impressed on her the difficulties he had to overcome to acquire invitations not only to Dublin Castle, but to the Viceroy's Drawing Room, the most important event of the season. He further impressed on her the great honour and importance of being presented to the Viceroy's representative, the importance of her behaviour, the importance making a good match, the importance of so many things. This, that and the other importance. Until her head felt it would burst with all those importances. And Mama was no help. She was on Father's side, nodding in agreement with everything he said.

It wasn't until Margaret had begun her journal that she realised how much she enjoyed the freedom of writing – what she thought, what happened, what didn't happen, what she might have liked to happen. There was nobody looking over her shoulder insisting she formed her letters properly, made complete sentences, punctuated in the right places. Through her writing she came to truly understand William Pembroke's preoccupation with words.

When Margaret's eyes met those of a slender young man across the gilt-and-red expanse of the ballroom of Dublin Castle, her interest was piqued, but without expectation as young men were beyond her remit and she had no experience of them.

From birth, her father had predetermined her future. She may have railed against other restrictions, but she was philosophical about whom he would chose for her to marry. It was the way it was for daughters of wealthy professionals in Ireland of the 1800s.

Still, *as the handsome figure in the dark-blue coat walked towards her across the ballroom, she hoped. As an avid reader of Jane Austen's romantic fiction, she likened him to Mr Darcy stepping out from the pages of 'Pride and Prejudice', albeit he was fair rather than dark-haired.*

As he approached, she rose from her seat and, oblivious to her mother's gasp of incredulity, went towards him and stood, waiting. Her silken gown from Paris was in a soft blue with elegantly slim sleeves.

Not for her the simpering mannerisms of the young girls of the period.

He bowed low over her hand 'Michael Mulchinock,' he said without elaboration. Afterwards she swore she felt his lips burn through the fine fabric of her glove.

'Margaret McCann,' she replied solemnly and with equal brevity. She gave a slight dip of her right leg — not really a curtsy, but the movement created a becoming ripple in the skirt of her gown.

They looked at each other gravely, unsmilingly.

Of one accord as the music struck up, they moved to the centre of the floor, she ignoring her dance programme on which no line remained unclaimed, while he was indifferent to her programme's existence. They revelled in the sensual music and saucy steps of Herr Straus's waltz.

Impervious to her mother's agitated fluttering of her fan — after all she was her daughter's official chaperone — Margaret and Michael remained together, either dancing or sitting out, but aware only of each other. They were decorous, nobody could accuse them of being otherwise, but they were distant to outside overtures.

As Michael handed Margaret back to her mother, he bowed deeply and said, 'Please inform Mr McCann that I shall call upon him tomorrow afternoon.'

❀ ❀ ❀

When her knock went unanswered, Mary opened the door of the

parlour and entered the room, carrying an arrangement of cherry blossom in a copper jug. As she placed the copper jug on the bureau a sound alerted her.

Mrs Mulchinock was sitting in her armchair almost hidden by its wings, an open book resting on her lap.

As she turned around she dashed at her cheeks with a lacy handkerchief. Mary crossed over to her and rested a hand on her shoulder.

'Oh, ma'am. What it is? What has you upset?'

Mrs Mulchinock sat up straighter and dabbed at her eyes. 'It's nothing, Mary. I'm quite all right.' She was amazed at the reaction of the girl. Never before had she experienced such forwardness and certainly not from servant. No, she amended, the word was not 'forwardness' – it was kindness, an instinctive kindness, the likes of which she had rarely, if ever, encountered.

Mary took a few steps backwards. 'I'm sorry, I shouldn't ...'

'It's all right, Mary.' She gestured to the journal. 'I was remembering my husband. I miss him.'

Mary took in the handwriting on the open page. 'Is it all wrote down?'

'Yes, I've written our story in my journal.'

Mary gave a little gasp, 'That's special, ma'am, but it must make for sad reading.' She was washed with the awfulness of Liam's death, the toll it had taken on them all, her mother especially, and the deaths of Hannah and Danny, but she sought to offer comfort, 'But hadn't you and the master a great love affair?'

'Where did you hear that?'

'Sure, doesn't everyone know?'

As Mrs Mulchinock was unable to think of a suitable comment, she settled for 'You are kind and there's not much of that around.'

'Can I get you a sup of tay?' For the women of the lane, tea when it could be afforded was the panacea for all ills. From what Mary had observed the Mulchinocks could afford to drink any amount of it morning, noon and night.

'No. I am quite all right. That is all for now.'

❀ ❀ ❀

That morning Mrs Mulchinock had broken the seal of William Pembroke's letter with urgent delight – a letter from him was a treat to be savoured. She had read its opening lines with pleasure, but pleasure changed to foreboding as she continued to the end of the page.

She reread it, slowly, one word at a time. It retained the same shock. He had left Ballinasloe but didn't plan to return to Tralee in the foreseeable future. He finished by assuring her that the shop was in the capable hands of M. Aubin. He offered no further explanation.

When she had slid her paperknife under the flap of Mr Keogh's letter its curt contents informed her that, as her son had behaved in an ungentlemanly fashion towards his daughter, he was no longer welcome as a guest in his home. Nor were any of his family.

From an effusive note she had received from Mrs Keogh some weeks previously, and from reading between the lines of today's letters she guessed that her son's exit from Ballinasloe had to do with the unrealised expectations of a betrothal.

From the time her children were babies her dearest wish was they would have as happy a marriage as hers. It didn't look as though that wish would be realised: Charlotte running away from her husband, Edward gaining a reputation for flirting with young matrons and William Pembroke's hasty retreat from Ballinasloe –

how could he have been so unaware? She sighed, overwhelmed. He was too wrapped up in words to the detriment of life going on around him.

Again she reached for the consolation of her journal. As she read, she relived the day in March 1818 that changed her life, amused at how she had indulged in the naughty pleasure of deducing her father's reactions and presuming to know how Michael would conduct himself. The words she had written all those years ago, imagining she was an authoress, like Jane Austen, took on a dream-like quality as the comfort of the past enveloped her.

On the morning following the ball Mr McCann dismissed his daughter's assurance that she had met the only man she would wed. He hectored her mama until she declared, her hand clasped to her heart, that if he did not desist, she would have a fit of the vapours.

Unknown to the other members of his family Mr McCann had foregone the pleasure of attending the ball to spend the evening going over accounts with his secretary, a nervous young man with a stammer and facility for analysis. The secretary's conclusion, delivered in his hesitant manner, was the same as before — he regretted to be the harbinger of such bad news but, in his opinion, Mr McCann was on the point of being declared a bankrupt.

Head bowed in his hands, Mr McCann sat behind the desk in the elegant house he had rented in Fitzwilliam Square for the Season, reliving his financial decisions of the previous decades. When he was a young man, after weighing up the pros and cons, he settled on trusting his money to Roche's Bank in Cork. As the number of private banks in Ireland fell he was certain enough of his own judgement to ignore the advice of the financial experts as to why he should transfer to the Bank of Ireland in Dublin. And now? He faced ruin. In these times — any time, indeed, lack of money was a disastrous situation — he and his family would be regarded as social pariahs.

His daughter and a suitor. His anger seesawed. How dare she! The impertinence of the young man arranging to call without as much as a proper introduction. Although he had somewhat modified his attitude when he discovered the young man in question was a Mulchinock, one of the Mulchinocks from his hometown of Tralee.

He summoned his daughter to his study and gestured to the chair on the opposite side of his desk. Margaret sat, unafraid, her hands resting lightly on her lap. Her creamy skin and dark-brown hair was complemented by the rich russet colour of her morning gown. New, he wagered, and from Paris he wagered further.

Pushing out his chair from the desk, he folded his arms across his ample belly, encased on that occasion in a waistcoat of gold-and-maroon brocade – Mr McCann too enjoyed wearing clothes made from luxurious materials.

The touch of his palms against the cloth reminded him of how much luxurious living cost, how much of an income it took to run his property in Kerry and to rent in Fitzwilliam Square for the Season – servants, upkeep, stabling, carriages, a wife, two sons and a daughter – all unused to doing without.

Uncharacteristically, he waited for his daughter to speak – usually he was the one in control, the dominant presence. He was one of the acknowledged leaders of the Irish legal profession, and in his household his every wish was met with alacrity.

Still he waited. If his wife was to be believed Margaret hadn't been shy about taking the initiative in the Castle. She had no right to have an opinion about whom she would or would not wed. Would that his sons displayed such a sense of initiative. Two gambling dandies he'd reared. But, egad, that was about to change, no matter what the outcome of his current financial fiasco.

At last he spoke.

'What did you find so admirable in that young man?' He was pleased with his choice of past tense.

Her smile danced into her eyes, but instead of answering she parried with, 'Pray, Father dearest, and what have you discovered about Michael Mulchinock?'

He was taken aback by her riposte but filled with admiration for her feistiness. Wench that she was, he was amused too by her humorous addressing of him as 'Father dearest'. For a girl she possessed unusual powers of debate and she wasn't shy about having attitudes. Had she been a boy he might have enjoyed developing such powers. But a girl, and such a comely one at that, had no need to develop an intellect. Heaven forbid, she might turn into a blue stocking.

Discovery about young Mulchinock wasn't necessary. He knew of the family's wealth earned from hard work — the ability to work to achieve financial success was a trait he admired. He also knew their social position was inferior to the McCann family. But Michael Mulchinock was an only child and West Villa's estate and holdings were considerable.

At precisely four o'clock Michael turned into Fitzwilliam Square. He was dressed fashionably in pale breeches, highly polished boots, a cutaway jacket in dark blue and a fine muslin shirt.

He looked joyously to the future with Margaret by his side. It never crossed his mind that he would not make her his bride.

Inside, the footman preceded him up one flight of the sweeping staircase and into a book-lined study. It was the best part of a minute before, pushing his eyeglasses up on his nose, Mr McCann raised his eyes from the brief he was studying.

'Sit you down.' He pointed to the chair occupied by his daughter some hours previously.

Michael would have preferred to remain standing — it would be the better to state his case — but with a slight lift of his eyebrows he did as he was bid. As he sat waiting while Mr McCann continued reading, he became aware of what he didn't know. He knew all he needed to know about Margaret, but he hadn't taken into consideration the temperaments of her family members, particularly her father from whom he needed permission to marry her, unless he carried her off. If it came to that he would.

So lost was he in thinking through the complications of eloping that he was a little taken aback when Mr McCann tipped back his chair and asked, 'You wanted to see me?'

'Yes, sir. To talk to you on an important matter.'

'So?'

'Did Miss McCann and Mrs McCann mention me?'

'Indeed they did.'

'Then you know why I'm here.'

Mr McCann was beginning to enjoy himself. 'You had better tell me.'

'I come to seek your daughter's hand in marriage.'

'What can you offer her that cannot be offered a hundred times more by others?'

'My devotion and love and a comfortable life. She will want for nothing.'

'She wants for nothing now. And she has suitors from titled families asking for her hand in marriage.'

'That I didn't know.'

'Discussions are taking place.'

'I do not need discussions or meetings. No dowry is necessary. Indeed, if you agree to us being wed soon, as a matter of honour and to prove my intent I will settle a sum of money on you immediately.'

Mr McCann jerked backwards. 'Do you have a sum in mind? Not that it's important,' he added hastily, 'but just so we know where we stand.'

During the intervening hours, Michael had not been idle either. The figure he mentioned was precisely the amount Mr McCann needed to ease his current financial predicament, generously rounded up to an even fifty guineas.

Mr McCann stroked the brocade of his waistcoat, 'In the circumstances and if my daughter is agreeable, I believe the matter can be speedily resolved.'

When the two men joined the ladies in the drawing room, Mrs McCann, sitting behind a handsome samovar, was the perfect hostess. As Michael sipped tea, he had eyes only for Margaret.

The following year the young couple were married. Their life was so blissfully happy that frequently Margaret wondered if it could continue. It ended on the fateful day when Michael was thrown from his horse.

CHAPTER 18

MRS MULCHINOCK WAS PLEASED. She had been right about bringing Mary upstairs. With the minimum of training, in less than a month, the girl was more than competent. Sitting at her desk Mrs Mulchinock watched as she eased the folds of the blue velvet curtains into place and ran the feather duster over the surface of a table. She wore her youth and beauty carelessly, as though they were eternal, as if age did not exist.

As their eyes met, Mary smiled, waved the bunch of feathers, and said, 'This is a lovely room, ma'am. All the blue.'

'Do you like colour?'

'Yes. And blue is my favourite.'

As she watched Mary adjusting the stance of a tulip, she was taken anew by her appeal and lightness of spirit. She was such a pleasant girl.

'Do you have a nice bonnet?' she asked.

'A nice bonnet. No, ma'am, I don't. Well, I do have a bonnet.

But it not nice. It's an old one of mam's.'

'Would you like one? A blue bonnet? To wear when you walk out with – your young man.' Just in time Mrs Mulchinock stopped herself from naming Paudge.

An expression of delight crossed Mary's face, quickly followed by a look of wariness. 'Where would the likes of me get such a bonnet? And I don't have a young man.' With a touch of mischief, she added, 'Or an old one either.'

'I have such a bonnet that I am unable to wear.' Mrs Mulchinock was puzzled. Paudge's courtship of Mary did not appear to be progressing.

'What has you unable to wear it?'

'As I am in mourning, I am confined to black.'

'Oh.' Mary's hand flew to her lips. 'I don't think of you as being in mourning. The widows who lived on the lanes keen like the Banshees of the race of the *Tuatha de Danaan*, thumping their breasts and wringing their hands, *ochóning agus ochóning*.' She stopped talking. 'Ooh, I am sorry.' Quickly she added, 'Ma'am'.

Mrs Mulchinock turned around to her desk – mistress and servant back in perspective. She would like to have Mary live in – but that had to wait – with Nora unwell and that husband of her so profligate, she was needed at home.

All the way back to Brogue Lane, resisting the urge to peep, but giving an occasional hop, skip and jump, Mary swung the silver hatbox backwards and forwards by its blue cords.

Once inside the cabin, she placed the box on the table, opened it slowly, peeped in and smiled in delight before reverently lifting out the bonnet from beneath the smooth folds of soft crumpled paper in the palest of blue.

'Look what I've got.' She placed the bonnet on her head, allowing the streamer ribbons to flow over her shoulders.

'It's lovely,' whispered Ellen.

'Oh, *a stór!*' Nora clasped her hands. She was taken aback at the beauty of her eldest daughter.

Mary's face was flushed with pleasure, her eyes darkened with joy and her hair, loosened from its confines, streamed down her back. The flower-trimmed bonnet looked so right on her.

'*Ooh,*' said Billy.

'Let me see, let me see!' cried Brigid. 'Can I try it?'

Mary handed the bonnet to Brigid.

Brigid was instantly transformed. She patted at the streamers before tying them under her chin in a big bow and twirling around the kitchen. She came to a stop in front of Nora, dropped a deep curtsy, took off the bonnet and returned it to Mary who twirled it around and around on her index finger.

'Mam, couldn't we even have a small kitchen dance?' Brigid pleaded.

Mary's unexpected gift had broken the humdrum of their lives.

Nora put a finger to her lips. 'Shush a while. We'll have to ask your father.'

Sensing he was being called upon, Willie looked up, his eyes blinking as they always did when adjusting from his world of leather and wax thread to the kitchen scene of family life.

He stood up from his table, straightened his shoulders, wiped his hands on his apron and moved towards Mary who was still twirling the bonnet.

'Where did you get that?'

Mary was taken aback at the roughness of his voice. 'Mrs Mulchinock gave it to me.'

'Are you sure of that now?'

Nora grasped the undercurrent of meaning in his question.

'Yes, I said Mrs Mulchinock. She gave it to me.' Mary looked fearlessly at her father.

'You'll not go cavorting in that. Give it back. No matter who gave it to you.' His voice was laced with suspicion and scepticism.

'I won't give it back. I will wear it.'

'You won't. Not while you're under my roof.'

Nora tightened with fear.

Mary stood her ground – the bonnet was hers, the only gift she had ever received and she would keep it and wear it.

Ellen and Brigid, wide-eyed, looked from their father to their sister.

'She has a right to it, Pa. And you've no right to stop her.' Billy's voice was calm and measured – it had deepened over the past weeks.

Father and son locked eyes. It was Willie whose look shifted sideways. The silence of the battle for male supremacy lay thick in the air and seeped into every corner of the cabin.

Willie dropped his eyes to the ground and retreated. He sat down heavily and picked up the shoe he had been working on.

Billy slammed out the door.

It was then that Mary knew for a fact and with a sensation of creeping dread that Billy's new-found confidence was stirred by outside influences. Given the right opportunities and chances he would grow to be a fine man, but if he took a wrong turning God only knew what might happen to him.

❊ ❊ ❊

Next morning she thanked Mrs Mulchinock for the bonnet. 'I will keep it for best.'

'Don't keep it 'for best' — enjoy it every day.'

'If I do I'm afeared it'll wear out.'

Mrs Mulchinock looked at her servant. She had never heard a more poignantly stated philosophy. There, in the girl's words, was the difference between those who had enough and those who were used to existing without.

❀ ❀ ❀

It was an afternoon of birdsong, humming bees and the sun shining from a blameless sky. Mary's mind was full of nothing more than the pleasure of being outside in the gardens, among the scent of crushed grass and thyme, gathering an armful of the first of the long-stemmed dog daisies. She rubbed her finger along their rough green stems with their sprinkling of tough little leaves, felt the satin delicacy of their white petals and the linen-like texture of their sturdy pollen-laden yellow centres that tickled her nose with their musky scent.

Paudge, who was checking on the privet hedges, watched her through a screen of yellowy-green leaves, thinking of the pleasures of being wed to her.

As though sensing she was not alone, she turned around, frowning as he stepped out. 'I didn't know you were there, Paudge.' She smiled shyly. 'You gave me a bit of a fright.'

In Mary's early days at West Villa she had sought out Paudge as frequently as he had sought her out. She asked questions of him and wanted his advice on this or that or was just happy to listen to him talk. But since his invitation to the dance platform she had become wary of him and grown adroit at avoiding him.

Perhaps it was the June sunshine, the daisies, traditionally carried by brides in Kerry, her smile, or just the pleasure of the summer silence and the long grass giving off puffs of pollen, but he said, 'As you must know, Mary, I've grown very fond of you.' He didn't wait to see her reaction to this or to hear her response before adding, 'I want us to be wed.' They were the words he had been thinking about for weeks and had practised saying out loud in the silence of his cabin.

Mary's features settled into amazement, her pulse thumped and her belly clenched in protest. She closed her eyes. She did not want this, any of it. She was unprepared for Paudge's proposal, unsure of what to say to him, uncertain of what to do about it. She opened her eyes. Her instinct was to dash the flowers to the ground. And to run.

'Mary?' His voice was soft.

How could she have been such an *amadán* as not to realise his intentions when he had suggested going to Clahane? How she wished for Hannah to confide in. She stood indecisive in the afternoon sunshine, her arms full of white daisies.

She did not want to be hurtful in her refusal, but by then she knew enough about Paudge and the way he went about his life to appreciate the importance of her answer. It would have to be decisive; she needed to make herself clear to him and to ensure that he understood exactly what she meant by her words.

'I am honoured, Paudge.' She inclined her head in a gracious gesture. 'And I thank you. But I cannot marry you.' Her voice took on additional firmness, 'I will not marry you. Ever.'

As he heard her words Paudge took his eyes off her. He clenched his jaw and pressed his teeth together so hard that they ached. He bent down, picked up a fallen daisy and twirled it between his thumb and finger.

Mary chastised herself for not realising the depth of his feelings for her, for not saving them both from this situation –

how could she have been blind to the soft way he looked at her. It was the very way Danny used to look at Hannah. She saw his upset and as it was not in her nature to be cruel or thoughtless, she amended, 'I can't leave the lane. My mam is ill and I am needed.'

As Paudge grasped at her excuse his features loosened. 'Maybe, when she's better?'

This was going from bad to worse. 'No. I said I won't marry you. I mean it, Paudge. And I beg of you, don't take this further. Don't call on my father.'

'But surely when your mother has recovered?' His voice was full of hope — he had only heard what he wanted to hear.

There was no point in continuing. Mary gestured to the daisies. 'I should be ...'

'Yes,' he said.

CHAPTER 19

A SENSE OF OCCASION surrounded afternoon tea at West Villa. The table was carefully dressed in embroidered linen; the lady-thin tea service was gold-rimmed and small silver spoons tinkled in its saucers. Mrs Mac oversaw the making and plating of triangles of thinly sliced bread and butter, finger sandwiches of egg, salmon and cheese, as well as buttery biscuits and slices of porter cake.

When women were present at these afternoon sessions they sat upright, with skirts arranged in careful fans across the seats of their chairs. The male guests were more relaxed, sitting back from the table and spreading their legs wide. Slender white hands and the broader male versions stirred sugar lumps into the tea, lifted cups to the lips and ate morsels of sandwiches and cake while conversing on family matters, local happenings and social gossip.

That afternoon, tea was set up in the parlour overlooking the lawns and flowerbeds. While Charlotte and her daughters were taking the air in their summer finery of lace and muslins and new summer bonnets, light and delicate as butterflies, Mrs Mulchinock was entertaining her brother-in-law, with Mary in attendance.

There was an air of great kindliness about John Mulchinock — he had a gentle, clever face that lit up as he asked caring questions and supplied thoughtful answers.

Had dear Margaret seen the display of French millinery at that new shop in Denny Street?

She had, indeed, and pronounced it 'Quite lovely'.

'Indeed, quite ravishing,' he added.

They were both perplexed by Daniel O'Connell's remark about 'a parchment union' and conversed for a good ten minutes about the way political coverage was handled in the *Kerry Evening Post*.

She had news of a reward of £1 for information on the four heifers stolen the previous week.

He wondered if she knew of a suitable pair of carriage horses for sale; she promised to make enquiries.

They discussed the pros and cons of travelling between Dublin and Limerick on the Grand Canal, and the value of a first-class cabin for fifteen shillings.

'I know, my dear, that you greatly admire young Queen Victoria.'

Mrs Mulchinock inclined her head. 'Indeed. I have constantly refused to commit to Irish politics, but one of my dearest wishes it that she will bring peace, prosperity and refined sensibility to Ireland.'

When their families became the subject of conversation Mrs Mulchinock dismissed Mary with her usual graciousness.

Then, Mrs Mulchinock poured out her heart to John about her upset and disquiet at William Pembroke's exit from Ballinasloe. Her brother-in-law was a sympathetic listener and a man with wisdom in his replies.

'There's nothing you can do about it, my dear, and if what you say is true we wouldn't want William Pembroke in an unhappy union. Situations mellow with time. And how is Charlotte and her lovely daughters?'

Mrs Mulchinock told him in succinct words that had him laughing. Before he took his leave he had succeeded in calming her and providing her with a solution to Charlotte's problem of caring for her daughters.

❈❈❈

Watching the efficient way Mary went about clearing off the remnants of afternoon tea, Mrs Mulchinock asked, 'Do you like children?'

Since coming to work at West Villa, Mary had come to realise that 'yes' was best when asked that type of a question, 'Oh, yes, ma'am.'

'Your brothers and sisters are no longer little?'

Mary wished she knew where Mrs Mulchinock's questions were leading.

'No, ma'am, they're not little anymore. Billy cuts turf and he is going to learn the trade from my father. And Ellen and Brigid have lessons in the school, and sometimes they get a bit of work selling bootlaces in the town or picking stones from the fields.'

'And you? What about you?'

Since being at West Villa Mary's head was increasingly full of thoughts and dreams and ambitions.

Some nights she dreamt that her family had achieved Mr O'Connell's promise of happiness and riches, their thatch was fresh, the cabin warm, the food bin stocked and drinks of tea and sweet milk a constant; other times her dream was of bookcases full of books written by Miss Austen and Mr Dickens waiting to be read; and on occasions her mind was filled with perfumed soap, cold cream of roses, pearl necklaces and the lengths of lace and fringing she saw in Mrs Mulchinock's and Miss Charlotte's bedchambers.

The wonder of dreams was that they cost nothing.

She wasn't about to speak of such matters to her mistress. She moved her shoulders uneasily and dropped her gaze. 'I suppose I've a bit of ambition, but mostly I just dream and I like to read.' That was as good an answer as she could come up with on the spur of the moment, and she hoped without too much expectation that Mrs Mulchinock might allow her to borrow some of the books.

Mrs Mulchinock suspected she was embarrassing the girl with her questions, but she also suspected that given the opportunity Mary O'Connor could be feisty and opinionated – not good traits for a servant girl, although she found her most pleasant to have around. She had heard nothing but praise for her from Mrs Mac, and she was a hard taskmaster.

'What do you dream of?'

'The roads to Dublin. I'd like to see the city. The organ grinders with monkeys. And the sea – wondering where it goes – I saw it the once out Fenit way.'

Mary's answer surprised her and confirmed the validity of her brother-in-law's suggestion.

She'd hand the matter over to Charlotte – it would be good for her to have the responsibility.

As Mary reached the door with the tray, she asked, 'Has Paudge spoken to you, said anything to you?' She flinched a little at the baldness of her own question.

'Yes, Paudge has spoken to me. But with Mam unwell I am needed at home.'

❁ ❁ ❁

During that golden hour of the evening when sunshine gilded the weeds and grasses that grew in the cracked mud, Mary met Father Sheehy at the entrance to Brogue Lane. He was leaving and she was returning. When he saw her, he shuffled something under his soutane, his eyes shifting sideways. His '*Dia dhuit*,' was so hearty that Mary wondered what he'd been up to.

She didn't have long to wait. As soon as she pushed in the door of the cabin and stepped into the kitchen, she saw her father seated at the table, the jar of poteen at his elbow; one mug was half full and another one empty. She took it in and knew. If she was in any doubt, Willie's ineffective effort to hide the jar and his mug confirmed her suspicions.

'You gave him the boots?'

Willie's face hung uneven in the flicker of tiny flames from the fire. 'That's my business.'

'It's all of our business. Not having enough affects us all.'

'We have plenty.' He flattened his skimpy fringe of hair against his forehead.

'So he didn't pay you. He still owes you money for the other pair.' Mary's voice rose shrilly. '*And you gave him drink!*'

She stopped at that. There was no point in railing over his attitude towards the clergy. It was Father Sheehy who was wrong – a priest should know better than to take goods without paying.

More than anyone he was privy to the aching poverty and hunger of so many of his parishioners. That the O'Connors had a little more than most did not mean he should rob her father of his due.

She used the bellows to blow the fire to a few weak flames, fetched a cauldron of water from the yard and set it to boil. Potatoes and buttermilk as usual, but Billy had brought in a couple of mackerel and she had the few carrots Mrs Mac had slipped her.

'Father Sheehy was discussing you.'

Willie's tone had a conciliatory ring and Mary wondered what was coming – nothing good she'd wager. 'Discussing me? What was he saying?'

'Your future.' Willie stroked a rectangular piece of leather.

Mary was about to say that her future was none of Father Sheehy's business when she thought better of it. There was no point in antagonising her father who was so influenced by the clergy.

'And what of my future? What did the two of ye decide?' She kept her voice light as she washed the mugs by holding them by their handles and scooting them backwards and forwards in the basin of rinsing water before returning them to the middle shelf of dresser. She placed the well-depleted jar of poteen at the back of the cupboard, and began putting bowls, mugs and cutlery on the table.

'He was saying you'd make a good wife. Needn't be a dowry – that a man'd pay a good bride price for you.'

As Willie spoke, his eyes narrowed, and when Mary looked over at him she saw that he was watching her closely, as though in anticipation of her reaction.

She rested her hands on the table. A crawl of worry ran up her back, but she wouldn't show fear. She looked at him squarely and spat out each word, 'A good wife for a good bride price. And no need for dowry.'

'You've changed since you went to the Big House.'

'And glad I am to be changed. To know I do not have to be bartered.'

'You know Paudge.' He tossed his head. 'And you likely know what I'm about to say?'

Mary clenched her fists. The seed of unease at the thought of marriage to Paudge had sprouted and grown. The idea of being attached to him for life! Her thoughts scurried like a mouse as she sought to scramble together reasons for her father as to why she shouldn't or wouldn't marry Paudge. But her mind remained blank with anxiety.

Paudge. She thought she'd made her position clear to him and that he'd honour it. She should have known he wouldn't let the matter rest — he knew his worth, it was a regular topic of conversation in the kitchen — he was well in with the Mulchinocks and he had his own cabin on the estate. He was a good match. But she had hoped he would respect her decision.

Willie continued talking at her. She could see from him that he was enjoying the power of his words and the information he was conveying.

'Paudge has spoken to Father Sheehy about a match with you. Anyways, it's way past time you were wed.'

Paudge may have been less of a servant than most at West Villa, but he too was in servitude to the family. If she married him, she would be answerable to him, and her life would lack any possibility of choice or chance — her dreams would never have an opportunity to be realised.

Her body felt heavy, cumbersome, as though her pockets were laden with stones, and her father continued talking, his tone growing more accusatory with each word.

'Paudge spoke to you. And you never said a word!' His voice

rose further in outrage. '*You told him to wait until your mother was better!*'

'I did not. I told him I would not be wed to him. Ever.'

By then Willie was shouting, his face red and his eyes angry. 'Your mother was always well enough for you to be wed to the right man! Paudge comes with good prospects!'

She would not let her life slip from her control as Hannah's had. 'Da, I beg of you, don't listen Father Sheehy.' Whatever about enlisting her mother's help by asking her to intervene, with Father Sheehy involved there was little hope.

'He's a priest.'

'I know he's a priest. He doesn't like me.'

'He will do his Christian duty by you.' Willie spoke in his sanctimonious way.

She tossed her head. 'I will not be wed to Paudge. Or to anyone.' Her slowly spoken sentences were gored with emotion.

At that moment, Nora pushed in the half-door.

Inwardly Mary groaned, bemoaning her mother's bad timing, but Nora was taken by a fit of coughing that consumed her thin frame and had her leaning against the wall for support as she located her kerchief and held it against her mouth. How fragile and ill she looked!

As father and daughter moved to her aid, she brushed them away, and the matter of Paudge was rested. But Mary knew it was only a matter of time.

❋ ❋ ❋

Charlotte seldom ventured below stairs. From childhood she had been uncomfortable among servants, and unsure of how to deal with them unless it was to issue orders. She was annoyed at having to resolve her daughters' care. But there seemed to be no alternative and Mama was adamant that she had to deal with the matter.

She paused on the threshold of the kitchen – elegant in her green day dress with its heavily boned bodice and layers of petticoats bulking out the skirt.

'Mrs Mac. I want to see Mary. Get her to come to the nursery as soon as possible.' Her voice fluted authority.

'Certainly, Miss Charlotte.'

Mrs Mac told everyone to stop gawking and to get back to work. She sent Lizzie to find Mary who should be in the back pantry.

Miss Charlotte looking for Mary. Not good, nothing to do with Miss Charlotte boded good, Lizzie decided, with a mean little skip of hope. Mary this. Mary that. And her only in the door of West Villa a wet week.

Mary was seated at a long strip of a table. Several pieces of silver were laid out on the green baize cloth covering it.

Lizzie paused in the doorway, the pinch of her features softening as she watched Mary. The sun from the small window slanted a dancing golden light. Whenever she thought of Mary it was enviously as nice, always with a smile and willingness to help.

They were of the same age. While Lizzie was in service a whole two years longer than Mary, it was Mary who had bettered herself with upstairs duties – now seldom having to scrub potatoes, drag water from the yard, or be put upon with Mrs Mac breathing down her neck.

When Mary saw Lizzie in the doorway, she smiled at her and held aloft a silver teapot by its handle. 'Beautiful, isn't it? Imagine the pleasure of taking tay from it? The Mulchinocks are so lucky.'

Lizzie gasped at Mary's boldness. 'The likes of us will be a long time waiting for a sup of tay at all.' Remembering why she was there, she said bossily, 'Miss Charlotte wants you in the nursery. Now. You're to hurry. You'll have to finish that later.' Lizzie enjoyed her moment.

Mary frowned, her expression becoming troubled – there was too much happening too quickly in her life. From the little she knew of Miss Charlotte she hadn't warmed to her, although she'd be hard put to give a reason. 'Do you know what she wants?'

'No, but you'd better hurry along. Her ladyship don't like to be kept waiting. It's likely nothing.'

Lizzie sounded so doleful that by the time Mary reached the nursery she had herself persuaded that Lizzie knew the reason for her summons, that her 'nothing' was likely a huge something and not a good something, either.

Charlotte turned from where she was standing by the small fireplace. There was no sign of her daughters. She had a superior, petulant face. Her expression at the best of times was forbidding – it was now creased with worry. Looking Mary over with critical eyes, she came straight to the point.

'I understand you're familiar with children, Mary? That you helped raise your younger brothers and sisters?'

'Yes, Miss Charlotte.'

'And you like children?'

What was it with the Mulchinocks and their questions about liking children?

'Yes, I do.' Adding, 'Doesn't everyone?'

Charlotte looked at her sharply. She was not as sure about Mary as her mother was, but it wasn't as though she had choice. Despite credentials and references lauding Florence's experience and ability with children, as far as Charlotte could see she had no control over her daughters. They weren't learning, they were vocal in their dislike of her and growing more disobedient and unruly by the day. She herself would not know where to begin with the organisation of their lives.

She spoke abruptly. 'From tomorrow you'll be in the nursery with my daughters. I presume you do know how to care for young girls?'

'Yes, Miss Charlotte. I do.'

As Mary returned to the kitchen, Lizzie stepped out from a corner, her expression bright with inquisitiveness, 'What did she want?'

'Guess.' Mary laughed as she skipped along the corridor.

❀ ❀ ❀

As luck would have it, on her way home that evening she met Mr Foley moving slowly along the Quay with an armful of books.

'I'm going to be in the nursery with Miss Charlotte's daughters. Doing lessons with them.'

He stopped, shifted his books to an easier position. 'Well, well.' He appraised her. 'A touch of the governess already.'

'Are those schoolbooks?'

'Yes, the latest from the Commission. Are there textbooks in the schoolroom?'

'I don't know.'

He held two canvas-covered books towards her, 'Early mathematics and a first Reader – have a look at these. And I've sent a letter to Dublin inquiring about teacher training.'

Mary rewarded him with a huge smile.

A governess. That's a start, she thought, as she pushed in the door of the cabin.

CHAPTER 20

'WHAT ARE YOU GOING to learn us today?' Anne asked.

'What am I going to *teach* you today,' Mary corrected.

'A thory?' Margaret's little voice was hopeful.

'Please,' Anne added.

Stories, when Anne and Margaret sat on either side of her on the sagging couch that they called the story couch, were much in demand. Mary read tales of derring-do from old chapbooks or made up adventures about a misfortunate donkey called Hi-Haw who put in long hours in the bog saving turf.

'First you must button your boots.'

Anne's fingers flew as she fitted the tiny bone buttons into their buttonholes.

Margaret sat on the floor, her plump little fingers refusing to match button to hole. Her hair had come loose from its velvet ribbon and her face was flushed.

'Can't you do it? Pleath, Mary,' she begged with tear-filled eyes. Her slight lisp was accentuated when she was upset. She knew most of her letters, but had difficulty pronouncing several of them.

With Mary's help the task was eventually accomplished, 'Thory now, pleath.'

She looked so woebegone that momentarily Mary was tempted to give in. 'First lessons. Then stories. What are the three Rs?'

'Reading, Riting and Rithmetic,' Anne counted off, using her fingers.

'Good. Now we'll recite our tables. Correctly.' Mary spoke firmly, going to the tall cupboard standing against the back wall of the nursery. As well as slates and pencils, she'd discovered a generous supply of paper, ink, inkstands, pens, slates and slate pencils, and an unexpected cache of powder paints.

'I hate tables.'

'Miss Margaret, you mustn't hate.'

'Anne does. She hates Florence.'

'I am sure she doesn't ...'

'I do so.' Anne was adamant, without apology.

Not wanting to get into an argument, Mary placed her index finger across the child's lips.

As she took it away, Anne asked, 'But suppose we can't remember?'

'Then, Miss Anne, I will teach you.'

'Me too. I can't member.'

'And you too, Miss Margaret.'

'And if we still don't know will you smack us?' Anne was matter-of-fact.

Mary was horrified at the thought of laying her hand on either child. 'I won't ever.'

'That's good to know.' Anne nodded, replicating one of her grandmother's most frequent gestures of approval.

Life in the nursery was good in a way that Mary had never anticipated — imagine advancing from kitchen skivvy to upstairs maid and then to nursery maid with, 'a touch of the governess' within the space of a few months? She studied the books Mr Foley had given her, was able to cast her mind back to her early days in the schoolhouse and, when doing lessons with the girls, she called on her experience of learning tables, doing simple sums, singing out spellings and basic reading. Mr Foley had grounded his students well in the basics of education, and Mary had the ability to impart what she had learned.

She was enriched by her new skills and knowledge, and as most of her time was spent between the nursery and the upstairs, she was able to avoid Paudge with ease. Though, best of all, she enjoyed teaching the little girls what she herself had learned in the classroom.

Her duties were varied — snacks at eleven o'clock, walks in the gardens, caring for the girls' clothes, brushing copious amounts of mud from their cloaks and boots, laundering and ironing their dresses, petticoats and the white pinafores and the smocks they wore to protect their day dresses. Unlike her predecessor, she did not allow their laundry to accumulate — she washed and ironed most days, thus avoiding the worst of the horrors of West Villa's formal washdays. She took pleasure in moving the heavy flat iron over the delicate materials — easing out creases, crisping ruffles.

She knew how to bring entertainment to the girls' lives too, introducing them to games from her childhood: Cat's Cradle, Share the Ring and Blind Man's Bluff. In a corner of the back yard she chalked out squares for hopscotch and set up a rope for skipping. Most of the time her charges were quiet and well-mannered, obeying her instructions without argument, although Anne was not without opinions that Mary encouraged her to voice.

CHAPTER 21

AFTER HIS SPEEDY EXIT from Ballinasloe William had journeyed by coach to Galway where he took lodgings near the Spanish Arch. At Hector Keogh's insistence he had been gone from the house within two hours of that most embarrassing of meetings, and without the opportunity of seeing either his wife or his daughter to make his goodbyes.

In Galway he was hoping to meet up with Daniel O'Connell – who was reputed to be travelling around the West, fundraising and rallying support – or if that didn't work out he planned join forces with some of the Liberator's supporters, and offer his services.

Despite what he'd heard at that soirée in the Stephen's Green Club, and the enthusiasm of Mr O'Connell's followers, William found Galway a glum place, seemingly impervious to the Liberator and all he stood for. He heard it said, in all seriousness, in one of the taverns, that commercially and economically the

West of Ireland hadn't recovered from the effects of the Battle of Aughrim. And that had taken place more than a century before.

On an evening when he got into conversation with a silversmith, he ended up with an invitation to visit his workshop a few miles into Connemara.

The aesthete in him was taken by the man's delicate filigree work, especially his Claddagh rings. As somebody interested in history, he was intrigued to discover that the rings dated from Roman times, and in Renaissance Europe they were used for betrothals and weddings. The heart was the symbol of love, the crown loyalty and the hands encircling the heart represented friendship. He had placed an order for a dozen – six silver and six in gold. Displayed under glass on a tray of black velvet they would complement the existing stock in the shop.

❈ ❈ ❈

After spending some weeks moseying around the wilds of Connemara, William rode into Tralee unannounced and unexpected. His first call was to the shop on the Mall.

Like it was yesterday he remembered his mother's summons and the ultimatum she had delivered on that overcast March afternoon. At the time it was three years since the death of his father and he had done his best with the various tasks she'd assigned to him, but his best had never been good enough.

Time and again he had failed. While he was running the dairy the creamery contract was not renewed; the year he was in charge of the gardens the vines developed mildew; under his watch several head of cattle died in mysterious circumstances, and during his stewardship the fields of oats and barley yielded a poor crop. With each failed venture, he felt his mother's desperation and Edward's irritation. His brother's passion was land and the realisation of its potential lay within him deep, dark and uncompromisingly. 'I've always loved the land and it loves me,' Edward said over and over again.

As William had opened the door to the parlour in answer to his mother's summons, she had turned around from her desk, still holding her pen, and he'd noticed the worry lines around her eyes. Without asking him to sit, she came straight to the point.

'So far you haven't succeeded in contributing to the family.'

Never before had he been on the receiving end of such sadness and disappointment from her.

'Thanks to your mishandling of the family interests, William Pembroke, we have lost business. Our reputation and our name have suffered. And it grieves me to have to say this – but the situation is directly attributable to you.'

He had no defence. What she said was true.

Using her pen as a pointer, she continued. 'I have decided you are to have the running of the shop for the next two years. Talk to Edward about expenditure. It has never done well, so even you cannot do too much damage.' She turned around to her desk and from the rigidity of her back he knew he was dismissed.

Saddened by her attitude and unsure of what else he could do, he rode straight to the shop. Dampness was in the air, the sky was as grey as gulls' eggs enhanced by an arc of smoky cloud, but there was a surprising vibrancy about the Mall as iron-shod hooves rang on cobblestones while carriages, jaunting cars and heavily laden drays competed for space.

The exterior of the shop was gloomy and forbidding, the windows grimy, and the gowns on display were unfashionable and uninspiring. Inside was as gloomy as outside. He stood, unattended amid the drab merchandise, until two unappealing-looking girls emerged giggling from the back. He laid his whip on the counter and removed his hat. They were sisters, Dorrie and Bridie, employed by his mother. Giggling subdued, they watched him from cautious eyes.

Without knowing how or why, as he stood in the dark interior looking around he saw glimmers of potential and rashly declared, 'We can make this a success to rival any Parisian drapers.'

'Have you been to Paris, sir?' Dorrie's face was dirty, but she had an intelligent look about her.

'Yes. I have.'

'What's the shops like, sir?' Bridie asked.

He had their complete attention. The sisters listened wide-eyed as words flowed, his memories coming fast and furious. He was at his most flamboyant, gesticulating, elaborating, as though giving a grand performance, remembering his days in Paris with his father as though it were only yesterday. He told them of the boutiques along the boulevards with aisles of deep red carpet and the way materials, gowns and trimmings were strung out like latticed necklaces between the marbled necks of fluted columns. He spoke of perfumed confusion, sparkles of glass from the countertops, whirls of bright and pale colours, displays of elaborate cashmere and muslins from India, pale chemises in materials as soft and delicate as flower petals, the smell of garlic and furs, and saleswomen enquiring, *'Mesdames, vous désirez?'*

He finished with, 'And we will make this shop just as beautiful.'

Dorrie rubbed at her face and Bridie hid dirty fingernails behind her back.

They smiled as they looked around. 'We will, sir. We will.'

And so the three of them did.

He employed a signmaker to paint the board over the door in

dark green with gold lettering that read **Mulchinock –
Draper and Haberdasher** in big, bold letters. Next he set
workmen to gut the interior of the shop before painting it in
white and gold.

The only fly in the ointment of his achievement was Leggett the
Nailer, as he was known, son of the man his father had purchased
the premises from. William ignored his aggressive behaviour and
muttered threats as he hung around the doorway complaining to
anyone who'd listen that Michael Mulchinock had robbed him
and his with the paltry price he'd paid for the property.

William had taken the Bianconi coach to Dublin. He visited
warehouses sited along the docks and some of the grandest of the
city's shops questioning, writing answers and contact names in his
notebook. He made lists and scoured worldwide sources for the
best of materials and trimmings: fine cottons from Egypt, bales of
crackling taffeta from Germany, delicate muslins from India,
brightly coloured silks from China, soft woollen materials from
England, and a variety of elegant feathers, ribbons, braids and
furbelows, the likes of which had never before been seen in the
town of Tralee.

Within himself he discovered previously unrecognised and
unrealised qualities of leadership and ingenuity. He dressed the
sisters in boldly striped black-and-white dresses and frivolous
little caps, and trained them in dealing with customers. He
journeyed to France and returned having appointed a Monsieur
Charles Aubin from Lyons as manager. Finally he placed an order
from a packaging company in Cork for black-and-white striped
boxes in various sizes, and from another supplier he sourced rolls
of matching wrapping paper.

But his real stroke of genius was the employment of a
seamstress – an idea he remembered from his visit to Paris.

Mademoiselle Giselle worked in the rooms at the back of the shop, doing alterations and making up day dresses in fashionable checks, evening gowns in satins and silks as well as skirts, blouses and capes.

Within months the shop was running smoothly and orders flowing in. Young and not so young women descended on the Mall in droves, with the line-up of their carriages frequently blocking off the street. They sat on dainty chairs perusing the latest issues of *Nouveau Journal des Dames,* the bible of fashion, illustrating the newest fashion plates and patterns in Paris They were encouraged to linger, to browse and, invariably, either Bridie or Dorrie succeeded in getting them to make a purchase or two.

❀❀❀

Dorrie's professional greeting turned to warmth when she saw who stood on the opposite side of the counter examining a bolt of blue silk that had been delivered that morning.

'Welcome back, sir! Bridie, Bridie, come quick! Master William is back.'

And with that M. Aubin, Brigid and Giselle joined in welcoming him home, all asking questions at the same time. He showed Giselle the samples of embroidery he'd brought from Pembroke Quay, and he promised to return in the morning with the sketches he'd made during his visits to various drapers in Dublin.

'You're doing a great job,' he praised them. 'I haven't seen better or smarter stock on my travels.'

❀❀❀

With more than a touch of trepidation he rode through the archway and into the yard at West Villa, dismounted, tied his horse to the post and looked around. The air was scented with livestock and the smoke from peat fires, the place was neat and clean as always, to his right the door to the dairy stood open catching the afternoon sunshine and the swish and bump of the churn confirmed the making of butter.

Nothing had changed – it was as though he had never left, that he not been absent for several months. He liked that feeling and was comforted by the sensation of permanence attached to his home.

Going through the kitchen the first person he saw was Mrs Mac, who on hearing his footsteps turned from the range and clapped a hand to her heart, 'Lord save us, Master William Pembroke. Coming on me like that. You gave me quite the turn.'

'I didn't mean to.' He hugged her.

She stepped back, looking him over, and touched his cheek. 'You're way too bony. Way too bony. Does the mistress know you're back?'

He raised his eyebrows and shook his head.

❁❁❁

Mrs Mac wondered about the gossip and rumours that had circulated about the young master during his time in Ballinasloe, as shoes clack-clacking and skirts swishing she thundered up the stairs and along the corridor. She swung open the door to Master William Pembroke's bedchamber, flung back the shutters and heaved up the sashes. In the evening light the room looked sad and neglected – dust on the furniture, soot in the fireplace and rugs that needed a good beating.

She got Lizzie to brush out the room and to freshen the

wooden floor and mahogany furniture with dregs of cold tea. Before the girl had a chance to draw her breath, Mrs Mac had her staggering down the stairs with rolled-up rugs to be taken to the yard and beaten until the pale grey dust flew out of them in all directions, and then the grate had to be blackened and the fire lit. Mrs Mac herself made up the bed with the finest of linen and the softest of pillows and her finishing touch was a few twigs of fresh lavender on the night table.

❀❀❀

William found his mother in her parlour. Not even the top of her head was visible over the back of her wing chair as she embroidered a delicate green leaf, her needle with its silk thread piercing in and out of a rectangular piece of linen, each stitch executed to perfection.

'Mother, dearest.'

She jerked upwards, dropping her frame to the floor, her initial welcoming smile of delight turning to a cautious wariness.

Before either had a chance to speak of any of the thoughts that flooded their minds, Edward pushed in the door.

'Well,' he said, standing aggressively in front of William, his finger jabbing the air, 'I heard the Prodigal had returned. Now that you've dragged our name through the mud of the county and beyond, you've decided to come back.'

'Edward, please.' Mrs Mulchinock's head swivelled from one son to the other. 'Your brother is only home. Give him a chance to explain.'

Edward looked scornfully at William, 'I don't believe there can be an explanation for your behaviour.'

William pushed back the flop of hair from over his forehead

and glanced at his mother in an effort to access her reaction. He was disturbed to see she had that closed, guarded look that he recognised as her expression when she was upset.

'If you're talking about the ridiculousness of a betrothal with Alicia Keogh, there isn't an explanation. There was never a question of my wanting to be wed to her. The word betrothal was never mentioned until my last morning. Perhaps Cousin Hector misunderstood.'

'Don't be absurd!' Edward's voice was laced with contempt. 'A man as successful as Hector Keogh wouldn't make such an error of judgement. It's an honour for our family that he apparently considered you as a suitable husband for his only daughter.'

'Mama?' William looked hopefully towards her, a touch of the little boy again, as though looking for her protection.

Shield-like, her embroidery frame was back across her lap, the needle holding the green thread stuck into the centre of the leaf. He remembered the hours he had spent with her and Papa in this room, wrapped in the bubble of security and happiness that their presence provided. He could still recite the names of the various embroidery stitches he had learned at her knee – chain, stem, satin, cross, blanket and running.

'I don't know.' She stroked the leaf with the pad of her index finger before looking towards him. 'The situation is profoundly upsetting. I presume you know your father's cousin wrote to me stating that no member of our family is welcome in his home?'

On consideration William did not regard that to be much of a loss, but he was saddened. He hadn't expected to come home to a disappointed mother and a scornful brother. He tried to explain how the misunderstanding might have arisen, but they were impervious to his side of the story – Mama too distressed and Edward too sarcastic.

He knew he lacked experience in matters of the heart, but he also knew that neither by words nor deeds had he intimated to Alicia or her parents that they had a future together. Still, he was unable to shake off a feeling of foolishness as though in some way he had dishonoured the family, and he was angry at being judged and condemned by his mother and brother in his absence.

❀❀❀

The kitchen was full of the news of Master William Pembroke's return, and while Mrs Mac was running backwards and forwards remembering little extras for his room the gossip flowed uninterrupted.

'He went to buy horses in Ballinasloe – that pair of greys. But stayed on for weeks on account of Miss Alicia,' said one of the groomsmen.

'How d'you know?' Lizzie asked.

'I've a cousin, a groom with the Keoghs. Miss Alicia is the only daughter. She's a right beauty and there's talk of a match between her and him. They're much taken with each other.'

'So, there'll likely be a wedding.' Lizzie's small face brightened with excitement.

'Only talk, so far.' The groom enjoyed the novelty of being the centre of attention. 'Master William Pembroke can't live in Ballinasloe and she don't want to come to Tralee. I reckon he has a bit of a broken heart. But my cousin says he's sure to go back. It's a good match,' he finished sagely as though he had played a leading role in the brokering of it.

'How does your cousin know all that?' Mary asked.

'Didn't you know servants know everything, but seldom say anything?' He gave a little jig to take the harm from his words.

'Master William Pembroke is a poet. A real poet,' Lizzie announced.

'Does he really write verse?' Mary was enchanted at the idea of somebody she might see being a poet.

'What's all this going on about?' Mrs Mac was back, reasserting control. 'Mary, you should be in the nursery. Lizzie, get on with that ironing — be careful with Miss Charlotte's blouse, you know how particular she is. You,' she addressed the groom, 'are needed in the yard.'

❀❀❀

As Mary was looking through some of the old chapbooks that she'd taken down from the cupboard, Anne shrieked, jumped up, ran at the tall, fair-haired man standing in the doorway and threw herself at him.

Margaret followed her sister. The man bent down, lifted the girls and held them aloft, one on either side of him.

When Mary saw him, she remembered. She had never forgotten the sight of the young gentleman standing alongside Daniel O'Connell in Denny Street and his image had remained dormant at the back of her mind.

'Whoa, take it easy!' He placed the girls back on the floor, hunkered down to their level, laughing, hugging them and ruffling their hair. 'Well, let me look at the pair of you. Haven't you been busy growing while I've been gone!'

'I think I muth be very big,' said Margaret in her hesitant little voice.

He smiled at her. 'I'd say at least two inches taller.'

Anne tossed her head, 'Well, if she's two inches more, I must be up three and I'm much fatter.' And to prove it she stuck out her little pot-bellied stomach.

'No, I'm more fatter.' Margaret copied Anne's gesture. 'Look!'

Anne and Margaret chattered on, their chirpy voices forming words, asking questions.

'Who do we have here?' He rested his hand on Anne's head and looked across to Mary.

She felt a slow heat spread through her.

'Her name ith Mary and she minds us and learns us lessons.' Margaret's little voice was liltingly serious. 'Thometimes too she plays games with uth.'

'But only if we do all our work.' Anne gave an enormous sigh.

'And tell me. Is she good to you?'

Anne looked from Mary to Margaret and back to her questioner before giving a big smile that revealed missing baby teeth. 'Oh, yes.'

He addressed Mary. 'I'm William or William Pembroke as my mother insists. I've been away.'

'Uncle William, will you take uth riding?' In his presence Margaret had lost her shyness.

'And, pray, what do you say?'

'Pleath.'

'You're like Mary about saying 'please',' said Anne.

'Mary is quite right. All well-mannered little girls should say please when they're asking for a treat and say thank you when they're lucky enough to receive one.'

'Can we? Please, please, please!' Anne jigged up and down.

'Not now. I am busy.'

'But you're only back from being gone. You can't be busy. Yet.' Her eyes widened. 'Did grandmother catch you to make you do work?'

William glanced across at Mary.

His presence was making her feel fluttery, flustered, but her movements were calm as she laid out pencils and slates on the table.

'Come, girls. It's time for your tables.'

'I can do the add tables — like two plus two,' said Margaret.

'I can add more than she can!' said Anne.

'You're fortunate girls to have such a good teacher.'

With that William left the nursery as abruptly as he'd entered. As Mary listened to the echo of his footsteps along the corridor, it was as though he had left a part of himself behind.

She was not surprised that he was a poet — such a handsome poet. From the awe in Mr Foley's voice as he spoke of poets and their verse, she knew such men were special — although, she thought, Master William Pembroke was the kind of man who could be anything he chose. As the gentry could — unlike the likes of her and her family, the choices of the world were open to them.

He was more handsome than Master Edward whose attentions Mary found increasingly embarrassing. She was unsure of how to deal with him. She was experienced in rebuffing unwanted attention from local lads and doing so firmly and decisively — she'd smacked Paddy Jack on the ear when had tried to kiss her and elbowed Tommy O in the ribs when he had grasped a handful of her buttocks. They were not solutions she could apply to Master Edward without the likelihood of repercussion. The gentry were different. In so many ways.

When she tried to talk to her mam about it, Nora pursed her lips. 'What has he done?'

'He asks me for a kiss.'

'Might you have given him encouragement?'

'Oh, Mam!' Her exclamation was a cry of frustration. 'I

didn't, I wouldn't … I'm afraid of him.' Until that moment she hadn't realised that she did fear his power.

'It does the likes of us no good to get fancy ideas about the gentry.'

She was unable to interpret the expression on her mother's face. 'Ideas! Mam, I don't have ideas. Any sort of ideas. I don't know what to do.'

'Your da is right, *a stór*. It's time you were safely wed.'

Mary thumped the table so hard that the items of crockery danced.

CHAPTER 22

THE SMALL KITCHEN was crowded with men, women and children, old and young, and the merry sounds of *rí rá* merged with the fiddlers' rendition of the Haymaker's Jig and the thump of dance steps. Some people were up dancing, more sat tapping their feet, others leaned against the wall clapping their hands in time to the music and, eyes closed, Mrs Tangney was tucked into a corner ullagoning. Several huddled together trading gossip, and the inevitable few sat morosely drinking porter. Father Sheehy, propped up in front of a jar of poteen, looked particularly jovial and expansive.

Willie, with urgings from Nora, had finally agreed to Brigid's entreaties to hold a kitchen dance. The door of the O'Connors' cabin stood invitingly open, allowing the jollity to spill out and anyone who happened to be passing was welcome to join in.

Mary, with flying hair and rosy cheeks, danced with abandonment, giving herself to the joy of movement and music.

Nora, her face flushed with the pleasure of company, appeared by her side to whisper, 'Paudge is invited. Your father saw to it with Father Sheehy.'

As Mary was about to protest, Paudge, bending his head to avoid the low doorway, stepped into the kitchen, holding a brown satchel. His shirt was open at the neck and a handsome leather belt held up his trousers. As he came into the kitchen music and conversation stopped and, as though by magic, a passageway cleared for his progress.

He paused by Nora. 'I am pleased to see you are looking so much better.'

'I am, thanks be to the good Lord.'

He placed his satchel on the table, undid the buckles and took out a brown-paper-wrapped parcel holding a round of spotted dick and a slab of butter. There was also a jar of whiskey, from Mrs Mulchinock – a drink rarely seen in Brogue Lane where porter and poteen were consumed more for their ability to blur reality than for taste or conviviality.

Willie, his head bobbing up and down in a master-of-the-house way, shook Paudge's hand.

'You're welcome, Paudge Sweeney, indeed you're most welcome.'

Paudge handed him the whiskey.

'Billy, fetch the tankards,' Willie ordered.

Billy did as he was bid, tots were poured and Willie, holding onto the jar, drew Paudge aside to where Father Sheehy was sitting at the top of the table.

When the initial flabbergast at Paudge's presence died down, father, priest and suitor, their heads close together, traded sentences, and all the while the air in the kitchen was ripe with speculation. The more observant were aware of the seriousness of Paudge's expression, Willie's air of fierce concentration and the jovial smiles of the priest.

Mary was unsmiling, her fists clenched, her knuckles shiny white.

The idea of a match between the Mary O'Connor and Paudge Sweeney was catching and added an extra touch of spice to the evening. She was well known and well liked and, while he kept himself to himself, it was common knowledge that he was regarded as almost one of the Mulchinock family. He had his own cabin and held the enviable position of steward at West Villa.

The feeling of goodwill in the kitchen was palpable as the makings of the match were sensed. Somebody remembered 'poor Peggy' his mother, and the little ones, and the devastation wrought on the family by fever – over the years the story had grown more and more dramatic in the telling.

When music and dancing took over again, a solemn-looking Paudge partnered an equally solemn Mary for the 'Siege of Ennis'.

'I am glad to see your mother's better,' Paudge said as they danced.

'She's not that well. She won't ever be going back to West Villa.'

'But well enough for us ...?'

'No, Paudge. I've told you. I will not be wed to you.'

Mary walked away from him and began to to fill the kettle, dipping the cup in and out of the basin of water that Billy had brought in earlier.

Paudge stood by the wall, smiling slightly. Despite Mary's brusqueness he was heartened by his welcome and the overall attitude of approval he sensed in the kitchen, and he was not unduly worried by her words. He had advised both Willie O'Connor and Father Sheehy to go easy on Mary, to give her time to get used to the idea of being wed to him, insisting that he would formalise arrangements with her when he judged the time to be right.

Some minutes later, after putting his arm around Mary's shoulder in a proprietary way, having another few words with the priest and a hearty handshake with Willie, he left.

Gradually the festivities dwindled until only Father Sheehy remained. Then he too rose to leave, but when he reached the door he doubled back to pick up the bottle of whiskey. 'I'll take this, if I may?' He waved it in Willie's direction.

'Certainly, Father.'

'I think not.' Mary stood in front of him, hands out. 'It was a gift to *our family* from Mrs Mulchinock'. She emphasised the words 'our family'. 'She would regard it as rude and lacking in appreciation if we passed on her gift.'

Father Sheehy's lips tightened, but he put back the bottle on the table and refused Willie's embarrassed offer of 'one for the road'.

❀❀❀

In the aftermath of the kitchen dance Willie did not mention Paudge nor was there any further talk of a match or a betrothal. But Mary was wary, sensing the matter was simmering in the background, knowing she had no control over whatever negotiations might be taking place.

❀❀❀

It was one of those perfect days of early summer that start with a slight heat haze, then stillness before the reveal of the jewel-bright colours of nature. The sky was so blue that Mary felt she could taste it on her tongue. It was a day of hope.

It was too nice to remain inside. She would take the girls to the wishing well.

When she looked up from helping Margaret to button her boots Master William was standing in the doorway.

His nieces leaped up to greet him with cries of rapture, jigging about him, pulling at his jacket and jumping up and down.

'Mary's taking us to the wishing well,' said Anne.

'For a walk on our feet.' Margaret twined herself around his legs.

'Easy now.' He disengaged her arms gently. 'I need to talk to Mary.'

As he drew her aside, Mary felt a blush rise up from her throat and travel across her cheeks, but he didn't appear to notice.

'With your permission I had the idea of taking the girls fishing but, as you've already arranged a walk, perhaps I could accompany you?'

The girls were on either side of him, lounging against him, clutching at the material of his coat.

'Yes, please, Mary. Let him come.'

'Pleath, Mary.'

In their efforts to persuade her, the girls bobbed away from their uncle and stood in front of her with expectation writ naked on their little faces.

To hide her confusion at the unexpected turn of events Mary bent her head to check on the fastening of Anne's summer cape.

The girls saved her from having to reply by grasping at William's hands, one on either side, urging, 'Hurry, hurry,' while Mary followed behind the three of them.

They took the circuitous route to the well, rambling along the crunching gravel paths of the flower garden, bordering the vegetable beds, bypassing the dairy, crossing the cobblestones of the farmyard, with its complement of snuffling pigs, pecking hens and strutting geese, skirting fields planted with oats and barley where rabbits and hares burrowed into the perimeters, and the sounds of the girls' laughter echoed on the blue air as they ran backwards and forwards.

William had disentangled from his nieces and broken into step beside Mary. As they passed through the orchard with its wizened trunks of apple, pear and plum trees, a quartet of goats came wandering over, the male shaking his dirty beard. He laughed, bent down and shook his head in unison with the goat.

'An agitated King Lear,' he commented. Then he looked sharply at her, 'Apologies. Do you know what I mean?'

'Yes, sir. Shakespeare.'

As they walked the dewy grass, he talked of Shakespeare's plays and sonnets and she was powerful with happiness.

The well reached, the four of them stood silently, caught in the moment, while sunlight made diamonds of the water flowing from the well.

Mary spoke softly, 'It's said if you drink of the water you may make a wish.'

William took control. 'Anne and Margaret, lean in and cup your hands to catch the water. Drink quickly.'

'Try not to wet your clothes,' Mary added.

The girls scooped up handfuls of water enthusiastically.

Mary watched. 'Close your eyes, make your wish and don't tell anyone.'

'Have you made a wish before?' William asked Mary.

'No, sir.'

'Well, come on. Surely there's something you wish for?'

Mary made her wish.

William sliced his hand through the water, let the drops flow from his fingers and briefly closed his eyes.

'What did you wish for, Mary?' asked Anne.

'If I tell you, Miss Anne, my wish won't be granted.'

The child looked to her uncle for confirmation.

'Mary is right. But if your secret is granted, then you may tell.'

'I'm tired of wishing water. Can we go up to Clahane?'

William was amused. 'Clahane, Anne?'

'The platform. Sometimes Mary takes us. And at night when we're asleep she goes dancing at the platform. Don't you, Mary?'

Now he remembered. That was where he had seen her. It was why she was so familiar to him. Mary was the girl dancing in the dusk.

'Well, shall we go to the dance platform?' He was light in spirit and his bow to Mary was an exaggerated gesture.

The girls looked from one adult to the other and executed a few giggling steps.

Mary didn't know whether to laugh with the delight of the invitation, or whether to be embarrassed at the ridiculousness of the idea. She settled for a prim, 'Not now. We must get back to lessons.'

❋❋❋

'My sister has given me permission to take the girls fishing? Is that all right?'

It was a few long days since they had walked to the well and William's re-appearance in the nursery was quite unexpected, but so welcome.

As though I could object to them going fishing, thought Mary, marvelling at the polite way of Master William.

'You're to come too. I insist. And my sister has agreed – probably doesn't trust me with her precious girls. Thinks I'll lose them.' He raised his eyebrows as though inviting her to join in the joke, and he was enchanted at the way the dimple in her cheek deepened.

Mary was in a quandary. Never before had she received such an invitation, and she wasn't sure of how to handle the situation. Should she accompany the girls and Master William? Or should she stay and report for kitchen duties? Mrs Mac had made it clear that her place was in the kitchen when she wasn't occupied with duties for either the mistress or Miss Charlotte's daughters.

'Yes, you must, Mary, you must come with us,' gabbled Anne who was joined by Margaret jumping up and down in excitement at the thought of a day out with her favourite uncle.

'Can we have a picnic?'

'What a good idea, Anne!' said William.

He reached down, grasped the two girls under their shoulders and swung them around and around until they squealed with joy.

Puffing and red-faced, he returned them to the floor. 'Mary, can you organise a hamper for us?' Without waiting for her reply, he added, 'Meet you in the yard in half an hour. I'll keep the girls.'

This was going from bad to worse. Mary dreaded going to the kitchen to ask for picnic food, although not as much as she dreaded telling Mrs Mac of her jaunt. While tidying away the books and slates, she had an idea.

As she hoped Mrs Mulchinock was at her desk.

'Master William Pembroke is taking Misses Anne and Margaret fishing – he has Miss Charlotte's agreement, and he has asked me to go with them.'

'Yes, you must accompany them. If for no other reason than to keep an eye on the girls. My son is quite likely to forget all about them halfway through the morning.'

'He suggested a picnic.'

'That's a good idea. Get Mrs Mac to pack a hamper.'

Ask Mrs Mac to pack a hamper? Indeed. Mary could picture Mrs Mac's face as she made such a request.

❁ ❁ ❁

'Master William is taking Miss Anne and Miss Margaret fishing and they'd like a picnic. What do you think I should take, Mrs Mac?'

Mrs Mac lifted a lump of dough from the bread bowl, slapped it down on a floured area of the table, crunched her fists and started kneading, her knuckles making short shrift of the corn bread. Without letting up on her firm movements, she spoke, 'Does the mistress know about this?'

Mary was relieved to be able to answer. 'Yes, and she's in favour of it, though I have to go as well to mind the girls.'

Lizzie sniffed. 'Just as well. Last winter during the big snow the master had them down the yard making a snowman. When he came back in, he clean forgot about them and left them outside in the freezing cold.'

'Now, Lizzie. That's enough lip out of you.' As she talked Mrs Mac was shaping the dough into a round and with a knife she slashed a cross on its top. She placed the loaf on a floured tray, opened the door of the range and put it into the oven.

After wiping her hands on her apron, she went into the pantry and a while after returned with a wicker basket.

'It's only a few bits and pieces, but they won't go hungry.'

William and the girls were sitting waiting in the small cart.

Mary hadn't expected to ride. This was a treat. She pushed in the hamper in front of her and climbed up beside William. The sky was high and blue as he took hold of the reins and the ground blurred between humming wheels.

'My three fisher girls,' he called them, regaling them with how his father had taught him the art of trout tickling when he was little older than Anne. 'He was patient and, thanks to him, I've come to appreciate the peace of the slowmoving stream and the thrill of catching fish in the way fish have been caught from time immemorial.'

When they reached the approved location, William lay on his belly on the grassy bank, his hands dangling in the brown water. His jacket was thrown off and his shirttails had become loosened from his trousers. 'The fish like quiet and I like quiet.'

Anne and Margaret, their faces framed by new bonnets, were giddy with excitement.

Anne giggled when Margaret promised, 'We'll be quiet like a mouth.'

The girls couldn't resist giving each other an occasional shove. Mary controlled their exuberance by placing a warning finger to her lips.

After a while there was a small ruffle on the surface of the stream. Leaning in further William used his index finger to tickle a small trout into submission before lifting it out carefully and placing it on the grass. Immediately his nieces were on top of him.

'Ith's moving.' Margaret bent down.

'It's alive.' Anne knelt beside it.

'I need help with the hamper,' said Mary.

'Me, me!' shouted the girls jumping up, the fish forgotten at the thought of food.

By the time the hamper was unpacked and its contents spread

on a fine linen cloth William had caught three more fish. All four lay in a row, motionless on the bank.

Margaret frowned and her lips quivered with the inevitable question. 'How did they get deaded?'

William held out his hands, 'Look at my poor hands, they are frozen, quite frozen.' He wrapped his slim brown ones around Margaret's tiny white ones. 'Can you help warm them?'

The girls fell on William, enclosing his hands in their pinafores, chaffing them through the fine material, little fingers flying. After a while they stopped, red-faced and puffing.

'You have to help us, Mary. Uncle's hands are so big and so cold and we haven't enough rubbing left in us.' Anne's voice had a touch of petulant authority.

William looked amused, glancing from Mary to his nieces.

'If you blow on his hands, it might help. Big puffs,' Mary suggested, the dimple on her cheek becoming more pronounced as she tried to suppress her merriment, while at the same time tucking her hands out of sight – while their condition had somewhat improved now that she no longer spent hours in the kitchen, they remained the hands of a servant.

'You could help too, Mary,' Anne spoke grumpily.

'I must look to the picnic.'

❋ ❋ ❋

William was happy that afternoon, enjoying himself in a way he hadn't for a long time. He had always been highly entertained by his nieces – from the first time they had stood up and wobbled across the room on lumpy legs, poking their fingers into this and that, he considered them enchantingly mischievous, refreshingly troublesome, and worthy of all his attention. Now that they were somewhat older his opinion hadn't altered.

'You're the best girls ever. You've done such a good job at warning my poor hands that I can hold the trout now.'

He prepared the fish with quick, efficient strokes and a softly whistled tune, completely absorbed in the gutting and cleaning. Finished, he sat back on his hunkers and sent his nieces to gather twigs. In no time he had a fire going and the trout cooking spit-fashion.

He liked being outdoors, liked the way the delicate balance of the day was caught between sunlight and a vagrant breeze, liked the sounds of nature and the scent of woodland. He watched as a heron rose on slow wings and drifted lazily away while a coot splashed, and on the opposite bank he glimpsed the quivering blue flames of a pair of kingfishers.

He had never known anyone like this Mary who his nieces so obviously adored. She had him intrigued, fascinated, enchanted, charmed, enthralled – spontaneously verbs applicable to her flowed through his mind. Her hair dark as a raven's wing curled out from her cap as though escaping from its confines. Watching her every gesture, he admired the competent way she moved – reaching, bending, stooping as she had set out their picnic, unwrapping bread and butter, removing the cover from a jar of Mrs Mac's quince jelly, opening a parcel of sliced ham, pouring lemonade from a bottle.

❋ ❋ ❋

As Mary packed up the remnants of the picnic, moving slowly, thoughtfully, savouring each minute, an unknown bird soared in quivering flight on the upward thread of its song, its music triggering an unexpectedly deep emotion in her.

After the hours spent on the bank of the small river, she knew her life was changed forever. At last she understood the power of what Hannah had felt for Danny. She felt the same for Master William. There. She had acknowledged it. And when caution stepped in quickly, reminding her that he was the master and she was a servant, as well as the fact that she'd only known him for a few weeks, she ignored caution. She was remembering walking back from Clahane on the night Hannah had met Danny, and how sure Hannah had been that Danny was her love, her only love and that he would always be her love.

Thinking ... wondering – these days she did much of both.

She was a servant, albeit no longer a kitchen skivvy, but a nursery maid with teaching duties – almost a governess, the next best thing to being a teacher. But life on the lane had taught her caution. She knew she could not allow herself to be affected by feelings. And yet she was. As she joined together the edges of the picnic cloth and folded it into neat squares before placing it in the bottom of the hamper, she listened to the running and laughing sounds of hide and seek along the bank.

Her life, as she had known it, had been cut adrift from its anchorage in the lane – first West Villa and now Master William – every aspect of her being changing. She hadn't known of the existence of men like him: softly spoken, gentle of manner, with smiling eyes and quality clothes. But she did know that her thoughts about him must remain a secret locked deep in her heart.

William became a regular visitor to the nursery, usually arriving around mid-morning, receiving a rapturous welcome from his nieces, who, she suspected, enjoyed the novelty of having their lessons interrupted as much as they loved seeing him.

'If I may?' He would gesture towards the story couch that sagged as though in anticipation of him.

Mary's affirmation would be delivered with a nod and a blushing smile.

'I shan't disrupt,' he assured her on each occasion, and he didn't, but she felt him watching her.

He did watch her. It was why he came.

He was aware of her humour and how quick she was to praise, and equally quick to admonish. She dealt with the girls firmly and fairly, in an affectionate, open-minded way, using hand gestures to make or emphasise a point

'Well, I never saw a blue tree, did you?' she asked.

Anne nodded. 'When I dream, the tree is blue.'

'Well, that's the wonder of dreams. But do you know the colour of leaves in real life?'

'Green. All green. Or browny, reddy-brown. In winter the leaves fall off some trees.'

'And what's left?'

'Branches and twiggy bits.'

'Beautiful in their own way too.'

'I prefer trees to have leaves.'

'Of course you do. You are a clever girl. Your tree is nearly there. Listen carefully now and think before you answer.' Mary spoke slowly and mischievously. 'If you mix yellow with the blue, what colour will you get?'

'*Green!*' three voices chorused.

Mary threw wide her arms. 'But you, sir, are not here to be taught and you promised not to disrupt our lessons.'

'Let him stay. Please, Mary,' entreated Anne.

'Well ... perhaps, if he behaves.'

He laughed, stood up and bowed from the waist. He was

becoming unnerved by the racing emotions she evoked within him, and unable to decipher the way she looked at him. It wasn't flirtatious – having been on the receiving end of many a flirtatious look he was familiar with that style of a look. The way Mary looked at him was only in evidence for an instant, gone in a blink, dissolving into his nieces, flowers, paints, paper and scribbles, so shortlived that it left him wondering if he'd imagined it.

In her presence his world was a better place. That she was a servant in his mother's employ had no relevance to his feelings for her. He enjoyed being in her company. That was all. Or was it?

The poet in him was drawn to beauty in all forms – be it the glory of nature, fabrics and trimmings or a pretty face, although up to now pretty faces had been in the abstract sense to be looked at, seen and appreciated from afar.

Mary was more, much more than a pretty face. She had a way about her, a manner that drew people to her – his nieces were devoted to her; she impressed his mother and that was no mean feat, and Charlotte had entrusted her with the care of her daughters.

Pretending to be reading, but not even the antics of Oliver Twist could distract him, he watched her from lowered eyelids, deciding she had a special way about her, that there was something indefinable about her spirit. He gave himself a stern mental shake – he could not permit his fascination with Mary to develop. He could imagine his mother labelling it 'another scandal', and Edward's biting comments.

Scandal. Ballinasloe. Alicia. The Keoghs. He cringed each time he recalled his mother's upset, his brother's sarcasm and his sister's indifference.

Deciding on discretion – although assuring himself there was no reason for him to be discreet, William stopped visiting the nursery and turned his attention to the shop that continued to gather its own successful momentum.

***

The Mall was a constant cacophony of iron-shod hooves and wheel-rims on cobbles, shouts, catcalls and laughter. The street was frequently choked with coachmen, ostlers and footmen yelling, as horses whinnied, passers-by rapped on carriage windows and passengers waved at acquaintances across the street. It was a place of thriving commerciality.

He spent several days checking the stock and discussing ideas for improvement and expansion with M. Aubin.

One afternoon as he was about to leave, Giselle called him aside. The seamstress was dark and slender with quick bird-like movements. Her command of English was as basic as his French.

He listened carefully to her excited idea and repeated what she had said slowly, feeding out each word with precision to ensure there was no misunderstanding between them.

'So, thanks to Queen Victoria, there is a demand for a new style of petticoats,' he said. 'And you want permission to make them?'

She nodded enthusiastically.

He was inordinately pleased whenever he managed to interpret precisely what she was saying and to provide an answer that satisfied her

'Yes, you may order whatever is required. I am sure you know more than I ever will about the influence of the young queen on fashion.'

His permission was not enough for Giselle who produced samples of materials and finally resorted to pen and ink sketches.

'You understand? You now know?' she worried.

'*Oui, oui*,' he assured her, escaping from the room. 'No problem.'

She followed, beaming.

As he left the shop he was smiling, shaking his head in bemusement at his newly acquired knowledge. Just outside Dorrie caught up with him.

'Please, sir, you know the man they call Leggett the Nailer?'

William frowned. 'What about him?'

'He's worse now, sir. Standing in the doorway shouting about being robbed.'

There was no time like the present and William turned the corner and called to Leggett's rooms, climbing the several flights of creaky stairs to the attic of the old building.

As he raised his fist to thump on the door it swung open and the lantern-jawed man stood before him.

'What do you want?' He leaned forward threateningly.

William stood his ground. 'As I told you before, I do not want you hanging around the doorway of the shop frightening the staff and customers.'

'And what'll you do?'

'You'll have a visit from the RIC inspector.'

The shaky door was slammed in his face and Leggett's curses and threats followed him down the stairs.

❊ ❊ ❊

In his spare time William fished, read and continued to write, trying in vain to recapture his previous fluency with words. Although his thoughts flowed effortlessly on a myriad of subjects, they still came to the paper sluggishly, reluctantly, ponderously, without the delicacy of his former touch. He was in quiet despair at his inability to capture poetry.

And then one night as he looked out from the window of his bedchamber at the moon riding high in the sky, words and lines and images came jumbling at him, seeming to fall from the stars.

Hardly daring to breathe for fear he would lose the impetus, he crossed to the bureau, opened his writing case and took out a sheet of parchment paper. He put a fresh nib into his pen and dipped it into the ink. Sitting at his desk the words flowed effortlessly, dancing off the page as never before.

His inspiration was Mary.

CHAPTER 23

MARY WAS TEACHING Anne and Margaret the basics of subtraction. The concept for them of seven minus three equalling four was turning out to be considerably more difficult than she'd anticipated.

William's entrance was greeted with the usual cries of delight from his nieces, and a deeply dimpled admonishment from Mary not to distract her pupils. But she was happy to see him – after all, it had been ten days and one hour since he'd last called to the nursery.

'Look, Uncle!' Anne held out her slate. 'We're doing writing figures and Mary says seven take away three leaves four.'

'Yes, that is right.'

'I can't understand why it does. Is it true?'

'Of course it's true.' He turned to Mary. 'May I?'

She smiled and dipped her head.

'Wait until I show you something.' He took out from the

pocket of his jacket a fistful of brightly feathered fishing flies and spread them on the table. Their iridescent lights of turquoise, yellow and cerise caught the dancing motes of the morning sunlight. 'Count them, Anne, but don't do it aloud.'

'Me, me, too!' wailed Margaret.

William wagged his finger. 'Your turn will come.' He turned to Anne. 'Have you counted?'

She nodded.

'Now you, Margaret.'

'I'll count to my insides.'

'That's the way.' William's glance met Mary's in a look of happy conspiracy.

'You first, Anne – whisper the number you counted into my ear.'

As Anne did, William kept a serious face and then it was Margaret's turn to whisper into his other ear.

'Seven. You are both right. Now, Anne, you take away three.'

Her tongue stuck out of the corner of her mouth in concentration, Anne pushed three flies to one side.

'Now how many are left?'

'One two, twee, four!' Margaret beamed as her small plump fingers tapped each fly.

'There. And isn't Mary right?'

'Yes, Uncle.' Anne was all beaming smiles. 'Can we go out now? We know our subtract.'

William raised a quizzical eyebrow.

Mary kept her voice firm. 'No. It's lessons for the whole of the morning.' She was discovering that the girls were picky learners, enthusiastic about the subjects that interested them, but stubborn in their resistance to Tables and Arithmetic. Their attitude had Mary all the more determined to teach them. 'And we've yet to practise doing sums.'

'But now we know four and three and seven. It's enuff learning.' Margaret's plump cheeks pinkened in annoyance. 'We know that thum about seven.'

'But you still must learn your tables,' said William. 'Mary is your teacher. And now I'll leave you to get on with your lessons, but make sure you behave.'

William gestured to Mary to follow him. In the corridor he pulled over the door, leaving a crack of visibility into the nursery. 'Apologies for interrupting the lessons, but I need to talk to you.'

Her heart was thumping wildly, but she composed her expression. She looked back into the nursery. The girls were absorbed in stroking his fishing flies, holding them up to the sun, and, she was pleased to see, watching intently as the rays created a rainbow-like irradiance.

William's voice was low and his expression anxious. He seemed to be unsure of what he was about to ask, and she picked up on his anxiety.

'There's a dinner this evening. I believe my mother plans to ask you to wait at table. I thought you should know.'

'Why?'

'It's called an advance warning.'

'I haven't heard anything about it.'

'You will and it might be better if you refuse.'

Anne and Margaret had abandoned the lure of their uncle's fishing flies and the noise emanating from the nursery could no longer be ignored. Oblivious to the perils of hurting themselves, they were going head over heels in cartwheels of pantalettes and petticoats.

'I must go back in. The girls ...'

❁ ❁ ❁

Mary was puzzled and somewhat disturbed by the earnestness of William's request. Despite the numbers of people who visited West Villa, the overnight guests, musical evenings and supper parties, her duties had never gone beyond serving afternoon tea, and she thought it unlikely that it would change.

But as she was passing through the hallway, Mrs Mulchinock called to her. 'I need you in the dining room this evening. There will be some extra shillings for you and food to take home.'

'Serving at table?'

'Yes. You and Paudge. You're well able to.'

Mary fidgeted with her hands across the front of her apron, wishing she could take heed of William's warning, knowing she couldn't. And suddenly realising she did not want to serve at a table where he was present.

'Well, Mary?' Mrs Mulchinock's tone was uncharacteristically sharp.

'Yes, ma'am.'

'That's settled then.'

❋❋❋

In the kitchen preparations for the dinner were well under way. Mrs Mac was harrassed and her face was redder than usual as she chose fish for gutting, examined a joint of ham and issued orders.

'Lizzie, finish beating them eggs and sugar, cover the bowl and put it in the larder.'

'What's that?' Mary asked Lizzie. 'What are you making?'

'It's a trifle dessert for the dinner. Will we get a taste of it, Missus?'

'Certainly not. And you,' Mrs Mac pointed to Mary, 'don't be disturbing my kitchen. What are you doing here anyway?'

'I'm to be in the dining room tonight. And I'm not sure ...' Mary's voice trailed off.

Lizzie dropped the beater into the bowl and stood erect. 'I heard Master Edward ask the mistress about that, but Master William said,' she crimped her lips and spoke in her interpretation of a posh male voice, '"No, Mary is not to be asked."'

'Lizzie!'

Lizzie ignored Mrs Mac's admonishment. 'There's talk of a match for Master Edward – Miss Harriet Elliott, it's said. She's from out Ballyseedy way.'

'You shouldn't be listening to talk between the family, and you certainly shouldn't be repeating it,' Mrs Mac said firmly.

Lizzie placed a square of muslin over the bowl. 'I couldn't not hear, with the way the mistress was going on about it being time her sons were wed, and frettin' about the food and the serving-up, the way she does when she's upset.'

Mrs Mac gave a click of annoyance. 'Enough of that, Lizzie. And you, Mary, take a clean apron, tidy your hair, keep it tucked under your cap. Stand by the sideboard, hands across your belly and eyes cast down. Only look up and move when you are serving.'

Ripples of unease ran up and down Mary's back. So, it had been Master Edward's idea.

❀❀❀

Before the arrival of the guests Mary slipped into the dining room and walked around the table. She didn't know what was what, but that didn't stop her admiring the table dressed in white damask laid with silver cutlery, crystal glasses and porcelain dishes, and dozens of candles dancing light in the late afternoon. Mrs Mac had personally set it.

Mary and Paudge were in position at the sideboard when the diners were led into the room by Mrs Mulchinock She was escorted by her brother-in-law, and took her place at the top of the table with him seated to her left. Her gown was trimmed with ruffles of black lace and around her neck she wore a large gold locket on a wide velvet ribbon. A toad-like man, short and squat, sat to her right. He had escorted Miss Charlotte who wore a gown of cherry red and her usual petulant expression. Also among the guests, and accompanied by his daughter, was the overweight, wheezing RIC district inspector, in a bright red uniform, resplendent with gold braiding.

Elegant as Mrs Mulchinock's and Miss Charlotte's gowns were, Mary preferred the lavender blue, pale-green and rosy-pink gowns worn by the guests. They had wide skirts flowing from tiny waists, puff sleeves and bare powdered shoulders draped with lacy wraps.

The youngest and most beautiful young lady was golden-haired with cascading ringlets. She was resplendent in the lavender gown lavishly trimmed with frills and flounces. She simpered at Edward and flashed her eyes from behind her fan. Mary suspected she was Miss Harriet Elliott, the hoped-for match for him. As the harpist played haunting tunes, she played with her food, eating in a picky manner, pushing her fish from one side of her plate to the other. Initially she drank tidily and behaved prettily, but as she allowed her glass to be refilled too frequently she slipped into giggling carelessness as she tried to gain Edward's attention.

He cut a handsome figure in a powder-blue coat with gilt buttons and pale trousers. The other men wore darker coats:

plum, green and navy without gilt buttons and William had the addition of a dazzling brocade waistcoat.

Edward paid scant attention to Harriet, concentrating instead on the attractive woman seated to his right, raising his glass to toast her, whispering in her ear. She had filled her plate with generous portions of goose stuffed with caraway. As she ate, she laid an occasional possessive hand on his arm.

In all likelihood, Mary decided, she was in her thirties but, because of the ease of their lives, the gentry looked younger than they were. The woman was self-possessed with a tinkling laugh and wore a pink dress with strands of creamy pearls around her neck and wrists. She had a high intelligent forehead and a simple upswept hairstyle, and she listened intently and contributed animatedly to Edward's conversation.

Determinedly, Mary did not glance in William's direction. He was seated between the woman who interested Edward and the inspector's daughter, the pretty young girl in green. This was a new side to William, a William who was unknown to her.

She wished she had been able to heed his warning: the glory of the dining room and the sophistication of the guests heightened differences between them that were not so obvious in the nursery. She hadn't known how handsome he would look – so in control, so 'Master of the House' with his fingers in constant motion playing with his wine goblet as he conversed with his table companions.

Mrs Mulchinoch paid equal attention to the gentlemen on either side of her, looking from one to the other with interest, commenting every now and then on whatever topic was under discussion, but allowing them the sway of conversation and directing questions to the other guests.

John Mulchinock had a commanding voice and Mary picked

up snatches of conversation about the economy of Europe and the need of a workhouse in Tralee. The woman in pink spoke knowingly about a performance of *She Stoops to Conquer* at the Theatre Royal in Dublin, but a muddled comment of Harriet's about Queen Victoria's lying-in was ignored.

The toad man, Mary decided, must be Miss Elliott's father, from the way he kept casting quick sparrow looks down the table at her. With her carry-on, no wonder he was anxious.

Paudge served table silently, efficiently, ghosting between the ladies and the men, eyes down, shoulders rounded, punctiliously pouring wine, passing dishes and retrieving napkins. Mary assisted him but, aware that she was nervous, he allowed her to stay in the background most of the time. She was grateful to him for his kindness.

The voices rose and fell in chatter, to the background of floating notes from the harpist, a thin man with straggling grey hair and long slim fingers who was tucked tidily into a corner.

Eventually it was time for Lizzie's dessert trifle, a concoction of cake, sherry, custard and cream decorated with jellied flowers. To end the meal there were elegant stands of grapes and peaches from West Villa's conservatory and a platter of cheeses from the dairy.

It took all of Mary's powers of concentration to keep a tight rein on the conflicting mix of emotions that threatened to overwhelm her while she observed the interactions of those around the table – accepting that she would have no idea of how to conduct herself in this company. In the nursery she was in control, a situation that appealed to her, but here, in the dining room, her role was that of a servant, and that was not the way she wanted her life to be. She was tired, so tired, her tiredness accentuated by new feelings of insecurity. Shifting her weight, she dropped her hip and felt her feet throb. To take her mind off her discomfort she strained to make out snatches of conversation and was rewarded by hearing Edward refer to the trifle as an 'Empire dessert'.

When it was time for the women to withdraw to the drawing room, leaving the men to their port, brandy, pipes and cigars, Paudge took her aside. 'You did well.' He didn't meet her eyes. 'You look to the menfolk. I'll do the ladies. They're the more contrary.'

Still she stood, easing out her back against the handsome sideboard, knowing she was an unseen presence, invisible to the men gathered around the table. Now that the ladies had withdrawn and the harpist had stopped playing, it was easier to hear the conversation, through the puffs of cigar smoke and the clinking of raised brandy glasses.

The toad man was holding forth on land prices, boasting of his ownership of large parcels of land around Ballyseedy – 'the first wife's money, you know' – while bewailing the state of the country's economy and the drop in land prices. It must be his second wife, she decided, who was the focus of Edward's attention.

William and John Mulchinock were deep in conversation – talking about a man called Thomas Moore – she'd heard that name, but she couldn't remember where or in what connection.

'Mr Hazlitt says Mr Moore's writings are a shower of beauty, a dance of imagery, a stream of music!' John Mulchinock's voice rose in admiration as he made his point.

Mr Moore must be a poet.

'And I would take such praise a step further to say his poetry seduces the taste and enervates the imagination.' As William spoke in his polite manner, he glanced in her direction and winked.

His action was so unexpected that her consternation was

manifested in the blush she could feel suffuse her face.

Finally, Edward rose. 'I believe it's time we joined the ladies.'

He led the men from the room. Mary took a deep breath and allowed it to escape slowly. It was over.

She began clearing the table, stacking glasses, plates and cutlery with the bundle of crushed napkins, prior to fetching trays from the kitchen.

The door to the dining room opened and Edward stepped in, closing it behind him.

'Mary, you brightened the dining room tonight.' His was smiling, his voice thick with wine and brandy.

She turned her back on him while she snuffed out the candles, but he caught her around her waist, his hands grasping, pulling at the cotton of her dress.

'Don't do that.' She slipped from his grasp and worked her way around the table with him following. 'If my mistress, your mother, found out, I'd lose my position.'

'Nonsense!' His voice was robust, his face flushed as he grabbed at her arms and pushed. The table pressed into the small of her back as he leaned closer, his breath wafting tobacco as well as drink. 'How about a little kiss now? Sure aren't you going to wed Paudge? And you can't be shy about kissing him.'

She turned away from him, her nose wrinkling in distaste, her cheeks flushing with anger.

He caught her by the shoulders and turned her around, bringing his face close to hers.

She struggled free, raised her hand and slapped him across his face. 'You may consider it acceptable to take liberties with me, but I don't!'

She wriggled past him, out the door, into the corridor and down the stairs to the kitchen.

Paudge was stoking the range. There was no sign of Mrs Mac.

'Paudge ...' she began, reluctant to turn to him, unable to protect herself and unsure of how Edward would react, but feeling she had no other option.

'Yes, Master Edward, and how can we help you?' Paudge looked from her troubled expression to over her shoulder.

Edward had followed her. She had never before seen him in the kitchen. She preferred not to think of what could have happened had Paudge not been there.

'I wanted to thank you and Mrs Mac for all the hard work you put in tonight – you too, Mary. Mrs Mulchinock – my mother – is well pleased.' How cool and unflustered he sounded.

'I'm pleased you found everything was to your satisfaction, sir.'

Mary had never heard Paudge sound so formal, so in control.

As the sounds of Edward's footsteps died away, Paudge said, 'I suppose he was trying to take the liberties with you that he regards as his right?'

Yes, Mary thought. That was exactly what Edward was doing.

CHAPTER 24

ONCE PAUDGE SET HIS MIND on a course of action he followed it through doggedly. Although raging at Edward's attitude towards Mary, confrontation was not in his nature and he decided against tackling him or questioning her. He had a good idea of what had occurred and he also knew that Edward regarded such behaviour as his right.

The more he saw of Mary, the surer he was that he wanted her as his bride. While he did not want to scare her off by hastening the formalising of their betrothal, in view of Edward's recent behaviour he decided it was time to move the settlement on to the next stage.

Just as the O'Connors had finished the rosary, The Glorious Mysteries that evening, and were rising from their knees, there was a firm knock on the upper half of the door.

Willie nodded to Billy to unlatch it.

Paudge stepped into the kitchen.

He looked around hesitantly, scrunching his cap in his hands. He had come determined to formally ask for Mary's hand in marriage and, hopefully, to have the matter settled before he left. He took a parcel from his satchel, looked from Nora to Mary and handed it to Nora.

'It's some of that apple cake you like.'

The O'Connors were silent, unsure of the situation. Mary felt the skin peel from her heart; Billy looked lively, as though about to ask a question, but remained silent; Brigid and Ellen chewed on their fingers; Nora rocked backwards and forwards by the fire and Willie flattened his hair against his forehead.

'Paudge, why are you here? Is everything all right?' Mary asked.

'Yes, Mary. I've called to talk to your father.' He turned to Willie. 'May I have a few minutes of your time, sir?'

Nora looked from Paudge to Mary and back to Willie. In living memory nobody had ever called Willie O'Connor 'sir' but, as though to the title born, he rose to the occasion.

'Certainly, Paudge. Mary, be a good girl and wet the tay.'

Mary busied herself making the tea as Nora set the table for the two men.

'Excuse us,' Nora then said, inclining her head graciously to Paudge. 'We have to call on Mrs Tangney.'

'Oh, of course,' said Paudge.

'Come on, you lot,' said Nora.

'I don't want to,' said Billy.

His sisters echoed Billy's refusal – with the instincts of children they sensed a momentous something was about to occur and they wanted to be present.

'Yes, you will. All of you. Mary, you too. Come along. *Now. Immediately.*' Nora pulled her shawl from the hook and wrapped it firmly around herself. She was seldom forceful, but there was no arguing with her when she used that tone.

Mary set the teapot on the table and followed her mother out the door, with an uneasy backward look.

'I expect you know what Paudge wants with your father?' Nora said as they walked along, the children trailing behind.

She kept her voice low but spoke in a formal way, quite out of character, that Mary found unnerving. They both knew full well what Paudge wanted.

'Something to do with the mistress, I suppose,' fibbed Mary. 'Somethin' to do with my work – or maybe she's just asking about you?' A creeping feeling of dismay threatened to overwhelm her.

Since the evening of the dinner Paudge had been kinder than ever to her but he had said nothing further about being wed and she had hoped he had relinquished the notion. Also, her father's talk of betrothal had become general rather than specific and, anyway, she had been too wrapped up in thinking about William to pay attention to much else.

'You know your father has been looking into making a match for you, for this past while.' Nora stated the obvious.

'If I get married – and perhaps I won't ever, it will be to someone I chose and who chooses me. You know that, Mam. I won't be bartered, haggled over. I've told Da that.'

'You can't be like that, *a stór.*' Nora's voice wobbled. 'Mary, time was when you'd listen to my advice.'

'It's different now, Mam.'

Nora tried a different tack. 'Do you think Paudge might be – you know, formally asking for your hand?'

'I suppose anything's possible,' Mary said in an offhand way. 'But Paudge can ask all he wants – he won't get my hand or any other part of me.'

Nora shivered, but she spoke gently. 'It's a good match. He has a good position. And he's highly thought of, almost one of the Mulchinock family.'

'But I don't want to marry him. And I won't.' Mary was on the cusp of telling her mother about William but, as the words were on the point of flowing from her, she thought the better of it and clamped her lips shut.

'It's up to your father.' Nora pushed in the door of Tangney's cabin. 'It has to be. You know that.'

'Well, well,' greeted Mrs Tangney, standing up plumply and bossily from her place by the fire with her usual midwifely air of authority. 'You're welcome, I'm sure.'

She bustled around, wetting the tea, cutting into a loaf of soda bread and putting out her blackberry jam. It was said that no matter what hour of the day or night you called on her, Mrs Tangney had a loaf of fresh bread and a jar of homemade jam on the go.

'Outside, you lot, while I talk to your mam and Mary.' To their disgust, she gave Billy and the two girls wedges of warm bread and jam and shooed them out the door.

As always Mrs Tangney's tea was strong, thick with sugar and flavoured with sweet milk. Her eyes darted backwards and forwards from Nora to Mary.

Mary couldn't warm to her and had never quite trusted her.

Hands wrapped around her mug and with her elbows on the table, Mrs Tangney leaned forward. 'Did you hear about poor Mr Hennessey?'

'No. What about him?' The tone of Nora's voice betrayed her dislike of him. Likely Mrs Tangney was about to announce something like another windfall of money from his son in America.

Mary composed her features as Mrs Tangney turned to her.

'You and young Hannah were always thick afore she married Mr Hennessey. And with that Danny Stack fella too.'

'Yes. We were friends.' Mary wondered what was coming – nothing good, she was sure.

Mrs Tangney blew across her mug and took a sip of tea. 'Mr Hennessey is dead. *Dead*.' She thumped the mug back on the table. 'God help us all. Found in his cabin he was.' She blessed herself piously, her big hand moving from forehead to breast and left to right across her shoulders. When neither Nora nor Mary reacted as she had hoped, she continued, 'His head was stove in. Stove in, it was!' she repeated, tapping at the back of her own head to emphasise the point.

By clamping her lips tightly Mary controlled the vomit that threatened to spew from her, the way it had on the night Billy had told her about Hannah and Danny being found at Blennerville. Her heart was racketing so hard that she feared it might leap from her chest. She was glad her sisters and Billy remained outside. Billy especially – it was safer to have Mrs Tangney still think of him as more a child than a man.

❀❀❀

On their return to their cabin there was no sign of Paudge, just Willie snoozing by the fire, his hands across his belly, his breathing rising slowly and evenly.

Nora looked at him as she unwound her shawl. Her husband. As though she'd had a choice in the matter of whom she married. As though her father had paid heed to her wishes.

Willie was just a young fellow when his father died, but he'd been learning the trade. The day after the funeral he had risen early, and an hour later his mother found him stitching the uppers onto the sole of a boot. From the beginning he was regarded as a hard worker with a rising reputation as a skilled shoemaker, and it was known that he never had a problem meeting the rent.

It was also known that he was interested in young Nora Flynn – his mother gazetted the fact up and down the lane. Mrs O'Connor was a pushy woman who idolised her only son and encouraged his industry. She was shrewd too – she had made it her business to find out about the girl: Nora Flynn had the makings of an obedient wife, a daughter-in-law who wouldn't throw her out of her own home and who'd care for her in her old age. She negotiated her son's marriage with unrelenting thoroughness, assuring Old Man Flynn that he didn't have to put up a farthing of a dowry. Not one brass farthing.

As her father had pointed out when Nora railed against marrying Willie, there was security for her in the match, more security than he had ever been able to eke from the rocky field for his wife and brood of children. He had a soft spot for his eldest daughter – and he told her he'd be sorry to see her leave, but he had insisted on the match.

Willie opened his eyes and looked at Nora, his gaze blurring with fondness, then he closed them again.

She had always known that he cared for her more than she had ever cared for him, not that he was in the habit of showing affection. Once married, she'd put thoughts of the other one from her mind. She had been a good wife to Willie, never denied him his rights and for his part he'd never raised his hand to strike her.

Nora sat into the old chair by the fire, waiting for Willie to come fully awake, hoping they might talk together, that he would tell her what had been said with Paudge and pay attention to her opinion on the matter of Mary being wed.

She had always wanted Mary to have a better life than hers – Mary more than Brigid or Ellen – but she was fearful of her eldest daughter's outspoken ways. She lamented that in all likelihood Mary would have no choice but to follow in her footsteps of a made marriage and a lifetime of carrying and dropping babies. She knew Paudge from boyhood; she had seen him grow from a frightened boy to a respected man. He was a good prospect. Wed to him Mary would never want nor, she'd swear on the Bible, would he ever raise his hand to her.

Nora seldom allowed herself to remember. Long ago she had put the past firmly behind her. But with all this talk of a match for Mary her own memories had come swarming back.

Like it was yesterday, recollections of that Thursday unfurled, rolling slowly through her head.

Seated by her own hearth all these years later she could still feel that sensation of restlessness that was settled like a cloak about her, the heat in her belly, tremor in her hands as she picked the stones from Hennessey's fields – even then more than twenty years ago Hennessey was a man of power. Times when she felt unable to breathe, she'd jump on his horse and take off across the fields, her hair flying behind her, her bare heels pressing into the mare's flanks, urging her to leap over the ditches, to jump low walls and to glide over hedgerows of bramble.

Hennessey, backside leaning against the wall of his cabin, *dúidín* clamped between his lips, cap pulled low over his forehead, would watch her take off and return through narrowed eyelids. He never chastised her, never said she shouldn't take the old mare, and while his lack of admonishment made her uneasy, she took it as a silent permission.

Then, on one occasion, the horse didn't make the ditch and Nora ended up on the ground, winded. Raising her head, she saw the horse calmly grazing and as she eased onto her knees she found she was staring at a well-polished boot. The owner bent down, offering his hand and, as she rose to her feet, he looked down at her. He was the gentry. Her skirt was torn, her blouse awry and her feet bare.

'Careful. Take it easy. You may be hurt.'

She had never known such concern.

She pushed back her cloud of hair that was said to be the colour of a fox's tail. 'I'm not hurt.' In the presence of the gentry she knew it was never good to be hurt, sore or ill.

'Well, well. There's bravery. And who are you?' His voice was richer and warmer than she thought a voice could be – if voice had a colour his would be the colour of a chestnut.

'Nora, sir.' She laughed with joy at the morning.

He bent down and lifted her chin so that she was looking straight at him. 'And do you often ride?'

'Whenever I get the chance.' There was a touch of impishness in her reply.

'Well then, let us ride together. Tomorrow morning. Nine o'clock.'

And with that he put his boot into the stirrup, leapt easily into the saddle and was gone so quickly that Nora wondered if she'd dreamt of him and his fine black horse. As she rode back to Hennessey's farm the hedges hooped with briars shimmered in the light and crows rose into an unbroken belt of trees meshing together in a plum-coloured haze.

Next morning just before nine o'clock, she was picking stones and setting them in piles, her head full of seeing the handsome gentleman again.

Mr Hennessey came to stand beside her – he was cutting slivers from a slab of tobacco. She eased onto her haunches as he spoke.

'If I catch you on my horse again, you or yours won't get another hour's work out of me. Know that.'

Less than a month later she was wed to Willie O'Connor. She dreamt of rescue until the very moment of her marriage vows. During the ceremony she delayed each response, and as she forced them from between her lips a sigh ran through her as though her soul had slipped away from her.

Two years later and three babies lost, the gentleman came into the dairy where she was scrubbing out the separator. He was Thomas Mulchinock, Master Michael's cousin, and he didn't recognise her.

❀❀❀

'Can we have a cut of the cake?' Billy asked hopefully.

'Yes, yes, please, please!' echoed Brigid, and Ellen gave an optimistic little jig.

Mary cut the apple cake into chunks and handed a piece to each of her sisters and brother. Her parents' silence was unusual, although the air was thick with questions waiting to be asked. Hoping to ensure their silence remained intact, she stood with her back to the remains of the fire – sitting down was more likely to promote conversation.

'Well, I'm to bed.' Nora rose, looked to Willie.

Mary was relieved when her father stood up.

But he moved to her side and rested a hand on her arm in an uncharacteristically intimate gesture. 'We can all sleep well tonight.'

She held her breath, suspecting what was coming, hoping he wouldn't speak, wouldn't make the expected announcement.

Brigid gouged out another piece of apple cake and stuffed it into her mouth.

Willie was the type of man who took being the recipient of news seriously and being its purveyor even more seriously. The opportunity for drama seldom presented itself to him and on the rare occasions when it did he played it for all it was worth.

'Paudge was here to formally ask for my permission to court Mary with a view to marrying her within the year.' He beamed at each member of his family in turn.

Nora looked worriedly from her husband to her daughter and Billy gave a manly tug on his recently acquired braces.

Brigid licked her fingers. 'If you get a wedding bonnet, Mary, can I have your blue one?'

The kitchen was still, just the flame of the one guttering candle running shadows across the ceiling.

It seemed an age before Mary spoke and when she did her voice was pitched low and without inflexion.

'I'll tell you all one thing and I'll tell it to you for nothin'. I won't marry him. Paudge knows that. I've already told him so. You must accept my decision, Da.'

❊ ❊ ❊

Mary felt utterly *trí na ceile* with the confusion of her life. Now that Paudge had formalised his proposal, there was no need for the family to remain silent about the betrothal, and she wouldn't want William learning of it from hearsay or gossip. While they were not in the habit of conversing on personal matters, she felt it appropriate that she should be the one to tell him. But it wasn't something she could state in a baldy way – the words and the occasion needed to be right.

CHAPTER 25

MR HENNESSEY'S DEATH was the talk of the county. There was a feeling of uneasiness around the town at the RIC's investigation and fear of the militia becoming involved. Even the most innocent would dread the thought of being questioned by representatives of the Crown.

Everyone wondered who might have perpetrated such a deed and the likely repercussions if that person were caught.

Many could name a list of likely suspects – over his lifetime Mr Hennessey had made many enemies. But nobody did. Eventually news filtered down through the streets, laneways and taverns that officially it had been decided the most likely explanation for Mr Hennessey's death was that he had fallen down in a drunken state – perhaps a bang against the wall of his cabin accounted for his head injury.

An acceptable solution having been reached, a sigh of collective relief ran through the townsfolk.

Few people mourned his passing.

❀❀❀

While life on the lanes was constantly full of ups and downs, life at West Villa ran smoothly and efficiently until the unexpected occurred. As had happened on the morning Mrs Mac met Mary halfway up the avenue, the news bursting out of her that little Miss Margaret was ill, and the mistress and Miss Charlotte had sent her to tell Mary to hurry.

Mary ran up the remainder of the avenue, through the kitchen and up the stairs into the bedchamber the girls shared.

She took in the situation at a glance – the child was ill with a fever, her head rolled on the pillow; she burned to the touch, her eyes were too bright, her cheeks too rosy and her breathing laboured as she tossed and turned in her little bed.

'I would have thought Dr Moriarty would be here by now,' Charlotte was grumbling. She was holding a bowl of water and a cloth and was dabbing at Margaret's forehead.

'He'll be here. As soon as he can.' Her mother was optimistic, with her usual attitude of no-argument sureness. 'Charlotte, do let me do that.'

'No, Mama, it's my duty. She's my daughter.' She gave Margaret's cheeks an ineffectual pat.

Mary excused herself and rested her cool hand on the child's forehead. 'Miss Margaret will be all right,' she assured them with more assurance than she felt. 'But we have to get down her fever.' She checked the water in the bowl. 'This is not cold enough. It needs to be cold as possible.'

In the kitchen there was a wake-like atmosphere, with Mrs Mac rubbing at her eyes and Lizzie sobbing.

'Is there any ice here?'

'Ice?' said Mrs Mac. 'What in the name of God ...?'

'No – I'll get some.' Lizzie ran to fetch a block of ice from the small icehouse at the back of the yard.

Back in the bedroom, Mary pulled the bedclothes back off the little girl. She sat her up, crooning softly, telling her that she'd make her better, but that she'd have to help by being a brave girl.

When Charlotte saw the chunks of ice in the water, she was outraged. 'Mary, what do you think you're doing?'

Mary wrung out a linen cloth in the freezing water. 'I know exactly what I'm doing, Miss Charlotte. I've done it before and it saved my sister. We're used to dealing with fevers in the lanes. If we don't get Miss Margaret's fever down she could go into spasm.'

Tears ran down Charlotte's cheeks and she gulped noisily.

'I hope you do know what you're doing, Mary,' said Mrs Mulchinock. 'We've been sponging her for the best part of an hour. To no avail, I am afraid. Are you sure we shouldn't wait for the doctor?'

'We should, ma'am. But we don't know when he'll get here.' Murmuring softly to the child, Mary bathed her forehead, opened the neck of her nightgown and ran the cold cloth over her neck, behind her ears and finally at the back of her wrists, stopping every now and then to wring the cloth out in the water again.

As Margaret began to look a little more alert, she mewled like a kitten.

'There's a good girl. Now lift up your arms. We'll have you better in no time.'

Mary removed the child's nightgown, slipped a towel under her and laid her back on the bed where she continued sponging her with the icy cloth.

Margaret began to bellow her indignation.

'*Stop, Mary! Stop!*' commanded Charlotte.

'That's enough,' decreed Mrs Mulchinock.

Ignoring their protests and the cries of the shivering child, Mary continued sponging. At last she was satisfied and, drying her off, she called for a fresh nightgown. As she was easing it over the child's head, the doctor appeared in the doorway.

'Well, well. What do we have here? A special little girl who's so sick she needs a doctor?'

'Oh, doctor, we've been beside ourselves with worry. Margaret's in an awful state.' Charlotte scrubbed at her eyes. 'We fear it might be brain fever.'

Dr Moriarty opened his medical bag, took out what looked like an ear trumpet and applied it to Margaret's chest. Bending over the child he put his ear to the instrument and, while she accepted his ministrations passively, her mother and grandmother looked terrified.

'It's called a stethoscope,' he explained, straightening up and holding out the 'trumpet' for viewing. It's the latest in medical inventions. That ice has worked.' He turned to Charlotte. 'I believe your little one is over the worst.'

CHAPTER 26

EDWARD WAS IN A BAD MOOD; he had always taken rejection and criticism hard: the lovely Mrs Elliott who had hung on his every word and laughed at his witticisms throughout the dinner at West Villa had greeted him frostily when he'd ridden all the way out to Ballyseedy House to call on her, and he'd received a letter from her that morning intimating that he was only welcome to call as her step-daughter's suitor.

Casting around for something on which to vent the gloom of his venom, he flicked through a set of current ledgers. Ah, as he thought – incomplete.

He burst into the nursery – a stocky, sturdy figure wearing a maroon cutaway coat and dark trousers, and stood just inside the door. His face was like thunder and he held a sheaf of papers in his hand.

Anne and Margaret went uncharacteristically quiet and Mary stood motionless, holding paintbrushes, as William rose and crossed the room to his brother. Mary had seen little of Edward since the night she'd slapped him and, to her relief, there had been no repercussions.

'What's up?'

Edward waved the papers. 'What do you think?'

William was calm in the face of Edward's annoyance, holding out his hand, taking the papers and looking quickly through them.

'What's the problem? These are already entered in the ledger, most probably in the old one.' His voice was quiet.

Edward's face reddened and he glowered. He slammed out of the nursery and thumped along the corridor, his footsteps leaving an angry echo.

William made a wry face. 'I apologise for the intrusion.'

'Uncle William, what does "intrusion" mean?' asked Anne.

'"Intrusion" means interruption. I have interrupted your lessons. And now I had better not intrude on your lessons any further this morning.'

William caught up with Edward in the dairy where he was being unnecessarily obnoxious – taking the lids off milk cans, sniffing, looking under muslin, picking up and putting down the wooden butter bats. The dairymaids had retreated to a corner and were watching him, scared.

'May I have a word with you when you're finished here?'

Edward, his mouth a tight, angry slash, asked, 'Why? What's so important?'

'When you're finished.'

Edward slapped a lid on a can. 'Whatever you have to say, say it to me now.'

William had always felt uneasy and disadvantaged when Edward was in one of his dark moods, and he would prefer not to have an audience, but he wasn't about to back off.

'I do not think you should interrupt our nieces' lessons.'

'And what do you think you are doing?'

'Mary has no problem with me dropping in occasionally.'

'So it's "Mary" now, is it? Well, I hope we're not in for another scandal.' Edward remembered the cowering dairymaids. He waved a dismissive arm in their direction. 'Get out. This is not your business. Nothing to do with you.' When they'd scuttled past him with bowed heads, he continued. 'That girl is the type of servant who creates scandals.'

'What do you mean?'

'Men running after her. And Paudge planning to marry her.'

'Where did you hear that?'

'From Mama. Hasn't she told you? He's already spoken to her. The deuced nerve of him — wanting to know about his future prospects at West Villa. Likely she put him up to it.'

William was unsure of how to respond. Edward's words made no sense to him. He thought of his easy friendship with Mary. He had presumed and hoped that it meant as much to her as it did to him. Now he wondered. He felt an icy bleakness, a shiver across his shoulder blades.

Edward stabbed at the air with his forefinger. 'Remember poor benighted Alicia Keogh and be careful you don't give Mary any more ideas than she already has. I'm sure you've noticed she's in the bud of untouched womanhood.' Edward's dark eyes burned in his ruddy face.

William resisted a most uncharacteristic urge to punch his brother in the face.

'Instead of dabbling in politics, as I hear you are, I can find plenty for you to do. Politics have been the ruination of this country for 700 years.'

'The power is in politics.' Seldom had William spoken so determinedly.

'And what would you know of real politics?' Edward sneered in disbelief.

William took a deep breath. 'I know enough.' He bit on his tongue to prevent himself from saying more.

'I hope you don't. Remember we Mulchinocks have always prided ourselves in avoiding becoming involved in politics. Well?' He stepped closer and prodded at William's chest with the butter bat. 'No, the power is not in politics. And never will be. It's in the land.'

William had heard similar sentiments time and again. Edward was possessive about every blade of grass in every one of West Villa's fields.

Edward slammed down the bat and brushed past William, his head held aloft, his back straight.

❂❂❂

William had Paudge bring around the buggy with the fishing gear. As he picked up the reins, he bit back the question he burned to ask him.

Sometimes the two men fished together, mostly in companionable silence, but not on that day. William craved his own company, wanted only thoughts of Mary to accompany the clip-clop of the horse's hooves, the swish of a line being cast, the music of the stream.

Fitting a plump worm to the hook on the end of his line, he settled comfortably on the damp red earth. Coppery sunlight filtered through the trees, swallows dived after insects and water washed his mind in a gentle musing way that took him into unexpected backwaters of thought.

As he hauled in a wriggling trout, the solution to what he had perceived as an insurmountable problem was so obvious that he laughed aloud. But first he'd visit the rose garden.

❀ ❀ ❀

It was one of those lilac-scented evenings of lingering light as Mary walked down the avenue. As was her habit when she reached the curve in the avenue she turned to look back at the windows, the eyes of the house, wondering at the secrets they held. Then with a skip in her steps she continued towards the gates.

William moved out from the shadow of the trees and, not for the first time on seeing her, his breath caught in his throat, although he was unprepared for her sense of exuberance beyond the servant's uniform. The way she strode, swinging a small blue bonnet by its ribbons. Freed from her indoor cap her hair caught the last rays of sun, dark tendrils gleaming and dancing.

When she saw him she stopped walking.

He took a few slow steps towards her and handed her a rose in half bloom. 'This is for you.'

She took the rose, held it to her nose and smiled.

'And I thought I might accompany you a little of the way?' As she didn't move or say anything he wondered had she heard him right. 'That's if it's acceptable to you?'

'That would be most pleasant, sir.' She ran her index finger along the petals. 'This is beautiful, thank you, and it's a beautiful evening too.' Her heart was thumping hard enough to leap from her body and she wondered how she had managed to summon the words to her lips.

They walked side by side through the wide gates, along the boreen, the dust thick and swirling with the warmth of the evening breeze.

They were wrapped in silence, locked in their own thoughts.

The initial step had been taken, but the next step was the determining one.

Because Mary found it difficult to believe what was happening, she dug the nails of her left hand into the soft skin of her palm. When the pain forced her to stop, it was still happening – she was still holding the rose Master William had given her, he was still walking beside her, she could hear the shush of her skirt around her ankles, the shoo-shoo of her boots in the dust, both overridden by the sound of his firm tread.

Then she was remembering Hannah and Danny and their love for each other – the way Danny would touch Hannah's cheek with the palm of his hand, how she'd take that hand and bring it to her lips. And the violence of their death which had been discussed, analysed and referred to again and again around kitchen fires, over the counters of shops, during card games, while drinking pints of porter, even from the pulpits during Sunday Masses.

The quietness between Mary and William was as companionable as silence on the brink of happenings can be.

William was remembering Alicia's absorption in the suitability or otherwise of Limerick lace for trimmings, the shade of silk lining for a cloak and the fit of a certain pair of boots from Paris. The ridiculousness of those thoughts when there were so many other thoughts he wanted to put into words to Mary had him breaking the silence.

'May I ask what you're thinking about, Mary? You're very quiet.'

She turned towards him, pleased to banish from her mind memories of Hannah and Danny. 'Of course you may ask for my thoughts, sir. Indeed, I believe, it is your right. But I won't tell you.' The lightness and humour in her tone took the sting from the words.

Seeing the present situation from her perspective, he felt humbled. Birdsong was all around them. A cluster of swallows, chattering and chirping, alighted on a branch overhead in a perfect progression, like a piece of knotted grass fallen slantwise.

They stopped to watch.

'They're still here,' she said softly. 'The swallows.'

'So they are,' he agreed

'Until the end of autumn.'

'Yes.' He glanced at her. 'Mary, it is not my right to know your thoughts. But it would be my privilege if you chose to share them with me. For my part I was thinking how different you are to Miss Keogh. I stayed with her family earlier in the year while I was in Ballinasloe.'

They were walking again, their steps slow and rhythmic, hands swinging loosely by their sides.

'She's the young lady you were visiting?'

'I was not specifically visiting any young lady, although I was a guest of the Keogh family for several weeks.'

'It's said in the kitchen there's a match in the making.'

'Well. With all due respects, the kitchen couldn't be more wrong. Is that what you talk about?'

'Oh, no, sir. It sort of came out ...'

He laughed. 'It's all right. I don't mind. But I want you to know there is no match between Miss Keogh and me, nor will there ever be.'

'Oh.'

'Oh, indeed. And yes. She compares most unfavourably to you. And that's what I was thinking.' He wondered might she say something to him about Paudge.

The dimples in Mary's cheeks danced. 'And that's good, sir?' Her voice was impish.

'Yes, good. Very good. And there's another thing, Mary O'Connor.'

'Yes, sir.'

'I never again want you to address me as 'sir'. I never want to hear you say the word 'sir' when talking to me.'

She dipped her head. 'How should I address you?'

'Just William – it's what I'm mostly called, although my mother uses my full name of William Pembroke and would have everyone do so. My sister has a habit of shortening my name to William P. But is plain William acceptable to you?'

Her heart felt as though it might burst from her chest. 'William. It's my father's name and my brother's too – well, Willie and Billy. Pembroke – that's an elegant sort of name. It suits you. Where did it come from?'

'It's the surname of my godfather.'

'William.' She'd so often spoken his name in her mind. Now she had his blessing to say it aloud. She savoured the sensation of saying it, her lips rounding the letters before they slipped out from her.

He loved hearing her say it.

At the start of Princes Quay she turned to him. 'It would be better, William, if I continued on my own.'

He bent towards her and whispered into the curl of her ear, 'As you wish, Mary. And I will see you tomorrow.'

Wearing the deep flush of her feelings like the warmest of blankets, she continued up along the maze of lanes to Brogue Lane.

✿✿✿

When William Pembroke strolled into the parlour his mother looked up from her desk with a smile. His presence never failed to melt her heart. Over the past weeks she had been pleased to notice that he seemed happier in himself and his happiness was hers. She had long forgiven him for what she considered to be the Alicia Keogh debacle – he was such an innocent, wrapped up in words, so unwise in the ways of the world.

However, it was well time he and Edward were married and raising families of their own. It was a subject she had discussed with her brother-in-law, and they were in agreement that had Michael lived he would have expected their sons to be married by now. Edward frequently talked about marriage and fulfilling his destiny, but so far there had been little sign of any sort of fulfilment. Although after Harriet's behaviour at the dinner, she was in accord with him when he said he'd 'rather die than marry that Miss Elliott'.

It had taken three generations for the Mulchinocks to evolve from 'trade' and to be regarded as 'landed gentry' – with the amount of acreage the family now controlled, the family was certainly 'landed'. Charlotte had 'married well' and, at the time, Margaret had thought, for love. She hoped her sons would choose their brides from socially suitable families of the Roman Catholic persuasion, marry for love and be happy.

Looking at William Pembroke, tall and slender, smiling with that unruly flop of hair falling over his forehead, she remembered the wild nights of passion when he was conceived. How she and Michael loved, their devotion to each other never wavering and the delight they took in the intimacy of their closeness. Theirs was a true love match, growing in strength over the years, a marriage of minds as well as bodies.

'How are you, Mother dearest?' William glanced at the opened ledgers. 'I thought we might take a turn around the gardens. But I see you're busy.'

She stood up, brushing down her skirts. 'Never too busy for you, son.'

He looked out the window at the sunlight playing on the lawns, the late roses in luscious bloom. 'The gardens are beautiful this year. You make our home.'

The warmth and spontaneity of his comment touched her. Michael used to make similar remarks.

'Shall we take that stroll?' she said.

As they walked the perimeter of the flower garden, stopping every now and then to admire the pinks, reds, yellows and white of the tea roses, she was aware of William's animation, his sense of happiness and awareness.

'The ground is quite dry – we should mulch.' He touched a bloom and its petals fell. 'And dead-head.'

'From the time you were a small boy, you've cared for and protected beautiful things.'

'Well, yes.'

'I'm too busy, so involved with worrying that sometimes I'm inclined to ignore the blessings of nature.'

She watched as he stopped by a bush of pink moss roses, each with the characteristic darts of green on its petals. He took a small knife from his pocket. Carefully he sliced through the stem of a blossom in full bloom and presented it to her with a flourish.

'I look forward to seeing this captured in your silken threads.' Then, as she buried her nose deep in the scent, he took the opportunity to say, 'Mary O'Connor is doing good work with

Anne and Margaret. They're learning well. Charlotte seems pleased.'

'Yes, she is and that's a relief. I hear you're spending time in the nursery?'

'Edward telling tales? Yes, I enjoy the simplicity of being with my nieces while they learn.'

'Mary O'Connor has turned out well. She's a pleasant girl and most agreeable to have around.'

William nodded and smiled.

'I suppose you know Paudge has plans to wed her.'

William's heart felt as though it might leap from his chest. Edward first, now his mother. He clamped closed his lips and plunged his hands deep into the side pockets of his jacket.

His mother was aware of his change of expression, the way his features appeared to flatten out. And wondered why.

'I believe Edward may have mentioned it,' he said. 'But that rather depends on Mary, doesn't it?'

'Oh, William Pembroke! Of course it doesn't. A servant girl like Mary couldn't do better.' The turn of conversation and her son's reaction was giving her an uneasy feeling, as though she were missing out on part of a puzzle.

William frowned. 'Am I the only member of the family who didn't know of Paudge's plan to marry Mary?'

'I doubt that. It's not a secret. Hasn't she mentioned it to you?'

'No. Why should she?'

'I thought that perhaps because ...'

His voice sharp, he asked, 'Were you going to say because of the time I spend in the nursery?'

'No, dear.' She was disturbed by his reaction. 'Let's go back to the house.'

'No, I must go.'

'Perhaps some tea first?'

'No, I won't.' He left the garden in uncharacteristic haste through the side gate.

With William Pembroke's departure, she found she had lost her enthusiasm for profit and loss accounts. She returned to her desk and started to close over the ledgers. She had done enough for the day. Before his interruption she'd been about to look at the credit and debit ledgers for the shop on the Mall. As she glanced down at the neat rows of figures, she was startled. If she weren't seeing the amounts written in black ink on the white paper, she wouldn't have believed the success of the shop. How delighted Michael would be at his son's implementation of his dream.

She inhaled deeply of the rose William Pembroke had cut for her. What a pleasure it would be to capture its likeness in silken threads.

She sat by the window and picked up her tambour frame. Removing the piece of embroidery she was currently working on, she inserted a fresh square of linen into the frame, easing the material to tautness. From the well of her mother-of-pearl worktable she pulled out the miniscule drawer where she kept her threads in colour order – for the petals she would need to blend several shades of pink, and that flash of green would be best interpreted with a dark shade veering to a lighter one.

CHAPTER 27

MARY WAS HUNKERED DOWN on the floor, helping Anne paint a flower. Anne's creativity appeared to be best expressed from ground level. Mary did nothing to change the child's way of working, although with the enthusiastic scribbles, splashes and puddles of paint her execution of a flower was wide open to interpretation. But Mary's patience, understanding and encouragement were unfaltering as she suggested petals, stem and leaves, even mentioning the stamen of a plant.

Watching from his place on the story couch, William did not want to think of Mary belonging to another, of life without her. Yet he couldn't get it out of his head that during all the times they had spent together she had never once mentioned Paudge. On the occasions he wanted to ask her about him, when the question almost slipped out, he had held back.

❁ ❁ ❁

A few evenings later as they approach Princes Quay, a blackbird was in joyous song, the sounds fluting and floating on the still air.

She laughed at him and tossed back her hair. 'I am growing used to your company, William Pembroke.'

'I am pleased to hear that, Mary O'Connor.' She had created the opportunity and before it had a chance to slip away, he grasped at it. 'But what about Paudge?'

'What about him?' she hedged, pleased with his question. Now that he had asked about Paudge she could tell him.

'You must mean a lot to him as, I hear, he's asked for your hand in marriage?' His tone demanded the truth.

'Yes.' Her look was unflinching. 'He has.'

'And ?'

'I will not be marrying him.' She spoke firmly.

'Does he know that?'

'Yes, he knows. I've told him. We haven't spoken for some weeks now.' As William was absorbing the implications of what she had said with a sense of relief, with a wave of her arms she added, 'Anyways it's well past time the marriage laws of Ireland were repealed.'

He looked at her with incredulity. 'What do you mean, Mary?'

'If Mr O'Connell gets his way the Union between England and Ireland will be repealed. I don't see why the laws about marriage shouldn't be repealed to give women a say in their lives – for a start, the freedom to choose who they marry.'

William threw back his head and laughed heartily. 'Human nature cannot be repealed. And as far as I am aware marriages have always been brokered for women.'

'There, William, you are wrong. It hasn't always been so.' As she had spoken to her mother about the Brehon Laws and her opinions on marriage, she made those same points known to William.

He had held back from expressing his feelings to her because, behind the ease and breadth of their conversations, he had always sensed a reluctance within her to change their status quo of friendly banter. But while hesitant about rushing matters, he was hopeful that she reciprocated what was increasingly in his heart.

Her chameleon quality and the quick way she changed subjects made her a delightful companion – one minute it was Irish politics, the next his nieces' paintings, then she'd ask a question about flowers or something about Dublin city.

And on one occasion something more personal.

'I've something to say to you, William.' She looked troubled.

He held back from putting his arm around her. 'What is it?'

'It's hard to say.'

'Just say whatever it is.'

'That dinner at West Villa ...'

William put his hand over hers. 'I hoped you wouldn't have to ...'

'What? Serve you and your fine friends?'

'Well, yes, I suppose so.' His voice was hesitant as he turned towards her, searching her face. 'I wanted to spare you.'

'Your mother asked me. I had no choice. Sometimes people like us don't have a choice.' There was the hardness of truth in her tone.

'I know what you mean. And on my father's grave I vow you'll never again be in such a situation.'

Often they sat by the canal on a low wall, shoulder to shoulder. Their admiration for Daniel O'Connell filled many of their talks. Mary asked innumerable questions and William never tired of answering, creating word pictures of the soirées he had attended in Dublin, relating bits of political talk, light-hearted gossip, describing the elegance of the women's gowns, evenings spent at the theatre and musical events, emphasising how always at the entertainments Daniel O'Connell's message about the importance of Repeal featured. As he spoke, he liked to be turned towards her so that he could watch the expressions of interest, incredulity, humour and awe flit across her face.

When he confided in her how he and Rob O'Sullivan were organising a rally she reacted with quiet enthusiasm and the touch of humour he'd come to enjoy.

'It's good to see the likes of you helping the likes of us.' She gave him a mischievous look.

'It's about time,' he responded ruefully. 'Believe me, everyone will be the better for Repeal.'

'Will they?' She sounded dubious.

'We're canvassing throughout the town. Getting everyone involved.'

'You'll canvas everywhere? Even the lanes?'

'Especially the lanes and the alleys. To find out what are the women's concerns. We want to know what they think about Repeal. What they consider to be the most important issues.'

'The women don't have opinions, but if they did it's full bellies for their families they'd be lookin' for.'

'I suppose you're right.'

They were quiet for a while, locked in their own thoughts until he pulled his notebook from his pocket, removed a sheet of paper covered in his writing and handed it to her. 'Here – I wrote this for you.'

'What is it?'

'A poem dedicated to you.'

She dimpled in delight. 'For me? Will you read it to me?'

He was shy about reading the verse that had poured from his heart. 'It's not finished yet.'

'That doesn't matter. Please.'

Watching her intently, in a low voice he recited the opening lines of the poem he'd written in such haste on that moonlight night.

The pale moon was rising above the green mountain,

The sun was declining beneath the blue sea;

When I strayed with my love to the pure crystal fountain,

That stands in the beautiful Vale of Tralee.

She was lovely and fair as the rose of the summer,

Yet 'twas not her beauty alone that won me;

Oh no, 'twas the truth in her eyes ever dawning,

That made me love Mary, the Rose of Tralee.

Eyes shining, Mary clasped her hands. 'It's beautiful, full of beautiful words. Did you really write it for me?'

'I believe so. I cannot recall bringing any other love called Mary to the "crystal fountain".'

'I am your love?'

'Yes. You are my Rose of Tralee. And my love.'

She looked guarded, unsure. 'I'll treasure it. Keep it for always and ever.'

'Yes, for always and ever,' he repeated.

He was tired of prevaricating, of tiptoeing around his feelings. He felt they belonged together, he wanted to move their relationship forward, and the time seemed right. He hadn't felt such happiness, so complete, so sure of life since he was a child walking the land with his father, his small hand enclosed safely in his large protective one.

They continued in a silence that was filled with words that needed to be said and plans that ought to be implemented.

His verse had moved their relationship to a different plane.

He took her hand and moved closer to her.

Her touch was like a jolt of lightning.

His touch was the only thing she knew.

Their lives were reduced to that one point of contact. It had to mean something, her hand in his, his hand encasing hers. Deep within they knew that to believe anything else was a mistake.

When she turned towards him Mary read the look in his eyes as love – she didn't know how she knew it was love, but she was sure that's what it was. Time had expanded, swelled and grown to absorb her senses so completely that she was dazed by the world, and she felt more alive than she had ever been.

William was no longer in doubt as to their feelings for each other. He drew her close, their senses drowning in the mingling scents of late woodbine and wild stock.

'I want you to know, my Mary, that you have become very dear to me.'

How lovely to be addressed as 'my Mary', she thought. 'And you to me, William.' She said it bravely.

It seemed to them as though the world stood still, holding its breath.

As William cupped her chin in his hand and bent towards her, Mr Foley came around the corner, his walking cane making no sound on the grass verge.

He halted. Mary O'Connor from the Lane and the young master from the Big House at Annagh.

His heart sang at the rightness of their togetherness, their sense of intimacy, the handsomeness of them, but it only sang momentarily as he realised the likely repercussions of such a relationship.

The story of the Colleen Bawn – poor, ill-fated Ellen Hanley rose sceptre-like before him. And that hadn't occurred so long ago, either – it was only a little over two decades since the beautiful young peasant girl in County Limerick had married into the gentry only to be discarded and murdered by her husband. Even worse, Daniel O'Connell had defended the husband. The only good that came out of the whole sorry situation was that he hadn't won the case and John Scanlon hanged. It was the talk of not only the county, but also the country and beyond.

Not that young Mulchinock bore any resemblance to that scallywag John Scanlon. But the gentry were the gentry. That was the way it was and the way it would always be. From birth they had been reared to band together to defend their rights and privileges.

He moved forward again and Mary, seeing him, stepped a little away from the young man.

She smiled shyly but widely. 'Good evening, Mr Foley.'

He looked from one to the other, raising his hat graciously. They were comfortable in each other's presence in a way he rarely saw — it made him wonder how far their relationship had progressed.

William approached, his hand outstretched. 'Good to see you, sir. I was going to call on you. Rob O'Sullivan and I — we're organising a rally for Daniel O'Connell. We hope you'll support us?'

Mr Foley nodded. Of course he would lend his support.

He moved on, feeling uneasy about what he had seen. If he could have seen Mary and William a few nights later as they danced at Clahane, he would have worried even more.

 # CHAPTER 28

THE SOUNDS OF THE FIDDLE playing 'The Rakes of Mallow' with joyous abandonment drew Mary and William to the dance platform.

Mary was greeted with warmth by young and old, while William was looked over with reservation. It wasn't so much that the majority of those present knew he was the young master from West Villa, but rather that he was accompanying Mary O'Connor, that they were so obviously together.

Many a hopeful lad from around the townland held a candle for her and would have grasped at any opportunity to be her dance partner. Several had invited her to accompany them to the platform and to various kitchen dances, and always she'd refused.

As she and William moved through the dancers, their aura of completeness prevented intrusion.

In the same way as Michael Mulchinock and Margaret McCann had danced in Dublin Castle nearly a quarter of a century ago, Mary and William danced only for themselves. As they stood on the edge of the platform, side by side, after a particularly strenuous 'Walls of Limerick', William drew Mary close, encircling her waist with his arm and of one accord they moved off into the deepening dusk.

Her heart soared at the feel of his hand through the fabric of her blouse, his touch so tender, yet so much in control, and when he kissed her his lips were both soft and firm. As she breathed him into her soul her heart fluttered and soared.

'We can have a future together,' he whispered into her hair.

His emotion rushed over her like a storm, over the nape of her neck, her back, every delicate hair on her skin responding to him as a frisson of happiness ran down her spine. She was fired with hope, to the extent of imagining their life at West Villa, being together in those beautiful rooms, being with him for always.

She touched the palm of her hand to his cheek, '*A chroí* ...'

He interrupted by putting a finger to her lips. 'I will speak to my mother and to your father, but first I want you to be sure you're happy to wed me.'

In the pale, high light of the Kerry evening, Mary felt as though she could die of happiness. Again she remembered Mr O'Connell's speech about the happiness of Repeal. Hers was the happiness of love. The thought of a future tied to William was tantalising beyond imagination. Being wed to him would be as much a meeting of minds as bodies – he treated her as his intellectual equal, sharing his world with her – forever she would be surrounded by opportunities to learn, to know, to experience, and all the while being loved.

'You haven't answered?'

'I will wed you with joy. And be a good wife to you, but ...'

'But what?'

'We've only known each other for a short while.'

'No. I've known you for a long while. From the evening I saw you dancing here. June, two years ago.'

That was the night when Hannah and Danny had met. She pushed thoughts of them to the back of her mind.

'And I believe I've known you a while too — since seeing you in Denny Street with Mr O'Connell.'

'That was way back in January.'

'Yes, quite a long time ago.'

'That's settled then.' He drew her close and whispered, 'I promise to be a good husband to you.'

From his pocket he withdrew a small velvet pouch and opened the drawstring. Little did he dream when he had bought the rings in Spiddal that within a few months he would be using one as a pledge of betrothal. Taking hold of Mary's left hand, he placed the delicate gold ring on the fourth finger — the heart finger.

'Now we're officially betrothed. And I want the world to know.'

Mary ran her index finger across the ring. Her heart felt as though it was pumping out joy. And then she thought of her mistress and how she'd take the news. Not well, she was sure — and Master Edward and Miss Charlotte, William's people at West Villa and hers on the lane, all had to be taken into consideration.

William was saying, 'Tomorrow I'll call on your father and tell my mother. We'll wed soon.'

It was all happening so quickly she could scarcely gather her breath. Too much, too soon. Her natural practicality and cautiousness had her suggesting, 'Perhaps we should keep our plans to ourselves until after the rally? You need to get that over you first — it needs all your attention right now.' And announcing their betrothal to his family would need all his attention too.

'But that's weeks away.'

'Yes. And we can wait.'

He was giddy with joy. 'We could always elope? Run off, come back wed. Present the world with a *fait accompli!*'

She spoke firmly. 'We're not going to elope – it's a dishonest way of being wed.'

William thought back to that evening in Dublin Castle, how as he stood watching the dancing couples he determined that he would only wed for love. To love and to be loved. And now it looked as though such a future would be his.

When he kissed her again, Mary felt her resolve weaken about keeping their betrothal a secret, even about eloping. One part of her wanted the world to know of their love, to have their feelings for each other out in the open, acknowledged – yet another part urged prudence. As she was weighing the one part against the other, she was relieved to hear his decision.

'You're right. I'll wait until the day after the rally to speak to our families.'

Exhausted as she was with happiness after William had left her, Mary stood for a long while looking up at the glittering stars, their distance and pinpoints of light giving her a sense of the depth and power of love.

❀ ❀ ❀

William took canvassing seriously, believing in the efficacy of one-to-one contact. He and Rob spent productive hours bringing the message of Repeal to the men and women of the town and beyond, listening to their fears and easing their worries about the potato crop failing again and the return of the dreaded typhus and cholera.

On an evening when a light shower of rain turned into a downpour, the drops heavy, they turned up the collars of their coats and ran up the street to seek shelter in the tavern where they'd first met Daniel O'Connell. The place was dark and quiet with a few men standing along the bar. They ordered porter and stood, elbows on the counter drinking, waiting for the rain to subside.

The men at the bar were talking politics, and the friends began to pay attention when they heard William's name mentioned.

'I hear young William Mulchinock is as close to Daniel O'Connell as a pig's squeal to its snout,' one of the old timers spoke without looking to right or left.

After a while another, drinking deep of his porter, said, 'And who've thought a Mulchinock would be a Repealer?' With sloppy movements of his hand he made the Sign of the Cross. 'His father'd turn in his grave.'

'He's a damn sight better man than that brother of his.'

Another pushed back his hat. 'And the word is he's supporting Maurice O'Connell in the election.'

'It's well time the power of the Denny family was broken.'

'Young Mulchinock has the making of a politician.' It was the man who'd blessed himself.

'He's a quiet one and I hear he's been havin' a wee word or two with tenant farmers, suggesting it would be to their benefit – to all our benefit – to show up at the rally.'

'When's that?'

'Saturday week. God help us. A bit of hope's what the people need.'

Rob nudged William and pointed along the counter. William shook his head and indicated the door. Outside the rain was still lashing down in zigzags of engorged drops.

'Why? Why didn't you make yourself known?" Rob asked, vainly seeking a modicum of shelter by pressing into the wall

'They didn't recognise us. It wasn't the time or the place.'

'There's not much point in canvassing in this weather.'

William stepped into a doorway and consulted a rough sketch. 'I'll go around the back of the Potato Market. I'll manage alone. You've done enough for the day.'

'That's worse than the slums of Dublin.'

'All the more reason to give a bit of hope to the "poor craythurs" – as Mrs Mac would say.'

'Yourself and Mrs Mac!' Rob cuffed him on the shoulder as he turned for home.

The further William moved from the main streets and the deeper he ventured into the back lanes the more conscious he was of the sounds, sights and smells of poverty, his awareness heightened by the relentless rain: the thin cry of a distressed baby, likely from hunger, he thought, ramshackle hovels existing cheek by jowl, the living quarters of too many squirming lives, and the dank smell of vegetables piled against the walls. While Brogue Lane was not as miserable as these lanes, he was glad to be giving Mary a better life, glad too that he was in a position to help her family.

He was reminded of the time his mother had marched them along the laneways of the town. She was a wise woman, but she couldn't have known how he would use the experience of that afternoon many years later while canvassing.

A young woman holding a baby on her hip answered the first door he knocked on, a small child hiding behind her skirts.

'I apologise for disturbing you, ma'am, but if you've a few minutes I'd like to talk to you.'

'You want my husband.'

'No. You. If that's all right?'

She nodded.

'Have you heard of Repeal?'

She shook her head

'Have you heard of Daniel O'Connell?'

She nodded vigorously and almost smiled. 'The Liberator? Yes. Sure isn't it due to him that we can practise our faith?'

'It is indeed. And if he succeeds in changing the Repeal law, all our lives will be better.'

'Ours too?'

'Most certainly.'

'How do you know that, sir?'

'Trust me. And come to the rally. Bring the children and your husband.'

As, finally, he turned towards West Villa he was pleased with his evening's canvassing. The people of the town he loved were eager to grasp at hope and he was equally eager to supply it to them.

CHAPTER 29

'WHERE'S MAMA? I WANT to show her my drawing.' Margaret was waiting inside the hall door, sucking on her thumb.

'She's gone out for a while,' Mrs Mulchinock said softly as was her way when addressing her granddaughters.

'When will she be back?'

'Well now, I think it'll be when she comes through the door, and won't that be lovely?'

'I did a drawing too.' Anne was aggrieved as only Anne could be when she felt Margaret was getting more attention than her.

Mary removed Margaret's thumb from her mouth.

'Thank you, Mary, she has that habit.'

'She'll grow out of it, ma'am.'

Mrs Mulchinock threw Mary a grateful nod and retreated back into her parlour to her letter writing.

'Where's Mama? I want my mama.' Margaret's plump cheeks crumpled. '*I want my mama!*' Her voice rose to a wail. Since her fever she had developed insecurities that fluttered about her like moths.

Before Mary could offer reassurance, Charlotte pushed in through the door. Her face was scratched, her skirt muddy, her bonnet awry and her hair streeling.

The children backed into the wall with frightened expressions as Mary went to her. 'Miss Charlotte, are you all right?'

'No, I am not. *Can't you see I'm not all right?*' She brushed at her skirt and jacket ineffectually, while her voice rose on notes of hysteria.

'Come, Miss Charlotte. Come in here.' Mary ushered her into the drawing room and looked back into the hall.

Anne was standing still as a statue, wide-eyed with fright, while Margaret sucked on her thumb furiously.

Alerted by the commotion, Mrs Mulchinock emerged from her parlour, brushed past Mary and went to Charlotte.

Mary took the children by the hand and brought them to the kitchen.

'Could you mind Miss Anne and Miss Margaret for a little while, Mrs Mac?' She placed her index finger across her lips to warn Mrs Mac not to ask questions.

Mrs Mac seated the girls at the table while Mary fetched a basin of warm water and some towels.

When she returned to the drawing room, mother and daughter were standing by the fireplace, in agitated discussion.

'I find that difficult to believe. These are our people. We're helping them.'

'If you saw them today, you wouldn't think so, you'd realise they don't want our help. I've said it for weeks. There's a feeling of unrest around the town.' Charlotte tried tidying her straggling hair with ineffectual fingers. Her face was more badly cut and marked than initially had been apparent.

'What happened?' Mary had a sense of foreboding.

Over the past while there had been reported sightings of the Whiteboys, murmurings about the politics of Repeal and mutterings about 'the power of the gentry'. Despite her personal happiness that had her floating on air, Mary felt uneasy, although she was unable to pinpoint the cause. She put it down to the town's unrest as it waited for the rally.

'I was attacked just after I left the soup kitchen. In the laneway. That's what happened.' Charlotte spoke haltingly, spacing out each word as though trying to make sense of the situation.

'Why? Do you know who it was?'

Charlotte shook her head

'Have you any idea? Was there a problem in the kitchen?' Mrs Mulchinock was beginning to return to her capable self.

'No. Nothing … Well, at the time, I didn't think anything of it …'

'What? Think what? Charlotte, we must get to the bottom of this.'

'It may have been because of what one of the women said … Tangney I believe is her name.' Her voice was uncharacteristically hesitant.

'Who is she? Do you know this person?' Mrs Mulchinock addressed Mary.

'If it's Mrs Tangney, she's the midwife, delivers most of the babies around the town. She has no need of free soup.'

'What did she say, Charlotte?' By the sharpness of her voice it was obvious that Mrs Mulchinock's patience was growing thin.

'Something about the disgrace of townspeople taking charity from the likes of us.' Charlotte glanced at Mary.

'Tell me exactly what happened,' said her mother. 'Take your time.'

Charlotte swayed. Her face was a ghastly colour, with cuts, scratches and dried blood a horrible travesty. She sat on the edge of a chair, put her face in her hands and sobbed noisily, her aloof dignity, such an integral part of her, no longer in evidence.

Mary was shocked at the rawness of her emotions and her lack of control. She lifted the basin of water she had placed on a table, and as she stooped down she was aware of the comforting security of William's ring moving on the narrow cord between her breasts.

Mrs Mulchinock's white hands rested on the back of the chair.

Gradually, as her sobbing subsided, Charlotte dabbed at her eyes with a scrap of a lacy kerchief. She took a deep breath, sat upright and exhaled deeply.

'We were serving the soup as usual. There was a good crowd, some men too with their pails, even a few children. There was a pleasant enough atmosphere as they queued, then somebody said something about Daniel O'Connell being back in Derrynane.' She sobbed again.

'All right,' soothed Mrs Mulchinock.

'The Tangney woman said he was a blackguard, getting off with putting his young servants in the family way. Somebody shouted it wasn't true, that he was a hero and a true defender of the Faith, that he'd set Ireland free, that it was his son Maurice who is the blackguard and him wanting to be the MP for Tralee. Mrs Tangney said her cousin was in service with the O'Connells, and she knew all about the goings-on of the gentry. And everyone looked at me.'

Mary had never heard Charlotte speak so volubly, so fluently or at such length, her words tumbling over each other as though desperate for release. She wished herself anywhere but in that drawing room.

'What happened next?' Mrs Mulchinock sounded determined to get to the heart of the matter.

'There was a lot of shouting, people agreeing and disagreeing with each other, and a bit of scuffling. The schoolmaster – Mr Foley – came into the hall. People listen to him. He told me to leave, said he would calm the crowd and make sure the soup was distributed. I got my jacket and when I went into the lane three young boys followed me. They hurled insults and jeers and had a supply of stones and rotten potatoes.' Charlotte sniffled.

'What were they saying?'

'Something about the Whiteboys. And landowners and the gentry getting their due.' She frowned in concentration.

'Not the Whiteboys again. Haven't they caused enough damage to this family?'

Mary's heart dropped at the venom in Mrs Mulchinock's tone.

'Charlotte, do you know who the boys were?'

Please God, Mary offered a silent prayer, do not let Miss Charlotte be able to name the boys. And, please God again do not let Billy be one of them.

'No. I don't remember seeing any of them before.'

'Were they in the hall?'

'No, there were no boys of their age in today.'

Mrs Mulchinock, ever practical, asked, 'How did you get away?'

'The master came into the laneway after me. He cuffed the boys on their ears, made them apologise to me, and sent them on their way, telling them that he'd be calling on their fathers.'

'So he knows who they are.' Mrs Mulchinock spoke in that considering manner of hers.

Mary's heart dropped further.

'I believe so.'

While Mary swabbed Charlotte's face, Mrs Mulchinock drummed her fingers on the table.

'This matter is not finished with. I intend to summon Mr Foley. To hear his side of this.'

❀ ❀ ❀

Mr Foley was pleased to find Mary and Billy together, and even more pleased to find Willie missing.

Throughout an unpleasant meeting with Mrs Mulchinock, during which she had not invited him to be seated, he had refused to divulge the names of the perpetrators who had frightened her daughter. It took his considerable powers of persuasion to convince her that he'd given the scallywags in a good dressing-down, to assure her that the matter was dealt with and such an incident would not occur again. He had finished by reiterating how grateful the townspeople were for her beneficence – 'beneficence' he considered to be the perfect word to describe her many charitable acts.

He still had a few questions he wanted to ask young Billy O'Connor, a few matters he wished to have clarified.

'Were the Whiteboys involved in that incident on Monday when Mrs Mulchinock's daughter was attacked?' As he spoke he watched Billy intently.

Billy flushed but met his eyes. 'I had nothin' to do with it. The Whiteboys hadn't either. I'm sorry for wha' happened to the lady.'

'I am glad to hear it, and I'm more than relieved that you'd no part in that disgraceful behaviour.' He wagged his finger. 'Remember we are judged by the company we keep. Now be off with you. I want to talk to your sister.'

Billy lathered out the door as though pursued by the hounds of hell.

Mr Foley and Mary exchanged conspiratorial glances of relief, perhaps tempered with a touch of amusement – Billy wasn't anything as tough as he made out to be.

Mr Foley looked fondly at Mary sitting across the table from him. She had been one of the cleverest pupils he had ever taught and, as well as growing into a beauty, she remained bright, quick and enquiring. She was the daughter he'd never had, and her ability was way beyond the role of a servant. But being involved with young Mulchinock? From his recent brush with the young man's mother he was in no doubt as to the ferocity with which she guarded the family, their home and their business interests.

He wished he had news from the teachers' training college in Dublin, but he hadn't heard back from the principal. A place on the course would surely take her mind off young Mulchinock. There was a touch of sadness about him as he sought for the best words to frame the warning he wanted to convey.

Before he had a chance to speak, she reached into her bodice and pulled out a thin leather cord with a ring on it. Her look of happiness was rapturous as she held it out towards him.

'William and I are betrothed. But it's to remain secret until after the rally.'

In the face of her announcement any warning of his would be redundant. But he shuddered at the thought of the reception she'd receive from Mrs Mulchinock. He had too much objective experience of the devastation love could wreak: the unfortunate Ellen Hanley, benighted from the moment John Scanlon clapped eyes on her – Hannah Cluskey and Danny Stack, their fates sealed with Hennessey's bride price – and now Mary O'Connor. The country was awash with the desolation of romances gone awry and repercussions from dalliances. Not that he thought young Mulchinock was dallying with Mary – his reputation was one of integrity – but still he feared. The gentry were the gentry. Always were. Always would be. When it came to the crunch they were protective of themselves and protective of each other.

He sighed, placed his hands on the table, fanning out his fingers. 'Have ye made plans?'

'What kind of plans?'

'Well … where you'll live?'

'West Villa, of course. It's William's home.'

'What about his mother? Brother?'

'William hasn't said. But it'll be all right.'

'And if it isn't?'

Mary's eyes widened and she bit on her lip. 'I don't know.'

'And I don't know what to say.'

She looked at him in an intense way. 'Say nothin', except to wish us luck.' Then, tucking the ring back into its hiding place, she surprised him with, 'Do you think women will ever have the same rights and powers as men?'

Looking at her earnest, intelligent face, he resisted the urge to laugh. In the circumstances, imagine her even thinking to ask such a question!

He reached across the table and put his hand over hers, answering quietly, 'Whatever about in the future, it will not happen in our lifetime. For now a woman's place is in the home, obedient to her husband and raising their children.'

The intimacy between them was broken as Willie stepped into the kitchen, his expression settling into a mask of displeasure. 'Master Foley. Filling me daughter's head with more nonsense?'

Mr Foley couldn't guarantee his civility to Willie O'Connor. 'Your daughter has a good brain. You should be proud of her.'

'Little use her brains will be when she's raisin' babbies.'

Mr Foley stood up, secured his hat on his head before raising it in an elaborate gesture to Willie as he left. The man would not be so cocksure if he knew of his daughter's betrothal.

Willie moved some swatches of leather on his cramped worktable drawn close to the small window to catch every vestige of light.

'Have you finished the curate's boots?' Mary asked.

'They're finished, and delivered to the priests' house, not that it's any of your business.'

'It's all of our business to get paid for the work we do. It's for the family. We won't eat otherwise.' She spoke more tartly than she meant.

'We've never not eaten. Anyways, it's different with the Church.' He stood up. His fist thumped the table. His eyes flashed. 'And you *will* marry Paudge!'

'I will not. Never.'

'What won't you?' Nora unwound the shawl from her head as she entered.

'Nothing,' Mary and Willie answered in uncharacteristic unison.

❋ ❋ ❋

Mary could not sleep. She felt as though the cabin was suffocating and strangling her, seeping into the pores of her skin. After an age of tossing and turning on her small section of the bed, she got up.

Her father, his head bowed in his hands, was sitting at the table, the jug of poteen in front of him. She eased towards the corner where her parents slept. Moving aside the curtain, in the half-light she saw that her mother lay awake, her body barely making a ripple under the blanket.

'Oh, Mam.'

Nora sat up and held out her arms. Kneeling by the bed, Mary went into them.

Nora stroked her bent head, whispering, 'Hush, hush, *a stór*. Everything'll come all right. Paudge's a good man.'

'No, it won't be all right,' Mary whispered. 'I'll not be marrying him. No matter what Da says.'

Nora's birdlike frame sat up straighter as she thought back over the past while – despite her determined outpourings about not marrying, Mary glowed with happiness. Hadn't she too experienced the rush of love?

'Are you in love with another?' The words were barely whispered.

'Yes, I am.' It was beyond time to tell her mother, but still she hesitated.

'Who is he?'

'It's William. William Pembroke Mulchinock,' she said it slowly, emphasising each syllable.

'The young master?' Nora eased herself upwards. She was faded and thin as a rail as though life was leaching from her, but her voice was stern, in a way that Mary wasn't familiar with. 'No good'll come of it, *a stór*, no good comes of cavortin' with the gentry.'

Mary laughed. 'We're not cavorting, Mam. William has asked me to marry him.'

Nora made a skimpy Sign of the Cross. 'You're not …? You aren't …?'

For a moment Mary didn't understand and when she did she didn't know whether to laugh or cry. She reached into her bodice and pulled out the ring and held it towards her mother.

'So you're not with child?' Norah spoke in an uncharacteristically straightforward way.

'No, Mam. I'm not.'

'And he's going to wed you? He's asked you?' There was a wealth of surprise in the questions.

'Yes, Mam. William and I are to be wed.'

Nora's smile was beatific, but only for a moment. 'Does the mistress know?'

'Not yet.'

'Listen to me, *a stór*. And listen well.'

Every muscle in Mary's body tightened as she waited for the onslaught of 'them and us', but her mother, the meek woman who was rarely heard voicing an opinion, surprised her.

'If you're sure – be with the young master. Leave the lanes. And don't ever look back.' Nora's cotton-soft voice was full of unaccustomed urgency.

'What'll I do about Da?'

'Leave him to me. I'll explain when the time is right.'

Mary threw her arms around her mother and whispered words of thanks into her hair.

CHAPTER 30

WITH A SIGH OF RELIEF Mrs Mulchinock closed over the door of the parlour and sat down by the fire. It was a chilly October afternoon and she was quite out of sorts. Much as she enjoyed following the activities of Queen Victoria, even John's recent gift of a copy of both the *Court Circular* and the *Court Journal* could not raise her spirits.

A knock broke into her thoughts and she looked up irritably.

Charlotte asked, 'Are you busy, Mother?'

'No. Come in, dear.' Mrs Mulchinock forced warmth to her voice. She knew she was lucky to be surrounded by her family – the economic necessity of these harsh times had forced the break-up of many families in the area – although on occasions like now, she craved the quiet of her own company.

She gestured to the chair opposite.

Charlotte sat, fussily settling her skirt, and, hands clasped together, she leaned towards her mother. 'I've decided – I'm taking the girls back to Cork.'

'Well! This is an unexpected decision. But I have to say it's the right one.' Mrs Mulchinock's sense of relief was obvious from her nod of approval and smile. On several occasions, tactfully and gently, she hoped, she had broached the subject of her daughter returning to her husband, but to no avail. Charlotte had been a stubborn child, marriage hadn't softened her obstinacy, and she had refused to disclose her reasons for remaining in Tralee.

Another knock and William Pembroke put his head around the door. 'I appear to have mislaid my book.'

'These days you look as though you're walking around with your head in the clouds,' said his sister.

'Perhaps, Charlotte, he's in love.' Mrs Mulchinock sought to inject a note of levity.

'William P in love?' Charlotte laughed.

His cheeks were lightly flushed as he looked around the room. 'No sign of my book.' He looked from his mother to his sister. 'Is everything all right?'

'Yes, I was just telling Mama that I'm returning to Cork.'

'It's about time. Your place is with your husband. And the girls need their father.'

Mrs Mulchinock was pleased to have his endorsement.

'Well, Cork is a much safer place than Tralee.' Charlotte turned to her mother. 'I can't get the fear of another attack out of my mind. I worry every time I leave the house. That soup kitchen is a dangerous place.

'Nonsense,' said William robustly. 'It's not dangerous. That was an unfortunate but isolated incident.'

'And there's the fright of Margaret's fever. I'll leave as soon as possible.' She stood up, smoothing down her skirts. 'Oh, and I'll be taking Mary with me.'

The periphery of Mrs Mulchinock's mind registered the sharp intake of William Pembroke's breath.

She spoke more brusquely than was her wont. 'You'll do nothing of the sort, Charlotte. Mary stays here. I've grown fond of the girl and come to rely on her.'

'Well, I want her to come with me. She's good with Anne and Margaret, as good – likely better – than any trained governess.'

'I am sorry, Charlotte, but I cannot permit it. Anyway, I believe she and Paudge are to be wed.'

'Paudge can wait.' Charlotte reached for the bell pull. 'Why don't we ask her? Give her the choice?'

William slipped outside.

Mary broke into a smile when she saw him as she was coming through the hall.

He put his finger to his lips. 'Shush and be quick. Charlotte is going back to Cork and she plans to take you with her. Perhaps now's the time to tell them of our plans?'

She touched his cheek, 'No, William, I don't think so.' She could imagine the family's reaction and, in truth, she wasn't ready to face it yet. 'It's best we stick to what we agreed.'

Mary's mind may have been racing as she entered the parlour, but it wasn't obvious as she gave her usual bob of a curtsy and waited just inside the door.

William followed her in a few seconds later, holding a copy of *The Freeman's Journal*.

Charlotte stood, her hands placed on the back of her chair, the better to take control of the situation. 'Mary, I know how attached you've become to my daughters and, indeed, they to you.'

Mary nodded.

'We're returning to my home in Cork, and I want you to come to take care of my daughters. Continue as their governess.'

William moved to the centre of the parlour and looked at his mother who was leaning forward as though about to do battle.

Mary kept her hands tight by her side, balled into fists. She looked first at Mrs Mulchinock, then at Charlotte, but she did not as much as glance in William's direction.

William's words were gentle. 'Mary, my sister wishes you to continue caring for her daughters – you are doing a splendid job and my nieces are devoted to you, but that would mean you would have to leave Tralee to live in Cork. And at West Villa we've come to see you as part of the family.'

Mrs Mulchinock sensed the same sort of vibrations as she'd experienced on the afternoon William Pembroke had presented her with the moss rose. She felt uneasy, caught up in a fug of scattering emotions. As fragmented rivulets of thoughts cohered there was a tug of memory and then it was gone.

'Well, Mary? What do you say? We haven't got all day.' Charlotte's voice was laced with its usual sharpness.

'Thank you, Miss Charlotte. I am honoured. But if it's all right with the mistress, I'll remain here.' With that Mary looked at Mrs Mulchinock. The formal part of the question answered, emotion burst from Mary, 'I love being at West Villa!'

Mrs Mulchinock looked from son to servant and back again, slowly, intently, as her expression began to settle into folds of understanding.

Looking only from mother to daughter, Mary nodded, bobbed imperceptibly and quietly withdrew.

'Well, of all the ungracious ...' Charlotte's rant went unnoticed.

Mrs Mulchinock was remembering that afternoon when Michael had called to Fitzwilliam Square to speak to her father. She remembered how he had looked at her with that lingering half smile and the light of love in his eyes. Now that she looked back, she had seen her son give her servant girl the same look, and she was filled with an understanding and a knowledge that she did not want to possess.

William Pembroke and Mary O'Connor. How could she not have noticed? How could she have been so unaware? So blind? The way he spoke of her, his recent contentment, the time he spent in the nursery and the manner in which way his face lit up when the girl was around. She thought that her awareness of the situation must have been on the periphery of her mind for some time, and she chastised her lack of action.

Pleading a headache, she asked her son and daughter to excuse her. Dreading the thought of the crack that threatened to penetrate the structure of her carefully controlled life she turned to her journal for comfort.

Her entry was succinct and to the point: *It is my belief that William Pembroke has developed an affection for Mary O'Connor, our nursery maid. I am unsure if she has inveigled a commitment from him. He is such an innocent. She is a clever girl. She has Paudge wanting to wed her. Could she be with child? William Pembroke's child? But no matter what, their relationship must end.*

She put down her pen, stood up and looked out to the garden, autumnal now with the leaves turning and only the dahlia beds splashing colour – reds, maroons, pinks and yellows. Mary would have to go from West Villa. There was no question of her marrying Paudge now. Best if she left Tralee. But, no matter what her feelings, as William Pembroke's mother and mistress of West Villa, she could not afford to act in haste and must behave as normal. However she would sort out the situation, she must be seen to be above reproach and must avoid alienating her son. She needed time. And she suspected time was not on her side.

CHAPTER 31

IT WAS SATURDAY AFTERNOON and only a few hours to the rally.

As was the way on the lanes, for days the menfolk had been consumed with political discussion and the implications of Repeal of the Union, whereas the women, with the exceptions of those William and Rob had managed to speak to personally, were blithely going about their usual business, ignoring the subject of politics.

In Mrs Mac's domain Repeal was spoken of in hopeful whispers, but only when she was absent from the kitchen, and Mary hadn't heard a mention of it upstairs.

Billy's words — when he spoke — had taken on a new defiance. Mary watched him worriedly, thinking he looked as though he might explode with anticipation. She understood the seduction of a group of idealists like the Whiteboys, and she warned him of the hazards of allowing his head to be filled with treacherous ideals and dangerous words, repeating William's belief that politics were best served with discretion.

That afternoon she was to collect Mrs Mulchinock's winter bonnet from the New Hat Establishment in Denny Street. She attributed the mistress's recent sharpness of manner and pernickety demands to sadness and loneliness at the thought of her daughter and granddaughters leaving West Villa, although, as yet, as far as she was aware, there were no obvious signs of them making a move to return to Cork.

After seeing to the girls' midday meal, she removed her apron, draped her shawl over her shoulders and tied the ribbons of her bonnet under her chin. She had not walked far down the driveway when she heard running feet and her name being called. Anne and Margaret, still wearing their nursery smocks, caught up with her.

'We'll come with you,' Anne beamed.

'Into the town,' said Margaret.

Mary hunkered down and put a hand on each small shoulder. 'You can't. I am on an errand for your grandmother and I have to hurry.'

'We can hurry you better,' Anne assured her.

'What would your mother and grandmother say if they found you missing?'

'"*Mary's minding them*."' Anne did a relatively good intonation of her mother's voice.

Mary took the girls by the hand and walked them back up the drive, in through the yard and into Mrs Mac's care.

❀ ❀ ❀

The autumn sunshine was pleasantly warming as she walked into town, and she paused to watch a skein of barnacle geese strung across the sky, like stitches sewn into the air – the first of the season, arriving early to winter in Kerry.

As she turned into Bridge Street, past the back lanes where children played in the gutters and lumpen women stood in doorways, the numbers of people already crowding the narrow cobbled area was unexpected.

Large and small groups of men marched with military precision, smaller groups straggled along, there were twosomes and threesomes and the occasional loner walking briskly, bands of women linked arms and sometimes a child darted in and out of the crowd. There was an air of optimistic jollity and good-humoured anticipation.

It looked as though William and Rob would have a goodly attendance. She was pleased for them, pleased that their canvassing would reap benefit.

And afterwards? The next day was Sunday. The thought of being publicly betrothed to William was a butterfly of joy.

Lifting her skirts, she dodged in and out of the crowd, hurrying – she needed to pick up Mrs Mulchinock's bonnet before the street was blocked off, and by the look of the gathering crowd that wouldn't be long. By the time she emerged from the shop, hatbox in hand, the street was thronged and the atmosphere had changed.

Some of the younger men had formed into aggressively moving groups – there were ripples of uneasy mutterings, a lot of pushing and shoving, and even an occasional pike, sword and stick being brandished. This was shaping up differently to Daniel O'Connell's rally in January. Mary looked around in nervous bewilderment – the aggression and latent hostility of the crowd was not what William expected, not what he and Rob had worked towards.

She sighted Billy and Mrs Tangney standing against a wall and made her way towards them.

'Do you know what's happening? The goings-on of the crowd?'

Mrs Tangney gave a raucous laugh. 'It's not enough to be having a rally this evening, but we'll also have that Leggett fella stirrin' things up again. He's been on the rant since morning.'

'Sure, nobody pays attention to the likes of him,' said Billy. 'He's harmless.'

'That's what you think, young Billy. Look at him. Going on and on about how the Mulchinocks took his inheritance. Mark my words, there'll be trouble before this night is out.' With that, she wrapped her shawl tightly about her person and moved away.

Mary looked over at Leggett, a dishevelled figure, leaning against a doorway. He was swaying backwards and forwards and mouthing indistinguishable words, drool running down his chin.

She saw Mr Foley who raised his arm and waved her and Billy over.

Mary was surprised to see Paudge standing on the corner of Castle Street, shoulders hunched, hands in his pockets. She hadn't thought of him as being a supporter of Repeal, or of having an interest in local politics. She'd last spoken to him some time ago, telling him she was honoured at his proposal, but repeating that she would never marry him. From his nod of sadness, she thought he'd finally accepted her decision.

Then William with Rob O'Sullivan by his side jumped onto the makeshift platform. Sombrely dressed in dark trousers and jacket with a gleam of white linen at his throat, William was a slim but imposing figure, smiling, using his hands to tamp down the clapping and cheering of the crowd.

The autumn sun was a ball of fire in the evening sky.

'*Hurrah for Repeal!*' someone cried and shouts of '*Repeal! Repeal!*' were taken up by deep-voiced men, the lighter tones of women and the little piping voices of the children.

William waited as the sounds of enthusiasm grew, ricocheting up and down the street. Then he signalled for silence and began to speak.

He had developed into a powerful communicator, and when he spoke he drew murmurs of assent from the gathering, holding its interest, and there was passion in his tone as he talked of the reforms of Repeal, repeating Daniel O'Connell's sentiments as he pleaded for support.

Mary watched nervously as Billy moved towards the platform.

'I have a question, sir. A clarification.'

What was Billy up to asking about 'clarification'? She was never sure about him, never sure at how he might react, erupt or what he might say.

William bent towards him and held out his hand, pulling Billy onto the platform. 'You are?'

'Billy O'Connor from Brogue Lane.'

'And your question?'

'Could you explain, sir,' Billy, his red hair brightening the purpling twilight, had a touching seriousness and attitude beyond his years, 'what exactly Repeal of the Union, if it comes to pass, will mean for the likes of us?'

Mary exhaled with relief.

William touched Billy's shoulder. Mary knew he had answered that question on dozens of occasions, in dozens of doorways, on dozens of street corners as he canvassed – it was the most asked question, but he answered Billy in a considering way as though it were his first time.

'*When* Repeal comes to pass, Billy O'Connor . . .' He waited for the ripple of optimism to die down before continuing. 'As we know only too well the Act of Union of 1800 linked Britain and Ireland. He has already gained Catholic Emancipation – and you all know the benefits of that?' His pause was filled with nods and rumbles of agreement. 'Now Daniel O'Connell wants to repeal that union – repeal meaning to abolish, do away with it. He wants us, the people of Ireland, to be independent.'

'Does that mean the English leavin' us alone?'

It was the woman from the lanes, the woman he'd told to come with her husband and children and it looked as though she had.

'We'd govern ourselves but still be linked to Great Britain – England,' he clarified.

'How? In wha' way?'

'Queen Victoria would still be our queen too.'

'I see.' She smiled and nodded in a satisfied way.

'Is that clear enough? Does anyone have another question?'

There were a few more questions.

Then, as William was reiterating how tirelessly Daniel O'Connell was working to achieve the dream of every true Irishman, a scuffle broke out towards the back of the group – manifested in yelps, grunts and curses. And then Leggett was running towards the platform, yelling about '*being done by the gentry*' and brandishing a pike. Three young men, little more than boys, moved towards him and tussled him to the ground. They took the pike off him and tried to lead him away, but in the ensuing scuffle he broke free of them and ran screaming obscenities through the crowd.

The evening light had yielded to twilight and the shadows created a bruising dusk. It was increasingly difficult to make out what was happening, although from the sounds carried on the still air it appeared that what had started out as one angry man had deteriorated into a fight involving many.

The crowd began to disperse – some of the younger men ran to the join in the skirmishing, more stood around the edge as spectators, but the majority skirted around the fighting which had spread up the street so that they could get to their homes.

William, his forehead creased with worry, jumped down from the platform and came to where Mary was standing. 'I must see to this. Stay here, my love. Don't move. I'll be back for you.'

Billy and Mr Foley had disappeared, and Rob was gone with William. Mary waited alone in the gathering darkness and after a while she climbed onto the platform from where she could make out part of the tableau unfolding along the street. Men and youths with raised fists and angry shouts were throwing punches at each other; the air was thick with swords and pikes and glowing sods of turf on sticks. Although as far as she could make out there was more yelling and shouting than the type of fighting that led to injury.

That was until a bloodcurdling scream ripped the sky.

Suddenly Paudge was alongside her. 'Mary, you shouldn't be here. Get down. It's turnin' nasty.'

'What's happened?'

'I don't know the details, but it appears that Leggett the Nailer fella is the cause of the trouble.'

'What about William? Where is he?'

'He'll be all right. Rob O'Sullivan will look to him. I hear there's fighting breaking out all over the town. Best you come back with me to West Villa.'

❈❈❈

Paudge brought Mary as far as the yard. 'You go inside.'

'What about you? Where are you going?' Mary was nervous at the turn of events.

'I'll be along shortly. Don't say anythin' to anyone.'

Mrs Mac was sitting alone by the fire in the kitchen. Mary placed the hatbox for Mrs Mulchinock on the table, removed her bonnet and stood, hesitantly looking around.

'What're you doing back here at this time a night?'

Mary nodded towards the table. 'It's the mistress's bonnet.'

'It could have waited till the morrow.'

'There's fighting broke out around the town. I'll be off home in a while.'

With a throw of her arm Mrs Mac gestured for Mary to sit opposite. She was knitting what looked like a very large shawl, her needles click-clicking harmoniously, the grey wool slowly and evenly unfurling from the hank resting between her feet.

Mary had never sat down with Mrs Mac, never sat by such a warming fire either and most certainly never been subject to such scrutiny – Mrs Mac's gaze roamed from her knitting to Mary's face. The kitchen was strangely silent and still without its complement of servants – a creak here, a settling beam of wood there and the lap of the flames – until a rattling in the yard, the sound of the gate creaking, followed by the clank of an overturning bucket.

Rob pushed through the door leading from the porch to the kitchen. He leant against the dresser, panting, his breath coming in ragged gasps – his coat was torn, there was blood on his shirtfront and he held a gun loosely by his side.

'Merciful God, sir, what're you up to?' Mrs Mac jumped up, scattering her knitting, the wool unravelling from its hank and spreading across the floor.

'What's happened? Where's William? Is he safe?' Mary's heart was racing.

Mrs Mac gave Mary one of her looks before turning to Rob. 'Master William Pembroke? Where is he?'

'There's been an accident, a terrible accident.' Rob passed a hand wearily across his forehead as he looked from Mary to Mrs Mac.

Mary knees went weak and the kitchen blurred. 'Is it William?'

'No. It's not. William's all right.' Rob pulled out a chair and sat down heavily at the table.

Mrs Mac rummaged in the cupboard, took out a flagon, poured some of the contents into a mug and handed it Rob. 'Brandy — sip it slowly and tell me what's happened.'

Rob gulped the drink. He put back the mug on the table, tightened his lips and again looked from Mary to Mrs Mac. 'The man they call Leggett the Nailer was stabbed. He's dead. And William is accused. There's a warrant out for his arrest and already there's rumour of a reward of 100 gold sovereigns for whoever turns him in.'

'Glory be to God on high. What's the world coming to at all, at all? Master William Pembroke? Fetch the mistress, Mary. *And may God help us all!*' Mrs Mac's voice rose in hysteria as she made the Sign of the Cross.

Mary ignored her instructions.

Rob caught hold of Mary's arm. 'William sent me to fetch you. Ye're to catch tonight's wine boat to France. It's best he leaves the country until this dies down. But he wants you with him. Paudge is bringing around the buggy and I've a couple of cloaks and a bag of coins for ye.'

'Mary.' Mrs Mac looked puzzled by the turn of events, but her voice was returned to authorative. 'You're to go nowhere. You'll remain here.'

Rob continued as though Mrs Mac hadn't spoken. 'Come on, Mary. Hurry. William's riding out Slieve Mish way before doubling back towards Blennerville, hoping to throw off the constabulary. He'll wait for us at the Cross.' He began to draw her towards the door.

Mary plucked her bonnet from the table.

'Mary O'Connor, where do you think you're going? Come back in. This instant. And fetch the mistress.'

'Missus, I'm going to see to William.'

'Master William Pembroke? You're going to Master William Pembroke?'

'Yes, Missus, I am. And I trust you'll pray for us.'

With that Mary was gone from the kitchen, through the porch and into the yard.

Shaking her head in puzzlement and more frightened and confused than ever she'd been, Mrs Mac made her way to the upstairs, trying to put coherence on the situation, dreading the news she was about to visit on her mistress.

As she raised her hand to knock on the door of the parlour, she heard shouting and cursing, and thumps and bangs, and the heavy brass knocker being hammered and hammered against the red hall door.

❖❖❖

Rob drove the buggy fast, the horse responding to his every touch of the reins. The night had turned cool rather than cold, and Mary's shiver was more of a reaction to the glitter of moonlight on the bushes and the stars pricking sharply through the sky.

Neither occupant of the buggy spoke. There was too little known, yet too much to absorb, and altogether too much at stake.

Mary thought of William with a price on his head; she thought of going all the way to France, perhaps seeing Paris, the place he had so often spoken of, describing its boulevards and balconies; she thought of Paudge's kindness and Billy's new maturity; she thought of her mam and her urging of her to leave the lane and the relief of having her blessing, and then she pictured her, as she was in bed that night, so frail, her body so feeble making scarcely a rise under the blanket.

Then William was riding alongside, his horse lathering sweat, wheezing great plumes of steamy breath.

Rob pulled the reins to a halt and stepped down.

William dismounted, came around to Mary's side of the buggy and reached in to touch her face. 'I couldn't go without you. Has Rob explained? I didn't do it, didn't kill The Nailer. But that won't save me. The crowd has turned.'

'I know you didn't – you haven't it in you to kill anyone.'

William extended his hand, his eyes seeking and holding hers.

She stepped down, grasping his hand tightly. As she did she remembered Mam coughing into the kerchief, the way she grasped at her hand too. Slowly, irrevocably, patchwork pieces of memory came together and merged to a whole that had her shuddering with the knowledge. She should have known – if she hadn't been so wrapped up in love she would have known. She stood surrounded by the darkness that settled deep within her soul, sure of nothing but a creeping numbness.

William drew her close, putting a protective arm around her shoulders.

Rob was talking to him in low urgent tones, 'It's better you don't make contact with anyone in Tralee. I'll go to Dublin, to the Castle, to try to do what I can to reverse this miscarriage of justice. When your name's cleared, we'll be in touch.'

'Talk to my mother – explain what's happened. And make sure to call to Mary's father as well.'

'Yes. I will. But you must hurry, William – they're holding the boat, but they won't wait for long.'

'I know. My thanks to you. We'll never forget what you've done for us. Go back, Rob. You can't be implicated. We'd better get going.'

Mary moved out of the arc of William's arm.

Separate voices clamoured in her head – some in accord with her flight to be with William, more in furious disagreement – after all she was the binding that held the O'Connor family together. Sceptre-like images of her fragile mother, her ineffectual father, Billy still finding his way and her sisters little more than children rose before her. She could not leave them, could not be away from them across the sea, in another country. They could not manage without her.

Silent sounds warred back and forth across her brain as she made her decision.

William bent towards her. 'What is it?'

She met his eyes. 'William, a *chroí*, I can't go with you. Not now. Mam is sick. I think she's dying. I can't leave her.'

'My Mary. Please. I cannot live without you.'

Rob was seated in the buggy, looking down at the reins as though finding untold mysteries in the flatness of the leather. When he spoke his voice was authorative. 'William. You must go. And now. The boat won't wait. If Mary won't go with you, she can join you later – I'll see to it – I promise to make all the arrangements. You can't be taken. You mustn't be taken.'

Tears ran down Mary's cheeks as she climbed back into the buggy.

With a leap William jumped onto his horse, brought it

alongside the buggy, looked down at Mary and held out his hand.

She ignored his hand and leaned forward, 'Be careful, William, *mo chroí*.' As though being careful was a protection. She swayed backwards and reaching into her bodice she grasped his ring, brought it to her lips and kissed it. Her face was peaceful, almost calm and the look in her eyes was timeless.

'Until we meet again thoughts of you will be forever in my heart.' William reined his horse in the direction of Blennerville, raised his hand as if to wave in farewell, then let the gesture fall to his side. With a slap of the reins and a push of his heels against the flank of the animal, he took his leave of her in a single glance – unconsoling, unaccepting, unreconciling.

He did not look back, nor did she call after him as man and horse faded into the darkness.

❈ ❈ ❈

Mary woke to a dark morning sleeved with black and a silvery dusting of stars. Her body filled with tremors, she made her way towards Annagh. Her legs dragged and she felt as though she were walking waist-deep in mud.

When she'd pushed in the door of the cabin last evening all was quiet. Everyone turned in. She'd slipped into bed beside Brigid and, exhausted as she was, it was a long while before she fell asleep, and when she did she was plagued with dreams of dark places and wide seas.

In the kitchen Mrs Mac and Paudge sat on either side of the fire.

Mrs Mac stood up, brushed down her apron. 'The mistress wants to see you.'

'But it's not yet seven o'clock.'

'Well, it's not as though you'll be wakin' her. She's been in the parlour all night with Master Edward. Not a wink of sleep did any of us get.'

In the hallway, candles still burnt in their sconces, angling shadows and emptiness. Mary's boots blundered along the floor, her hand skimmed the wainscot, and she avoided looking at up Michael Mulchinock gazing out at the world, but she felt his eyes follow her until she knocked on the door of the parlour.

Edward threw it open and looked back into the room. 'She's here. Mary O'Connor is here.'

To Mary's relief he stomped off up the hall.

Mrs Mulchinock was sitting by the fire, her eyes swollen and shadowed with tiredness, her face pale and her features crumpled. Strands of hair had escaped from the confines of their combs. She was wrapped in a thick woollen shawl of grey.

She was curt and to the point. 'I want you to tell me precisely what happened last evening.'

As Mary finished her account of the rally, omitting her involvement with William, their plans for marriage and the more recent proposal that she join him in France, Mrs Mulchinock stood up. Her cheeks were flushed livid and she tossed the shawl to the back of a chair.

Mary had never imagined she could be so angry.

'And I believe you had plans for a future with my son?' When Mary didn't answer Mrs Mulchinock pointed a finger at her. 'Well, did you?'

'Yes, ma'am. I did. We did.' It would be pointless to try to deny it or to begin to explain their relationship.

'I want you to listen. And to listen well. You are no longer in my employ. You are to leave. Now. You are never to return — never again will you darken the door of West Villa. And know that no matter what happens you do not have a future with Master William Pembroke. You never will have a future with him.'

Mary heard the words. They hung on the air, clouding it like swarm of flies. Alarm drew the blood from her skin. Her breath came harshly in and out, in and out, as if she'd been running. She could feel her pulse tapping against the skin of her neck as she absorbed her situation – she was no longer in service, she was without prospects, William was gone and all night long she had listened to her mam coughing.

The shriek that ripped from deep within her was reduced to an agonised moan as it left her lips.

'That is all. Go. Now.' Mrs Mulchinock turned from her and held her hands towards the fire.

The servants were coming and going in the kitchen, but nobody looked in Mary's direction as she walked across the flagged floor, through the porch door, into the yard and down the driveway. She didn't look back, mellow and beautiful as she knew the house would be in the morning light; she didn't wonder at what was happening behind the eyes of its long windows. Instead she reached into her bodice for William's ring, brought it to her lips and held it close as she walked back home to the lane.

❀ ❀ ❀

Over the next days the town was in a state of chaotic upheaval. The local RIC constables were everywhere, their very presence threatening. Roughly pushing through groups of people, truncheons at the ready, they caught at shoulders, punched arms and demanded answers to their questions of where was William Pembroke Mulchinock? Who was hiding him?

It was whispered behind hands that certain constables had not only visited all the Big Houses of the gentry throughout the townland of Annagh and questioned families and servants, but that they'd thoroughly searched various other premises including outhouses, stables and yards.

The rumour was that they had spent several hours at West Villa, but by all accounts their questioning and search there was sensitively handled. Because of his closeness with William, Rob O'Sullivan had been brought in to the barracks on three different occasions.

The occurrences on the night of the rally, Leggett's death and repercussions were talked of in an impersonal way within the cabin. Mary's grief at being separated from William was contained deep within her. Day after day she waited for the bang of a constable on the half door but, after two weeks, when it hadn't happened, she began to breathe easier.

She tended to her mother and began to take control of the family.

She pulled her father aside. 'Mam is sick and it's worse not better she'll be getting.'

He shook his head and picked up a swatch of leather.

She took the leather out of his hand and put it back on his worktable. 'I want you to listen to me, Da. And listen well. Mam has consumption and she knows it. She hasn't long. I'll be here, taking care of her. And we have to make changes.'

He looked at her in puzzlement, 'What changes?'

'I won't be returning to West Villa and there'll be no more talk from you about me being wed.' She waited for his reaction and when it didn't come, she continued, 'I'll do the books – write up the orders and payments. And I'll be collecting the overdue monies.'

Tapping at his head, he protested, 'They're all here – the orders and the monies.' With a touch of pride, he added, 'Always were.'

'Yes, I know, Da. And you're the best. But from now on it'll be all recorded here.' She tapped at the unused ledger lying on the table. 'And you need to start Billy, apprentice him on the less skilled parts of shoemaking.' As he opened his mouth to protest, she gentled her voice, 'He'll be a great help, Da, and you'll need him when the orders start to pour in.'

As she laid out their futures, other than an occasional shrug and casting of his eyes to the ground, Willie was surprisingly docile. He didn't raise any objections when she said Brigid and Ellen were to continue with their lessons and only after school could they sell bootlaces in town.

CHAPTER 32

THE CAPTAIN OF THE WINE BOAT had that devilish air of knowing more than he should. As William stood on deck resting against the railings, he crept up alongside him. He looked to the right and to the left, smoothed the front of his jacket and touched his index finger to the side of his nose before leaning in towards William. Gusting a breath of wine and garlic, he whispered, 'It's known you're making for France, but it is in your better interest to journey on to India.' Then, with a nervous look around the deck, he pulled up the collar of his jacket and disappeared down the ladder into the bowels of the ship.

William had no way of checking out the captain's credentials or his information so he had no choice but to take his message to heart. He had never felt so alone, so isolated. He could not contact Rob and he missed Mary with every fibre of his being. The fabric of his world had become unbelievably thin and scary.

His only possessions were the clothes he stood up in, his

notebook and the bag of coins Rob had given him. When anyone asked about his luggage he convincingly managed to account for its absence and his lack of possessions by saying he had been mugged and robbed, and he was so well spoken and so obviously a gentleman that he was believed.

A few days later he found himself at the docks in Calais, scarcely aware of the noise and the hurrying, bustling and confusion of the burly dock workers and sailors. A little way back from the water there was a small cluster of stalls. He was drawn to one manned by a young lad with an energetic attitude, a silver tongue and extravagant claims for his merchandise, and from him he bought a selection of cotton shirts, scented soap and cologne.

In the early afternoon, along with his fellow travellers, he boarded a small steamer bound for Alexandria. Evening light was fading into a violet sunset, staining the docks red, as he stood on deck watching a flock of gulls wheeling around the steamer. As the shallow light thinned, the day faltered and the boatmen released the warps securing the ship to the quayside. For a moment the steamer seemed reluctant to move, then it sighed quietly before sliding under its own power, out into the harbour as it put out to sea with a fair and gentle breeze.

Weeks later he was in Bombay – his journey there a nightmare blur of sea and sand, buffalo-drawn wagons, and inexplicable travel instructions received from a variety of mysterious sources.

He stepped down from the latest wagon at the place designated in a note that had been passed to him as he had mounted it several hours previously. He looked around, allowing the power of the city to impact on him: masses of people of all ages, shapes, sizes and colour, elderly *paanwallas* calling the delights of their aromatic morsels, watermelon-men piercing the humidity with their noisy cries, doe-eyed women and fragilelimbed children, spiced opulence combining with dirty poverty; oppressive heat laden with a sharp dust permeating everywhere. Bombay was another world, a world he had never thought to see.

Clothes clung to his sweat and his heart thumped under the command of this unknown climate. He was unsure and scared and lonely, but as he breathed in the sounds, sights and scents, it seemed to him that India began to nestle around him. And he thought of how much better it would be, quite an adventure, if only he had Mary by his side.

A European woman wearing a large, wide-brimmed hat touched his sleeve. 'William Pembroke Mulchinock Esquire?' she inquired. He was no longer surprised by such an approach – they had happened with frequency along the route of his journey. She introduced herself as Mrs Jackson, the wife of Colonel Jackson, a distant cousin of his late grandfather on his mother's side or so she told him. By then he no longered wondered at the hows or the whys of his situation. It was enough that there appeared to be a conspiracy of protection that he hoped would win out against the conspiracy of false accusation. At Mrs Jackson's request he followed her to a battered baroche.

Some forty minutes later the carriage rolled up the driveway of a rambling, one-storey house, sprawled against the backdrop of a gloomy banyan grove. The bungalow was constructed as an interlinking series of large darkened spaces and wide corridors cooled by blinds. Mrs Jackson led the way followed by a phalanx of servants who seemed to appear from nowhere and multiply en route.

The bedchamber assigned to William contained a hammock, a large double wardrobe and an archway leading to a private water closet. The bed was a luxurious affair with gauze curtains embroidered with gold thread, a fat bolster and a thin cotton comforter.

With a flourish of her arm, Mrs Jackson produced his personal houseboy. The boy stepped forward, bowing his dark head and putting together his palms in the traditional greeting. William liked him immediately. Another boy, small and skinny, sat in a corner of the room. He had the string of a fan attached to his big toe, and with a slow motion, he got the fan flapping and fluttering like an enormous moth over the bed.

A deep veranda encircled the bungalow, trailing exotic blossoms. 'Clematis, hibiscus and bougainvillea,' supplied Mrs Jackson as though reading his thoughts.

He saw tailors sitting cross-legged at one end of the veranda, needles varying in size from large to small with different colours, lengths and thicknesses of thread jabbed into their turbans; children, their childhood stolen, tatting intricate patterns of lace; and beyond the veranda youths and young girls ferried covered dishes of food from the kitchens; others waved fans; while more watered plants and the lawns that needed constant moisture to achieve a modicum of greeness, and under the eagle eye of Mrs Jackson even the dust that rose in spumes was watered into obedience.

'Such industry,' he complimented. 'Everyone working so diligently.'

Hands grasping the railings, his hostess surveyed her kingdom with a look of satisfaction on her plump features. 'Ah, but if you observe closely, you'll notice that a job which fills the time of one well-trained Englishman requires the attention of at least six natives.' Over the days that followed he would come to know how she delighted in explaining what she called the 'vagaries of India'.

During one of his rare visits to the bungalow the colonel announced that William should present himself to one George

Buist, editor of *The Bombay Times*. 'The interview is a mere formality, dear boy, as Buist is having difficulties with employing natives as journalists, and we hear you are a published man.'

William said nothing, but he wondered from where the colonel had got his information.

Lighting up one of his pungent cheroots, Colonel Jackson added, 'I've arranged rooms and servants for you in Borah Bazaar Street – an interesting part of the city.'

William heaved a sigh of relief. Grateful as he was for his hostess's hospitality and kindness, her inquisitiveness and concern were becoming claustrophobic. He suspected she was curious about the reasons that had brought him to India, although she never asked outright. And he hoped she wouldn't. He couldn't tell her the truth, she wasn't the type of woman to be fobbed off with a flimsy story, and he was no good at constructing falsehoods.

The colonel walked to the window and back again to face William. 'I understand your safe passage was at the request of Daniel O'Connell, the man they call the Liberator? You work with him? And are politically influenced by him?' The last two sentences were more statements than questions.

That was an unexpected turn of conversation and, unsure of where it was leading, William hedged. 'We share similar political hopes for Ireland.'

'Perhaps you haven't heard. Daniel O'Connell has been charged with conspiracy, sentenced to a year's imprisonment and fined £2,000. Rumour has it that his health is failing and dissension has broken out in the Repeal Association. All in all, a sorry situation.'

The colonel was better informed than William expected. It took all of his self-control not to react with dismay – dissension would break Daniel's heart. He settled his features. 'I am sorry to hear that. He's a good man – he cares for Ireland.'

The colonel gave a grunt of annoyance. 'Ireland has always been a thorn in the side of the Empire. But try explaining that to my wife.'

❈❈❈

The Bombay Times, established two years previously, was published twice a week on Wednesdays and Saturdays. It put William in mind of *The Kerry Evening Post* and gave him a pang of nostalgia that he quickly dismissed. The paper covered national and local events. Mr Buist gave William a free editorial hand – the only stipulation being, 'that the news you report on must be relevant to the area'.

William's work helped to fill his void of loneliness. He wrote under the name of William Pembroke and his stories became known for their factual accuracy, but they were written with compassion and from his personal viewpoint. The subjects he wrote about included the District Benevolent Society for relief of the poor which reminded him of his mother's soup kitchen; he tried to imagine Mary's reaction to a gentlewoman named Clara Rainitz being appointed as the first dentist in Bombay; and while researching the elegant splendour of the Bank of Bombay he wished Rob were with him.

He grew fond of the city of palm trees, battered by war, decimated by famine and pestilence and riddled by panics.

There wasn't a whisper of news from Ireland about his situation. He had heeded Rob's warning not to make contact, presuming that, if the warrant for his arrest were cancelled then the news of it would be filtered through to him in the same way as his travel arrangements. He missed Mary more with each passing day but held on to the hope that either she would join him, or his name would be cleared and he would be free to return to Tralee to marry her.

As he had done in Paris with his father and in Dublin with Rob, he walked the streets absorbing the scenes, filling page after page of his notebook with impressions: a young girl brushing forward the black satin of her hair; a mother sluicing water against her son's naked backside; an old man in a snow-white dhoti leading three goats with collars of red ribbons; women wrapped in crimson, blue and gold who belonged to white-toothed, almond-eyed men and gave birth to delicate children.

The only verses that flowed freely from his pen were a continuation of those he had written for Mary.

After a chance meeting with the commander-in-chief while dining at the Byculla Club he asked for and received permission to visit army outposts and to record his impressions of military activities. At each outpost he discovered a wealth of stories, and from then on, with the enthusiastic approval of Mr Buist, he concentrated on reporting about the conditions under which the British army operated.

He observed at first hand the courage of the soldiers and the results of battle violence – bloodied bodies, amputated limbs, brave men lying in agonies of pain, their suffering compounded by continuous bouts of cholera, dysentery, lack of medical supplies and shortage of food as well as the scourge of rain, heat and flies.

His reputation as a respected chronicler of army life in India grew. When he met anyone from Ireland he was adroit at sidestepping queries as to how he came to be in India and he blessed the stroke of inspiration that had him known as William

Pembroke. He picked up bits of news from home and was devastated to learn of outbreaks of cholera and typhus and the repeated failures of the potato crop.

CHAPTER 33

BETWEEN CONVULSING FITS of coughing that left flecks of blood at the corners of her mouth, Nora whispered the words — 'consumption' and 'white death' over and over, with the prayer-like devotion of one reciting the litany of saints. She had good days and bad days, although the knowledge of her disease dwindled the family to a constant nothingness. Father Sheehy was a regular visitor and Mary revised her opinion of him when she saw how solicitously he tended to her mother's spiritual needs, and her sense of peace after his visits.

The women of the lanes, led by Mrs Tangney, came in and out of the cabin, bearing gifts of food they could ill spare, tiptoeing about the outshot, peering around the curtain, making hopeful comments that Nora ignored.

'Look how beautiful she is, Mr O'Connor,' chirped a newly wed young woman. 'How rosy her cheeks and the brightness of her eyes!'

Indeed, with the flush of the disease and her air of acceptance, Nora was beautiful. The older women returned to their cabins, shaking their heads knowingly.

Mostly Nora kept her eyes closed as though shutting out the world. She asked for nothing and seldom spoke, although sometimes as Mary bathed her face and hands she would whisper, 'And how's the young master, *a stór?*' When Mary assured her he was well her smile was beatific. She did not ask why Mary no longer went to West Villa, and Mary did not speak to her of the events of the night of the rally.

'You'll be away soon, away to be wed?' she whispered early one morning, her eyelids fluttering, her expression appealing.

'But not while you're ill.' Mary was rewarded with a glimmer of a smile and a wash of relief over the tired features. By her every gesture Mary sought to reassure the sick woman that she would not leave her.

The weather turned cold and bleak with hard frosts every morning and icy drafts that bit at exposed hands and faces as Mary dragged herself and an empty bucket across the yard and returned weighed down with the full bucket slopping water over its sides.

Working from dawn to dusk – washing, cleaning, cooking, collecting the monies that were owed, holding the family together – only aggravated her worries about William. Such industry simply grew a skin on worry and crusted over it. I love and I am loved, she assured herself over and over, bringing William's ring to her lips.

❋ ❋ ❋

'Mary, there's a gentleman asking for you.' Willie relayed the information without inflection. Mary or her actions were no longer accountable to him.

Rob's expression was sombre as Mary ushered him outside. They leant against the freezing stone of the wall, their breaths hanging on the icy air.

'I went to Dublin, called to the Castle on several occasions and got to see various officers in charge of the case against William ...'

'What's happening?'

'Nothing. As far as I could ascertain there's no move to cancel the charge.'

'Why?'

'It's known that he was working alongside Daniel O'Connell. All we can do is wait and hope for a change in the administration.'

'Surely Mr O'Connell?'

'He has his own problems to deal with, and his health is failing. And you? How are you?'

'Why do you ask?' Rob's kindness was almost the undoing of her.

He looked into her eyes. 'Because you look unwell and William charged me with taking care of you.'

She turned her head from him and blinked rapidly. 'I'm all right. But have you heard anything at all about William?'

'No. And the most worrying part is that he didn't make the rendezvous with our contact in France.'

'So we've no way of knowing where he is, or if he's safe. Even if he's alive?' Gooseflesh rose on her arms. That she wouldn't, that she couldn't have left her mother to go with William made not knowing where he was and how he was all the worse.

Rob's touch on her shoulder was tentative. 'I am sorry, Mary.

But I don't hold out much hope.'

After Rob's visit her sleep came under a skim of dreams that scattered like birds, flying high in the sky, and she'd wake to the vast night, the fullness of cold and the long tooth of despair.

❀❀❀

Nora left life as she had lived, without a sound, without fuss or complaint.

On the morning of her death, when Mary carried in a mug of tea to her it was later than usual. With the exception of their father who was up and about and had got the fire going, they had all slept beyond dawn. For once coughing hadn't broken their rest. Mary paused by the side of the bed, thinking how peaceful and young her mother looked. Looking closer she saw the bright stain of blood on the pillow and when she touched her forehead it was icy.

After the burial, with the kitchen crammed with mourners, Mary slipped out and stood grieving in the blue gloaming for her mother, the loneliness of loss hitting her with a body blow.

Father Sheehy came upon her bent double, coughing. He rested a gentle hand on her head, 'My child.' His tone was compassionate, as was his expression. 'How long has this been going on?'

'It's nothin'. The cold weather getting to me.'

Having ignored the chills and night sweats that racked her body she was strangely comforted by his concern.

'You have learned much about the ways of people and life, and developed a new purpose, but you are returned to the lanes.' He spoke softly and she stood head bowed as he blessed her.

Her acceptance had her existing in the nothing of herself.

CHAPTER 34

WEEKS BECAME MONTHS and months turned into years as William settled into the beat of India.

Always he kept thoughts of Mary close to him and he missed Rob's companionship. Occasionally he wondered about his mother and his brother, and if Charlotte had finally returned to her husband in Cork. His memories of West Villa were fondly nostalgic and he thought benevolently of the shop and warmly of M. Aubin, Dorrie, Bridie and Giselle.

He felt abandoned by Daniel O'Connell. If the man was too ill to handle his case why hadn't some of his followers, many of whom William had come to regard as friends, come forward and spoken for him? But day after day he got on with living.

On an intensely hot, breathless afternoon with flies scribbling the air, as he walked through the medical tent he came across a young officer lying on a stretcher. He recognised the bloodstained body as a young lieutenant from Tralee. Looking down at the vulnerable freckled face he knew the devastation the news of his death would bring to his family. He was washed with such a sense of isolation, loneliness and homesickness that his eyes smarted. Impatiently he dashed the tears from his cheeks.

To report in a professional manner on the state of the military he had to be objective, composed, avoid becoming emotional or personally involved in the many situations he came across. And while mostly he succeeded admirably it did not mean that he didn't grieve for the bravery and courage of young lives lost.

As he stood looking down at the body, memories of his homeplace threatened to overwhelm him – the comforting loveliness of West Villa; the banks of the canal where he and Mary had sat talking of Daniel O'Connell; dancing at Clahane; her sense of humour as she spoke of 'the likes of you'. Mary. Always Mary. His love for her had grown with separation. Again he dashed his hand across his eyes, bit firmly on his bottom lip, made the Sign of the Cross and said a short prayer for the repose of the soul of the body that lay before him.

Major Howe who had entered the medical tent to pay his respects to his young lieutenant watched William's reactions. He knew of him by reputation. He had read many of his reports and was impressed by their clarity and accuracy. He was even more impressed and, indeed, intrigued by the look of him in person.

As William turned to leave, he touched his arm. 'You were acquainted with my lieutenant?'

'Not really, sir. But I know of him and his parents, the whole family.'

The major shook his head. 'He was Irish, from County Kerry, I believe?'

'Yes,' William answered shortly as he moved outside the tent.

The officer followed him. 'Unrelenting chaos.' He gestured

with his arm. 'It's how the military operates. And that's not a comment for quoting in your next article.' He offered William a slim cigar, and when he declined he lit his own and leaned companionably against a post.

William moved a few steps away from him.

'We have many Irishmen in our ranks, but how come an Irish civilian is reporting on the British military in India?'

William gave what he hoped was a nonchalant shrug.

'Dine with me tonight, young man, I could do with the company.'

It was more of an order than a request. William's unlimited access and freedom to visit the outposts where he sourced his stories was down to the approval of the individual commanders.

Major Howe dined in style – white linen tablecloth and napkins, crystal glassware and silver cutlery, but they ate the inevitable curry, albeit served by his personal servant with a flourish, and they drank the finest of wines.

After discussing the social changes to the British Empire that had come about since the Napoleonic Wars, predictably conversation turned to various Indian rebellions, a subject, William had discovered, that few of the officers he'd asked were willing to discuss.

'They highlight the shortcomings of the army, but regretfully entrenched interests prevent the implementation of the necessary major reforms.'

The major was feeling expansive – he lit a cigar and called for brandy.

'You have me curious,' he said then.

'And why is that?' William wished he could make his escape.

'Why the heir to the Mulchinock estate is reporting on the British military in India when his country is devastated by famine?'

William was taken aback that the major knew of his family. He wondered about likely consequences. Was there still a price on his head? Was the part Rob played in getting him away known?

He answered calmly — he had learned to control his emotions. 'We're a resilient nation. We've survived famine after famine.'

'Ah, but this one is different, they're calling it the Great Famine. There are reports of mass starvation, deaths, disease and emigration. By all accounts it's a disaster with your county of Kerry one of the worst affected. A natural event, it's being called. All because of the failure of the potato crop.'

William suspected he was exaggerating. The English did that, painted Ireland as miserable. He thanked the major for his hospitality, and escaped, breathing sighs of relief, into the night.

To the major's experienced ears, William's reactions did not ring true.

Some months later after a convivial night of dining at the Byculla Club, a porter handed William a message. It was from Major Howe requesting that they have a drink together on the following evening. William stood in the lobby rereading the brief note, certain it boded no good, but knowing he had no choice but to accept the invitation.

Next evening he arrived early at the Club, but the major was already seated in a rattan chair, half hidden by a huge fern, a snifter of brandy cradled in his hand.

'You asked to see me, sir?'

'Sit down.' Major Howe clicked his fingers and ordered another brandy. 'I've good news for you, son.'

Major Howe was positively beaming. Most of the news he

usually had to impart was of the bad variety.

He had been intrigued enough to ask a few judicious questions about William Pembroke Mulchinock. Eventually he was directed towards Dublin Castle, and in terms of the strictest confidentiality he was advised of the killing that had occurred in Tralee some five years previously on the evening of the rally for the promotion of Repeal of the Union. He was further advised that the file was marked 'No Further Action'.

He requested that the matter be looked into again and, after additional correspondence and legal advice, he pronounced himself unimpressed by the way the case had been handled. It appeared to be common knowledge that this man, Leggett the Nailer, as he was known, was a troublemaker, a nasty piece of goods, bound to have enemies. The immediacy and amount of the reward offered for young Mulchinock's capture was not only ludicrous, it smacked of conspiracy, as did the 'No Action' file which felt like a cover-up.

Certainly, he agreed in the correspondence that went backwards and forwards from Bombay to Dublin, there were bits of circumstantial evidence that pointed towards young Mulchinock, but nothing positive tied him to the killing. Indeed, it appeared he had been some distance away when the stabbing took place. It looked as though a serious miscarriage of justice had taken place, and at the highest level.

Although fleeing the scene and leaving the country could be interpreted as the act of a guilty man, the major was willing to stake his reputation that William Pembroke had not committed the crime of which he was accused. The major had impeccable family connections as well as considerable influence in the Castle and the paperwork to clear William's name was hurried through.

William was wary of Major Howe's assurance of 'good news'.

During his time in India he had discovered that one man's good news was not necessarily another's.

'The arrest warrant against you is cancelled.'

It was as though time had stopped for William. The brandy remained untouched on the table in front of him. He looked around the Club, at the tired elegance of the men and women who talked too loudly and laughed too heartily, registering the heavy smell of perfumes, oils and alcohol. Could it be true? Dare he believe it?

'What does that mean?' If it were so, he knew what it meant. It meant that he was free to return home, to the life he'd had to leave behind, but his brain refused to process the information. He needed to hear those words of freedom spoken aloud.

'The arrest warrant against you is cancelled. You will not be arrested when you step on Irish soil.'

William stood up, let out a whoop of delight that had frowning faces turning in his direction. He stooped down to the table lifted his glass, raised it to the major and drank the brandy down in one swallow.

'You cannot know, sir, what this means to me.'

'I have a fair idea. Go home, son, and get on with your life.'

CHAPTER 35

WILLIAM'S JOURNEY FROM INDIA back to Ireland was the same nightmare of buffalo-drawn wagons, sand, sea, sailing ships and decrepit carriages that it had been on his way out to India. But he was scarcely aware of the discomfort.

He would surprise everyone; he had advised no one of his return.

As the Bian journeyed through the countryside his excitement increased, as did his devastation at the destruction wreaked by the Famine. 'Great', the major had called it. William didn't see a modicum of greatness in the blackened fields that used to hold crops of healthy potatoes lying striped with dark foliage, the hide of the skinny cattle hanging loose and flabby, tumbled thatchless cottages and windowless cabins lining the boreens – but it was the hopelessness of the clusters of emaciated men, women and children standing along the roadside that brought tears to his eyes.

From what he observed from the windows of the coach the

famine wasn't over yet, but he was sure there had to be more to this famine that had annihilated his people and his counry than the blight of a potato fungus. He'd heard a group of men discussing the whys and wherefores of the situation in Ireland during the crossing from Calais to Southampton.

'Half the country wouldn't have died if the landlords hadn't insisted on shipping away the grain,' said a heavily built man.

'Yes, as well as seizing cattle, rack renting, evicting and torching of cabins. God help them.' The speaker was a thin man with the yellowed complexion of someone who'd spent too long in the tropics.

'God may have sent the blight to Ireland but it was the English who made the famine,' said a third man with a lugubrious sigh.

At the time William had dismissed his fellow travellers' theories as the exaggeration of inconsequential gossip, but travelling down the country from Dublin to Tralee he had seen and experienced enough of the devastation to know they had been speaking the truth.

As he dismounted wearily at Benners Inn, the men's conversation was still running through his head. Try as he might to push to the back of his mind the images of the starving people he'd passed on his journey, they refused to be dismissed.

Before entering the Inn, he stood looking up and down the grey, drab of the street, strewn with decayed cabbage leaves, dirty straw thrown over horse manure, shouting men, carts backing, horses neighing, ragged boys fighting and the braying of an occasional donkey. There was a chill around the buildings and the air was dim and liquid as slowly and gladly he adjusted to the forgotten sights, sounds and smells of his hometown.

He was hungry, tired and grubby from travel. He would eat, bathe and rest a little before going to West Villa ... or would

Mary be in Brogue Lane? He wondered about her as he had every day for the past years. But, now that he was back, he could be specific — wondering how she was, how she was managing and coping with her mother's illness. For the first time since leaving India he was nervous about his homecoming — speculating on how he might be received by his mother and brother.

He took a room in the inn and ordered bread and mutton and a flagon of wine to be sent up, and while waiting for his bath to be made ready he summoned a porter and sent him out to buy fresh linen. He idled the waiting time by standing in the doorway of the inn, watching the activity on Castle Street.

There appeared to be a kerfuffle near the corner of Denny Street. When William stepped out from the porch, he saw a group of straggling people coming along the street. A man in soiled livery pushed out behind him from the inn, looked up and down the street, blessed himself in more of an automatic than a pious gesture, nodded in William's direction and rushed back into the lobby where he loosened the inside shutters and began pulling them over the windows.

'What is it? What's going on?' William asked an old woman with a bowed head making her fragile way along by the walls of the inn.

She adjusted her stick on the ground, ensuring it had purchase, and looked up at him, her face lined in sorrow. 'Another funeral, sir. As if the famine and starvation wasn't bad enough, we've the consumption, cholera and typhus too. An awful affliction, them diseases.'

'I've lived here all my life, although I've been away for some years. Perhaps I know the person?'

'Likely you don't, sir. It's a pauper's funeral, a poor soul from the workhouse.'

So, Mama and Uncle John had succeeded. The workhouse for Tralee had finally been established. He wondered what other changes had been made in his absence.

The old woman was running a set of rosary beads through her fingers, murmuring prayers familiar to William from his childhood.

The coffin was drawing close. 'Who is it?' he asked. There was an edge to his awareness, a feeling that something was happening, something that was leaving an imprint on the atmosphere.

She lifted the crucifix of the rosary to her lips. 'It's Mary O'Connor, sir, from Brogue Lane. Willie O'Connor's daughter, the shoemaker.' She shook her head, 'God help us all, it's a pauper's funeral for the poor craythur.'

The street darkened around William. His body and mind were no longer connected, either with each other or with the world around them.

He had no idea of how to be, how to breathe.

Mary was dead. He sought to grasp the meaning of that. And what that meant. Dead. She was dead. He would never again see her; never again watch the dimple in her cheek deepen – never again hear her say his name – never again touch her. He was lost in an abyss of never again. He forced every thought out of his head until it was filled with nothing but the white light of grief.

William shuddered at the thought of Mary being buried with strangers in the plot of unmarked graves that were tucked into a disused corner of Rath Cemetery. A pauper's burial was dreaded by all and sundry, the nightmare of the poorest of people.

Immobility changed to panic and he dashed back into the inn. 'Where can I hire a horse?'

The animal could be brought up from the livery stables in about ten minutes, the innkeeper told him. William used that time to push his way through the crowd of mourners, to reach the coffin at the head of the cortege. He recognised young Billy — no longer so young, and he plucked at his sleeve.

'Is it true?'

Billy hardly registered surprise and his sombre, tear-stained face provided the answer.

Rigid as he was with grief, William sought to gather his scrambling wits. All he could focus on was that he could not allow Mary to be buried as a pauper. He stood in the middle of the street clapping his hand to his head as he sought a solution. The funeral must be halted.

Uncle John. He thought of his kindness over the years, his donations to the Church and charitable organisations, how no problem was beyond him.

'Billy, have the coffin taken to the church and wait for me there. Do not go ahead with the burial. Do you hear me?'

Billy nodded assent.

A young lad walking along the side of the street, leading a sturdy-looking chestnut coloured mare, called, '*Who's the horse for?*'

William claimed the animal and jumped onto its back. He whirled it around in the crowded street and headed towards Cloghers House in a gallop.

❀ ❀ ❀

John Mulchinock was attending to his post when William, unannounced, burst in on him.

'William, is it you? You're returned to us, thanks be to the Good Lord!'

The room swayed in front of William.

'What is it, lad? What's up? Are still you in trouble with the law? Is it your mother?'

William stood, suppliant, in his travel-stained clothes, and shook his head. 'No, it's nothing like that.'

Where to begin his explanation? Time was of an essence. Five years ago it was unlikely that his uncle would have known of his relationship with Mary, but he presumed that during his absence he would have become aware of it.

He moved towards the desk. 'Uncle John, can I ask a favour of you? Ask that you trust me?'

John Mulchinock stood up. He had lost weight and his beard was completely white, but his stature was as imposing as ever. He came out from behind his desk and placed his hand on William's shoulder.

'Tell me, lad.' He gestured to two chairs on either side of the fireplace.

He sat silently as William spoke, the words spilling out from him.

Finally, he said, 'Now I have but one question. Would it be acceptable to you to have Mary buried at Clogherbrien?'

William was quiet for a moment, remembering his youthful self, his plans with Mary for their future, before answering in the affirmative. Mary would be safe in the small cemetery behind that low wall on the road leading to Fenit. Fenit the place where once she'd seen the sea.

As John Mulchinock saw his nephew out, he touched his shoulder affectionately, 'I'll send news to your mother. She has been heartbroken.'

As William rode up the driveway of West Villa his mother was waiting on the steps with the hall door open behind her. She held out her arms to him and he ran up the steps to her. Grief-stricken as he was, he was aware that she had aged, almost beyond recognition. His home was changed too. An air of sadness hung about the place, its vitality gone from it and its occupants.

Mrs Mac was less authoritarian, but she still aired her opinions. 'It was like your mother, the poor craythur, lost the will to live after you went. She left the doing of everything to your brother, and spent her days in meditation and prayer, as well as embroidering the flowers Paudge picked for her.'

Edward worked all the hours of the day, Paudge was serious beyond belief, Lizzie had lost her chattiness, the housemaids, dairymaids and yardmen were all subdued, unsure of their futures, dubious in their welcoming back of William.

❀ ❀ ❀

Over the ensuing days, weeks and months and in all weathers, William spent hours by the side of Mary's grave, taking to her and reciting the verses he'd written for her while in India.

Occasionally Rob joined him, standing, head bowed in silent prayer.

On his last visit he rounded on William and berated him for ruining his life.

'Mary would not want this for you!' He cast an embracing arm around the graveyard.

'How do you know what Mary would want?'

'She had courage and she was a fighter. She never gave up believing in you.'

William sent him away with, 'We don't want you here.'

❀❀❀

The passing of time and having control of the family businesses appeared to have mellowed Edward. He feared for William's sanity and watched over him as one would a child, encouraging and supporting him in the erection of a handsome headstone to honour Mary.

'Despite the economic downturn the shop is doing well,' he said one day. 'I hear Giselle's gowns are still the talk of the town.'

William shrugged his indifference. He seldom called in to the shop and when he did he was not interested in further developments and paid scant attention to the latest fashions.

'You cannot continue like this, William,' said Edward.

'Like what?'

'The way you're going on.' He paused for a moment before continuing, 'Mary would not wish to see you waste your life.'

Up to then Mary's name had not been spoken within the walls of West Villa. It was as though she had never existed.

CHAPTER 36

AFTER THOUGHTFUL DELIBERATION, although without consulting his mother, uncle or brother, Edward contacted Hector Keogh in Ballinasloe and invited him, his wife and daughter to visit. He was both surprised and pleased when his invitation was accepted, and once again the kitchen at West Villa was agog with rumours.

William made no concessions to the entertainment of the houseguests, scarcely registering their presence. He continued to ride out daily to Clogherbrien, spending the daylight hours by Mary's grave. If he was drawn into conversation with the guests he answered in a distracted way and escaped from the company as quickly as he could.

Edward went to great lengths to be an affable host. He invited Hector Keogh to accompany him on his daily rounds, pointing out the areas of devastation wreaked by the famine, explaining the workings of the farm and elaborating on the family's commercial interests in the town. He organised for the Mulchinock carriage to deliver Mrs Keogh and Alicia to the shop on the Mall and left them in M. Aubin's capable hands with instructions to show the visitors the new stock of bonnets, trimmings and materials and to accommodate their purchases.

Despite her initial reservations about the visit, Violet Keogh found she was enjoying herself. She had wanted to refuse Edward's invitation, but her husband was insistent on accepting.

'The change will do you good, my dear. Do all of us good.'

His wife was constantly out of sorts, regularly professing her exasperation at Alicia's refusal to consider suitable suitors and her lack of interest in marrying. 'She's doing too much thinking and reading. Not good for a young girl.'

'She's become an intellectual, one of those bluestockings, I fear,' agreed her husband.

'Oh, dear.' Violet touched her eyes with a lacy kerchief.

But after a few days in West Villa, admitting herself invigorated by the change of air, Violet had reverted to her former social self. Meanwhile, Hector talked business matters with Edward who he considered far superior in all ways to William, so much so that he began to harbour hopes that perhaps there might be a match between Edward and Alicia, the idea growing on him in a pleasing way as he read meaning into the most minor of their exchanges.

After gentle pressing from his mother William agreed to make an appearance in the drawing room during afternoon tea on Sunday. His grieving had corroded his natural charm and he appeared to have lost the ability to converse.

Alicia's penchant for pastel frills had given way to plain dresses in muted colours with small white collars. She had grown plump and dogmatic with voluble opinions on the power of Irish literature, even quoting Lady Morgan's views on how weakened Ireland was by the Great Famine. William hadn't remembered her like that, but then memories of the time he had spent in Ballinasloe belonged to another world, and they'd scarcely spoken since her arrival.

That afternoon she ate heartily — idly he counted several sandwiches, some cake, a biscuit or two and three cups of tea.

Returning her cup to its saucer with a clatter, she leaned forward, 'Did you see much poverty while you were in India, William?'

William, who was crumbling a slice of cake in a distracted way, flicked the crumbs from his fingers and turned in her direction. 'From what I saw poverty throughout India is appalling, and the natives are badly treated by the British.'

'In what way?'

'Half-starved men, women and children carrying out heavy manual labour for a pittance or a few bowls of rice; servants overworked and children's eyes ruined from tatting.'

Margaret hadn't heard her son speak with such eloquence since before he had gone away.

'How very, very sad,' said Alicia in a caring tone.

Violet did not relish this turn of conversation. She had been relieved at William's absences from West Villa and, on the rare occasion when he was around, to observe her daughter's apparent indifference to him. Before coming to Tralee she'd worried that Alicia might still be infatuated, and she'd asked her outright, more to alleviate her own worries than out of compassion, but she'd only sniffed in a way that her mother later described as 'haughtily'.

'Poverty is an affliction of our times,' said William.

Alicia gave a little nod of understanding. 'As is starvation. On our journey from Ballinasloe the public roads were crowded with hundreds of poor souls toiling for six or sevenpence-worth of meal for an entire family.' She looked around the handsome drawing room, her gaze lingering on the well-stocked trolley of tea things. 'I suppose it's the same in Tralee?'

'We try to look after our poor.'

'The political situation is disastrous. And poverty is on the increase. You've read Miss Edgeworth?'

'She's writing fiction.'

'Yes, and she says it's impossible to draw Ireland as she now is in a book of fiction, that realities are too strong and party passions too violent.'

Margaret and Violet looked at each other in shared perplexity, neither having heard of Miss Edgeworth. Violet accepted another finger of Mrs Mac's porter cake and the two ladies talked animatedly about the cake's texture.

William rose, and made his excuses in the graceless way that he had adopted.

As he was leaving the room Alicia had the last word. 'It's said that an Irishman raises beautiful crops, carries his harvest to the nearest port, puts it on board an English vessel, and returns home to subsist on potatoes.'

At the door he turned around and gave a little laugh. 'Is it now?'

❈❈❈

A few mornings later Alicia knocked on the door of the bedchamber allocated to her mother and father, and without waiting for a reply she entered and stood just inside the doorway. Her parents hadn't seen much of her over the past days. Her mother was occupied with fittings for some new silk gowns and grateful to avoid Alicia's rants about extravagance, and her father had become obsessed with the workings of the dairy.

Alicia had her hands on her hips and was beaming.

'Mama, Papa, I have news.'

Violet, who was still in bed, settled her wrap around her shoulders and Hector tucked his shirt into his trousers.

'William and I are betrothed.'

Her parents were expressionless, as though frozen as she continued.

'We'll be wed and leaving to live in New York as soon as possible.'

Having stated her piece, she bestowed another beam on them and withdrew before they had a chance to gather their wits in reply

Violet promptly had a fit of the vapours, thrashing around in the bedclothes so violently that Hector went to pull on the bell to summon help.

'*Don't!*' At the thought of the scandal that would evoke she pulled herself together and sat up moaning, 'What are we to do?'

He did not answer.

'Your side of the family,' Violet pointed an accusing finger at her husband who was putting on his coat, and slowly doing up each button. 'Oh, oh! The shame of it!'

As he picked up the clothesbrush and ran it smartly across his shoulders of quality broadcloth, he acquired that set look of a decision reached. He replaced the brush on the chest of drawers, turned towards her and spoke slowly, annunciating each word while congratulating himself that he hadn't shared the details of William's disgrace with her. There would be no reasoning with her if she knew of his involvement with Daniel O'Connell, the shooting and fleeing to India with a price on his head. He preferred not to consider his attachment to the servant girl — he'd decided that sort of behavior from a gentleman must have resulted from a temporary aberration.

'There is no shame. Our daughter is making a good marriage — the joining together of two prominent families.' He gave a little smile, as though savouring the situation. 'We will hold our heads high and give Alicia a memorable day. Remember, my dear, that I have a position to uphold in Ballinasloe.'

Alicia found Mrs Mulchinock in the garden, gathering blooms from a pale-pink rosebush.

She watched, unobserved, as her hostess carefully cut each stem at an angle, handled it reverently, and ran the pad of her index finger along its flash of green before carefully laying it in the trug by her feet.

'Good morning, Cousin Margaret.'

Mrs Mulchinock straightened up and looked at her keenly. The timbre of Alicia's voice was unexpectedly cheerful.

'Good morning, dear.'

'I came to tell you that William and I are to be wed. And we'll be living in New York.'

Margaret stepped backwards on the gravel pathway, knocking over the trug.

'Yes,' Alicia continued. 'Mama, Papa and I will be returning to Ballinasloe today. There's much to be done.' With that she tripped along the path and entered the house.

Margaret followed her a few minutes later. She pulled on the bellcord and when Lizzie entered she told her to find Master

William Pembroke immediately.

It was close on half an hour before William joined her. She expected to see a change in him, but he was as she'd grown used to — untidy-looking, his hair too long, his linen creased and wearing a rumpled jacket and trousers. He looked around the room in that distracted way of his.

'Why, William? Why?'

'Why what?'

'Why are you going to wed Alicia Keogh?'

'Why not? She says they'll appreciate my writings in America.'

'But you aren't writing? You haven't written anything for months.'

'Perhaps I will.'

He came towards her and held out his arms and, as she'd done so often, she went into them and briefly the world was a perfect place.

'It's all such a mess, Mama. And it's better that I go.'

❄❄❄

Some two hours later Mrs Mulchinock stood on the steps with Edward watching as William escorted Alicia to the Keogh carriage. He settled her in without any gesture of affection, shook Mr Keogh's hand, nodded at Mrs Keogh, and looked after the carriage until it turned the curve in the driveway.

Mrs Mulchinock gave a little sob that she did not allow to develop.

Edward patted at her arm in an ineffectual way, 'It's all for the best, Mama. And this marriage is more than we could have hoped for.'

'But America!' she wailed.

'At least he'll be gone from Clogherbrien. Stop the talk that's going around the town.'

❀❀❀

The news from America came at irregular intervals. Letters written by Alicia marked the birth of their daughters, Alice and Bernadette, reported that William was gaining quite a reputation for his newspaper articles and lyrics, and that she had become involved in the anti-slavery movement. Another letter announced that *The Ballads and Songs of W.P. Mulchinock* was to be published the following year and that her husband's patrons included the poets Emerson, Longfellow and Whittier.

Mr Keogh boasted to anyone who'd listen that his son-in-law was a newpaper magnate; Mrs Keogh seldom left her bedchanber; Mrs Mulchinock prayed that her son had found happiness and fulfilment, and she wished with all her heart that she could get to know her granddaughters.

❀❀❀

On a bright autumn afternoon William returned to Tralee from New York. As he had done four years previously, he came unannounced and unexpected. Considering the coach too slow he'd left it at the last stop and hired a horse. He lathered the animal along Castle Street and tethered it loosely to a post before entering the inn and calling for wine.

He had become a heavy drinker and, although remnants of his handsomeness remained, he looked like a man closing down on himself.

As he sat drinking whiskey the innkeeper recognised him and

sent word of his arrival to West Villa. But, by the time Edward arrived in the town, William and a fresh horse were on their way to Clogherbrien.

Light was fading and the birds were in twilight song as Edward reined in his horse and looked over the wall into the graveyard. At first he couldn't see William, but by standing high on his stirrups he made out the figure of his brother lying flat on Mary O'Connor's grave, his arms stretched wide, and his hands scrabbling at the grass as though seeking to join her.

EPILOGUE

WILLIAM NEVER RETURNED to live at West Villa. He took rooms in Nelson Street and founded *The Kerry Star* – the newspaper closed down after two years. He suffered from depression and alcoholism and died alone in 1864. As he wished, he was buried alongside Mary.

AUTHOR'S NOTE

THE STORY OF MARY O'CONNOR (182?-1845) has been with me since I was a child on school holidays in Tralee where the chat in the kitchen was mighty. I didn't grasp half of what was going on in the story, but I understood it was about a romance between a young girl and a handsome Prince Charming-like man. And imagine there was an annual festival commemorating Mary's life! A festival that, on pain of committing a 'mortaler', my cousins and I were forbidden to have anything to do with. In case threat wasn't enough, while the town of Tralee was festooned in celebration we were banished to the seaside.

The First Rose of Tralee is a novel of the imagination, garlanding fact with fiction. In the interest of the story I have introduced characters that presented themselves to me as I wrote, and imagined voices, thoughts and feelings as well as taking creative liberties with names, locations and times. Researching and writing this book has been a trip down Memory Lane, a pleasure from start to finish.

I attribute the lyrics of the ballad titled 'The Rose of Tralee' to William Pembroke Mulchinoch as local lore has it, although it is elsewhere attributed to poet Edward Mordaunt Spencer. It is universally accepted that the music is by composer Charles William Glover who died a year before William.

BIBLIOGRAPHY

- *The Victorians* – AN Wilson, Hutchinson, London 2007
- *Miss Emily* – Nuala O'Connor, Sandstone Press, Ross-Shire 2015
- *Longburn* – Jo Baker, Black Swan, London 2014
- *Ireland Before the Famine (1798-1848)* – Gearóid O'Tuathaigh, Gill and Macmillan 1972
- *The Workings of the Household* – Lydia Morris, Polity, Cambridge 1990
- *Katey* – Lucinda Hawksley, Doubleday, London 2006
- *The Big Wind* – Beatrice Coogan, Michael Joseph Ltd, London 1969
- *The Whitest Flower Rose* – Brendan Graham, HarperCollins UK, London 1998
- *Under the Hawthorn Tree* – Marita Conlon-McKenna, The O'Brien Press, Dublin 1990
- *The Great Irish Famine* – ed. by Cathal Pórtéir, Mercier Press, Cork 1995
- *Great Irish Speeches* – Richard Aldous, Quercus, London 2007
- *British India 1772-1947* – Michael Edwards, Rupe & Co, New Delhi 1967
- *Shantaram* – Gregory David Roberts, Abacus, London 2005

Archival material from *Kerry Evening Post* 1840s
Various websites dealing with the Victorian era